FORWARD LEANING

By Addison LeMay

This book is dedicated to my wonderful wife

Nadine LeMay

Thank you for putting up with me baby.

Forward Leaning;

(1) Posture of a military unit when it has all its combat units, fully armed, fully equipped, fully briefed and just about to launch into combat operations.

(2) Just before a race or a fight, a person has their weight shifted forward and are leaning forward just before they spring into action.

CHAPTER 1

CHIAPAS, MEXICO, 2003

The silver Mercedes-Benz glides up the long driveway as nearby gardeners tend the many colorful flowers. Lawn sprinklers shower the lush green grass of a finely manicured mansion. The Mercedes parks and a smashingly handsome man in an expensive suit steps out of the car. Dr. Roberto Sovia walks into the open courtyard of the hacienda carrying a black leather medical bag.

Scantily clad women, dripping with shiny jewelry sip from expensive looking drinks while the sound of Mexican music blasts. One woman in a bikini snorts cocaine off of a glass table. Dr. Sovia approaches a tough looking security man in expensive clothes leaning against a wall with a sub-machine gun strapped under his shoulder.

"Where is he?" asks Dr. Sovia. The security man looks annoyed as he pushes himself off the wall and starts walking.

"This way doc," replies the security man who then leads Dr. Sovia into a dark garage. The stench of blood and sweat fills the darkness and Dr. Roberto Sovia feels a shiver of fear. The security man flips on the light switch and reveals a man sitting in a chair in the middle of the garage, covered in blood and looking frightened. The security man points at the bloody man, "Jefe said you could fix him up."

Dr. Sovia walks to the bloodied man and sees two disheveled and bruised children huddled together on a nearby beat up couch. "What's with the kids?" he asks.

The security man smiles cruelly as he looks at the kids. "Guests of Jefe Rosa," he replies. Dr. Sovia carries his medical bag to the children and kneels to examine them. The security man appears agitated and moves closer to them, "The fuck you doin?" Dr. Sovia ignores him and security man gets louder. "How long you think you can keep doin whatever you want? Huh? You follow orders like the rest of us!" Security man points angrily at the bloody man. "Now go fix Jefe's man over there!"

Dr. Sovia continues wiping the children's cuts and bruises without looking at the security man. "I'll help the kids first. Don't like it? Call someone else." The security man snorts and spits on the concrete. Dr. Sovia finishes his work, pats the kids on the head and then turns and approaches the bloody man. With his back to the security man he says, "you have the cash?"

The security man pulls out a roll of cash secured by a rubber band and tosses it on the concrete at the bloody man's feet. Dr. Sovia squats down, pulls the rubber band off the roll and counts the money. "Enough?" asks the security man.

"It'll do" Dr. Sovia replies as he pockets the money and turns and examines the bloody man."All right then, where were we?"

CHAPTER 2

ONE YEAR LATER

AFGHANISTAN, 2004

The sun rises above pine tree covered mountains and slowly illuminates a series of stone houses and walled compounds built into the side of the mountains a thousand years earlier. Chickens squawk and goats belch as villagers trudge through their morning chores. A speaker from the Mosque's muezzin screams out the morning call to prayer. Few answer the call. Nestled half way up the mountain sits the largest home for many miles. The massive stone villa boasts a ten-foot wall complete with an iron gate and armed guards patrolling the compound.

Crime runs rampant in Afghanistan and in a lawless land where might makes right. Here the strongest and smartest criminals amassed wealth and power at a rate that put America's "Robber Barons" of the 1870's to shame. These powerful crime lords sometimes used the power of Mosques to convince their followers the Warlord's were the instrument of Allah. Other times the Warlords of Afghanistan kept it simple and just killed, raped and pillaged their way to the top. All thirty -four of Afghanistan's Provinces had at least one if not multiple Warlords controlling territory they claimed was theirs. Almost always they were fighting the other Warlords over turf, drugs, money, trade routes.

There are over sixty different tribes in Afghanistan, and a dozen languages. Many people who call themselves Afghans cannot understand each other. Most do not like others from different tribes and the blood feuds go on for literally thousands of years. The hate runs deep and wide creating a river of intolerance, and violence that sweeps up the entire country in a chaotic current.

It is one of these Warlords that owns the biggest stone compound in the village. In the distance, a cloud of dust follows in the wake of a white 4 door Toyota Hilux Pickup truck as it approaches the village

A hundred meters up the mountain, concealed in the scrub- brush, two Special Forces Sergeants watch the compound through their scoped rifles. Their faces are painted with green camouflage and they are invisible to the naked eye. US Army sniper school trains its sniper students to be the masters of concealment. These two professional soldiers could have crawled for hours and gotten within feet of the compound without being seen by the enemy.

US Army Special Forces snipers are some of the most patient and effective killers on earth. In order to keep their movements to a minimum so as to not attract attention from human eyes, Staff Sergeant Johnny Span has a microphone button mounted in his glove. He squeezes the button with his thumb without moving his hand off of his rifle and speaks into his helmet mounted microphone, "Red Rhino, Blue Dog over."

On the other side of the mountain, inside the command Humvee bristling with radio and satellite gear, sits Captain Lance Erickson. He is the Commander of this Special Forces team officially known as Operational Detachment Alpha (ODA) 666. The radio crackles to life. He answers it, "Blue Dog, Red Rhino here, what's up Johnny?"

Johnny's voice crackles out of the radio speaker, "Red Rhino we got a white four door pickup truck approaching the village at this time."

Lance replies, "Ok Johnny, let me know if it's our man." Johnny's voice comes back over the radio, "Roger, out."

Lance, still sitting in his Humvee, consults the map on the laptop computer when the radio crackles to life again. "Red Rhino, Blue Dog over."

Lance grabs the radio handset and speaks into it, "Yeah, go Johnny."

"Ah, it's him boss, at the compound now", Johnny relays over the radio.

Lance sits up straight and asks excitedly into the radio handset, "does he have the hostages with him?"

Johnny peers through the scope of his rifle, carefully looking over the truck and calmly replies into his helmet microphone, "No-go on the hostages boss, it's just our bag man with the money.

"You sure Johnny?" Lance's voice says over the radio.

Johnny continues looking through the scope and says," not unless he's got all six girls packed into the cabin of that pickup truck."

"Yeah Johnny thanks for the early warning, keep me apprised of any developments." Lance switches the frequency on his radio and speaks again into the handset. "All right everyone looks like our guy is arriving now. No visual on the hostages yet but be ready to move."

It was two days ago that the six young, beautiful, American women disappeared. They were so full of vim and vigor and popular at their respective colleges in the mid-West of the United States. Two girls from each campus would make the trip to Afghanistan to bring relief to the women and children suffering in that war torn nation. They were tasked to be part of a humanitarian aid mission from the prestigious International Aid Organization. Their parents and school faculty publicly celebrated the women's sacrifice and courage. "Don't you think it's a bit dangerous for Western women to be in

Afghanistan right now?" was the question most of her classmates asked them. "What are you some kind of sexist?" was often the response of these young heroines, "You would never ask that of a man, would you? was often added. Off they went to Afghanistan and quickly vanished into its vortex of crime and chaos.

    Directly down the mountain from the hidden Special Forces Sergeants, the white pickup truck pulls into a gated compound. Armed men dressed in traditional Afghan garb wave the truck in as it parks in front of the stone villa. The front gate that separates the compound from the villa opens and two men in Afghan attire walk out. Aasif Ahmad, the informant, walks with Baraat Mansoor to the pickup truck.

    Baraat Mansoor proudly strutted while he walked and although he was not ostentatious in his gait, years of intimidating, oppressing, and killing had given him a confidence he could not hide. He was also the brother of the warlord and often took initiative in creating new revenue streams for the family. Baraat spent years building contacts in other cities as well as across the border into Pakistan and even Iran. Those contacts who with ease could buy or sell whatever Baraat wanted. Such skills were worthless in the West, where anyone could get whatever they needed by driving down to the store or ordering online. No such luxuries existed in Afghanistan, a country of twenty-four million people. The people's needs and wants did not stop simply because goods were not available. No it was Baraat's family's job to satisfy those needs, at an inflated cost of course.

In the year 1979, after two years of social upheaval and a highly un-popular, inept Communist government the people of Afghanistan had had enough, there was massive discontent. The Soviet Union, the enormous communist behemoth of a nation to the north, assassinated the President of Afghanistan and installed their own choice as President. This new President was from a "friendly-to-the-Russian's" tribe. The Afghani tribes fought for ten years against the Russian army and puppet government of Afghanistan. During this time, loyalties switched sides and so did Baraat Mansoor's crime family. They did anything to keep the profits coming in and themselves in a position of power.

The Soviet Army left in 1989 and right after that the country's civil war truly exploded. Tribes allied with other tribes, all shuffling for a better position to be in on the power when their team won. The various tribes, led by their perspective warlords fought for seven more years against each other. They plunged the land into a maelstrom of murder and violence. The country was paralyzed with little to no trade and hundreds of thousands of deaths. Cities were left without electricity, water or waste management. Their civil war brought the developing nation of Afghanistan, back to the middle ages. The nightmare continued until a religious order of students with lots of guns, known as the Taliban brought order to Afghanistan.

    The Taliban brought with them a stricter version of Islam, the dominant religion of Afghanistan. Men were no longer allowed to shave their beards. Women were confined to the home unless accompanied outside by a male relative. No more school or public life for women. Anyone caught violating these or any of the countless Draconian rules of the Taliban were often beaten and publicly executed. With the Taliban in charge, alcohol and of course drugs were prohibited. Televisions and most consumer products were forbidden. As with any type of prohibition, these rules simply drove up the levels of profit to be made selling the prohibited item. And of course the

Mansoor family profited handsomely from smuggling in what people were willing to pay outrageous prices for. This lucrative cash flow ended when the Americans came to town. Baraat truly believed that the Americans brought freedom for the people to import far too much. And now too many sinful goods were available to his countrymen. Goods that the Mansoor family had provided to only the rich and decadent were now available to everyone and inexpensive. As long as the prohibition remained, only those few destined for Hell after death, would be corrupted. It was those idiotic Arabs, paying rent and building roads in Afghanistan, who knocked down the Twin Towers on the other side of the planet. They brought the Americans that now poured into Afghanistan. "It might not be so bad if the Americans had behaved like the Russians," Baraat often said, "But all this choice and all this decadence." The American army took away the smuggling business and was putting the Mansoor family out of business. Kidnapping had become a burgeoning cash flow for the family. Baraat walked out to the pickup truck to collect his money.

Up the mountain, overlooking the compound,

the snipers watch Baraat casually and confidently walk to the truck. Johnny Span, still looking through his rifle scope calls the Captain over the radio, "Red Rhino pick up."

Back in his vehicle, Captain Lance Erikson answers, "Go Blue Dog, whatcha got?"

"Red Rhino I've got eyes on our little paid informant walking out of the house." Baraat was wanted by both the new puppet Afghan government and the US Army on multiple charges. When a known associate of the Mansoor family walked in to American (now called Coalition) headquarters, offering to sell information on the recent kidnapping, Lance's team got tasked with the mission to oversee the exchange.

Lance speaks into his handset, "Please tell me he's with our target."

Johnny smiles while looking through the scope and squeezes his radio button, "That's a roger Red Rhino. I am looking at one priority High Value Target. A Mr. Baraat Mansoor."

A slight breeze carries the ever present Afghan dust across the compound as Aasif approaches the pickup truck first. Aasif's eyes squint through the dust, his fingertips sweat and his heart pounds. All the effort, all the back door deals and meetings in secret, had come down to this moment. He was not supposed to use his cell phone according to some US Army Special Forces soldier named Dan. Dan kept telling Aasif, "don't text us, don't call us. Just follow the steps we told you to drop off the intelligence. The Mansoor's have people in the telephone company on their payroll," Dan warned him. "Well screw him," Aasif thought to himself, "I didn't get caught and I'm about to get paid."

Aasif gets close enough to touch the pickup truck and the tinted rear passenger window slides down to reveal an elderly, yet regal looking Afghan tribal leader named Imran Khan. His silver white hair makes him look far older than his fifties. Aasif gestures to Baraat Mansoor standing nearby and makes the introduction, "Mr. Imran Khan, of the New Afghan Provisional Government, please meet Mr. Baraat Mansoor, who needs no introduction."

Baraat approaches the open truck window and gets right to the point, "Will they pay?" Baraat asks.

Imran Khan scowls his face and waves Baraat away. "Where are your manners Baraat Mansoor? You sound like the infidels now." Imran Khan had respected the ways of the Afghan warrior of legend.

Manners and respect, like the old Italian gangster movies was Imran Khan's daily discipline. He had not risen to the near top of Afghan politics by insulting people. No, when the nature of this delicate tasking came up and the President of Afghanistan called him to handle this matter of national security, Imran was always willing to achieve ends. "Who are these girls that were kidnapped?" he asked the President.

One of Imran Khan's security men steps out from the front passenger seat of the pickup truck and shoves past Baraat and Aasif and opens the door for his eminence, Imran Khan.

Baraat realizing his faux pas tries to recover, "my apologies Mr. Khan. Please come this way." Baraat gestures with his arms to follow as Imran slowly eases himself from the truck.

"Of course, they expect me to see if all of your guests are in good health first," says Imran Khan.

Baraat spins around quickly, his eyes widely open and gesturing angrily, "are we savages to them? Do they think that all Afghan's do is-"

"Imran Khan gently pats Baraat on the

shoulder as he tries to ease the tension. "It is a great sum of money they have agreed to pay," said Imran Khan. "You are getting what you want." Imran Khan pulls a camera phone from his tunic. "Let me give them the photos they want." Baraat looks back at Imran, nods and smiles. They walk to the compound as Imran's security man attempts to follow. Imran turns and waves him back to the truck. "Stay with the money." The security man joins the other two security men at the truck.

The three Afghan men saunter away from the truck and pass through a solid metal gate into the villa. The gate clangs shut with a loud metallic sound. Armed men suddenly appear and seize Imran Khan and Aasif Ahmad.

"What are you doing?" Screams Aasif Ahmad as the armed men tie their hands behind their backs.

Imran Khan remains calm and merely stares directly at Baraat Mansoor. "There will be consequences for this Mr. Mansoor," said Imran Khan.

Baraat stares straight back at Imran Khan and replies, "yes, but they won't be paid by us. I assure you." Aasif attempts to wrestle away but he is held firm by the men. Baraat turns to Aasif and strikes him hard across the face. "And you, you filthy son of a whore! How long did you think you could betray us and not be found out?"

The look of sudden discovery and realization sweeps across Aasif's face as his lips quiver. He tries to lie, "no. No Baraat you misunderstand. I-" Baraat hits Aasif again and the armed men drag Aasif away while he screams for mercy.

The reach of Baraat's brother extended even further than his own. "The Grand Warlord," was how Baraat often referred to his brother. Sometimes respectfully, sometimes snidely with a hint of contempt. The warlord had government employees on his payroll. Government stooges at every level that for a few shekels a month, would give up their own mothers. Those few shekels were pennies compared to the information that was purchased from them. It was not even a day before Baraat learned from his brother of Aasif's treachery. Aasif sold out the family for his few shekels and Imran Khan was part of that betrayal.

Outside the villa, in the compound, Imran's men stand guard around the pickup truck smoking cigarettes, looking bored and hot. The silence is shattered by the distinctive cracking sound of AK-47s as Imran's men are slaughtered where they stand. Their bullet riddled bodies slump to the ground like rag dolls. Seconds later their killers emerge from expertly camouflaged spider holes, dug into the ground nearby. The killers proudly smile as they inspect the carnage they have just committed.

Up the mountain Johnny Span, still looking through his rifle scope sees the sudden attack. He speaks excitedly into his helmet microphone, "Red Rhino, RED RHINO! We got hostiles, it's an ambush, the VIP's vehicle is under attack!"

On the other side of the mountain, inside the command Humvee, Lance sits in the passenger seat and is reviewing his map when Johnny's frantic radio transmission jolts him alert. He grabs the radio handset and speaks into it, "Blue Dog, gimmie status on the VIP."

Johnny's voice comes through the radio, "Unknown at this time Red Rhino, permission to engage hostiles?"

Lance waves at his driver and shouts, "let's go! Go!" Then back into the radio. "Engage Blue Dog! Engage at will."

Lance switches the frequency on the radio again and shouts into the handset, "All units converge on the compound. NOW! Hostiles in contact!" As the Humvee pulls out of the orange grove, the Machine Gunner in the roof turret of the vehicle, Staff Sergeant Bob White racks the heavy bolt on the 50 caliber machine gun mounted to the swinging turret. Lance yells up to Bob, "Bobby, get that fifty up!"

Bob looks down at Lance through the turret hole and yells back, "I got it boss! We're up. We're up." Inside the Humvee the microphone handles and their wires swing from side to side as the Humvee turns and climbs the rocky road out of the orange grove and races towards the compound.

Lance Erickson, grew up in Findlay, Ohio, a small industrial town with three colleges. Lance grew up the son of a fairly wealthy business owner. The Erickson family never wanted for anything, and Lance made the most of his dad's money with all the football and hockey equipment dad could buy him. Lance was a jock all throughout his high school and college years. Good enough to get on the teams but not good enough for a scholarship. Not that that he needed one, he just did not want dad to have to keep paying. A certain inner compulsion to go his own way made Lance deeply desire to earn that scholarship to show the old man he did not need him. But alas, the scholarship was not meant to be. Since Lance watched other guys schlub their way through school by working nights and weekends, which would nullify his chances of playing football, Lance accepted his dad's largesse and let dad pay for college. It always burned him up inside and he felt like he was groveling to his father even though he wasn't groveling. Independence burned deeply inside Lance. Which is why it was astounding to Lance's parents when he joined Army ROTC. The discipline was a good thing his father reasoned, "but didn't Lance get enough discipline and team building playing sports?" Dad asked his son. "Yeah dad," Lance's reply came, "deep inside I am a warrior. Sports are great, but dad, I know what I want to be."

Lance was commissioned a Second Lieutenant after completing college and ROTC and went through all the Officer Basic Course BS to qualify as an infantry officer. Lance loved the physical and mental challenges of being in the field, conducting operations. Lance detested all the BS that went on back in the office, or the barracks or the motor pools. All the paperwork and rules and adherence to policy made Lance sick to his stomach. It was two years after his service to the Army began that he was able to try out for his dream; The US Army

Special Forces Assessment and Selection or SFAS also known as the School For Advanced Suffering. Eighty percent wash out in the first three weeks of Selection. Lance passed and was selected and after years of training and deployments to hot spots around the world, he was an A-Team (ODA) leader in a war. He was a warrior.

Back in their sniper hide overlooking the compound, the two Sergeants of ODA 666 patiently scan their fields of view for targets and calmly pull their triggers on their long range rifles. Baraat's gunmen one by one fall to the ground. One last gunman grabs the bag of money out of the bullet riddled pickup truck and races to the compound gate only to be cut down by the sniper's bullet feet from the gate's handle. Cash spews from the bag and is carried away by the Afghan breeze.

The four Humvee's of ODA 666 converge on the compound, smash through the front gate and park in tactical positions near and around one side of the villa. Lance and his soldiers jump out of their vehicles, weapons at the ready. Lance's Second in Command, Chief Mike Mastronardi, affectionately known as "Chief M" since no one can correctly pronounce his name, breeches the gate to the villa with a pre-fabricated explosive charge and makes a tactical entry inside, followed by a tight line of soldiers, their weapons up and at the ready, covering each other.

Lance's heart is racing as he analyzes the situation. High speed combat, this is what he worked so hard to become, a Special Forces team leader. Lance yells commands at his men, "Mike! Take Dan and Chris on the left side, we'll take the right."

The soldiers move further into the compound, in the middle of the dirt courtyard, tied to a stake is Aasif Ahmed, the informant. He is shirtless and his belly is cut open from his neck to his balls with his guts hanging out. A wad of US dollars is stuffed in his mouth. Bullets wiz past them and a soldier Sergeant First Class, Craig Oldfield cries out in agony. "I'm hit. I'm hit!"

Chief M screams out the obvious, "Craig's down! Craig's down." As he pulls the fallen soldier behind a wall and begins treating him to stop the bleeding.

Lance takes cover and speaks into his radio microphone, "Ritchie get to Craig, get him stabilized. I want him at the field hospital ASAP.

Mike, Call it in."

Chief M grabs his radio handset and yells into it, "Medevac 1 this is Devil's Child 5. I need a bird inbound, 1 critical wounded. How copy over?"

The radio crackles to life, "Little busy right now Devil's Child 5. Big shoot-out, we'll get to ya when we can."

Chief M stares at the radio handset and screams, "What the fuck are you people fucking kidding me??!?!"

313TH FORWARD SURGICAL TEAM, AFGHANISTAN

The giant spinning rotor blades of a US Army Blackhawk helicopter kick up a storm of dust as it lands on the rocky terrain of the Army field hospital. Soldiers drag wounded soldiers off the helicopter towards the hospital. A metal sign in Army Brown and green reads "313th Forward Surgical Team". A handwritten sign below that reads "Better not get hurt".

The Forward Surgical Team looks nothing like the hospital on the old show Mash which had green dilapidated tents. This field hospital is state of the art with inflatable buildings and truck trailers parked end to end to make a modern day facility with all the technological advances of any trauma center in the United States. Inside the corridors of the hospital, wounded patients lie on gurneys in the Trauma Ward. Nurses and Medics race from patient to patient. Dr. Roberto Sovia, who is now a lowly Private in the US Army and a Medic, is there prepping patients for surgery.

Major/Dr. Harvey Goldstein, forty-four years old and chief of surgery, pompously parades into the ward. Dr. Harvey Goldstein, the poorest kid in his Hebrew school, the butt of jokes from the other kids. It wasn't Harvey's fault his dad got sent to prison for cooking the books at his company, but the community didn't care. He would always be "Oh that poor little Goldstein boy". Harvey Goldstein, whose mom could only afford to send him to state school while his friends all went off to Harvard, Yale and all the other top undergraduate schools. Well, Harvey found his place in Army ROTC, Reserve Officer Training Corps. ROTC is the program that trains young future Army officers. When mom's college money ran out, the ROTC scholarship picked right up. Harvey never missed a class. He earned his right to be an officer, a college graduate and eventually a doctor. Harvey commands, and people listen.

Standing in the middle of the chaos of a rush of wounded soldiers in need of care, made Harvey feel like the powerful calm at the center of a storm. "Full house tonight people. I hope you all drank your coffee," said Major Goldstein. Everyone on staff, far too busy, simply ignores him.

Captain/Dr. Maria Paredo, thirty-three years old, marches into the trauma ward with her hands freshly washed and held up. Her gaze lingers on Dr. Sovia nearby. They gaze at each other for a beat before she finds her assistant. Sergeant Douglas, glove me up and let's get the first one into surgery. Sergeant Doug Douglas, twenty-four years old, scurries to Captain Paredo and stretches fresh surgical gloves over her hands as she walks backwards opening the door to the Operating Room with her behind.

Major Goldstein spots Dr. Sovia staring after Dr. Paredo and starts snapping his fingers and shouting. "Private Sovia!... SOVIA!"

Private/Dr. Sovia is still staring towards Maria when he hears his name and walks to Major Goldstein who is now coughing. "Who was that sir?" asks Dr. Sovia.

"New Doctor on staff," replies Major Goldstein. "Hey Sovia! Keep your eye on the ball here."

"I am sir." replies Dr. Sovia. Major Goldstein looks at him disapprovingly and changes his tone.

"Scrub up Sovia, I want you assisting in the O.R. And no bullshitting around tonight!"

"I don't bullshit around sir."

"Are we back to that Sovia?" Major Goldstein retorts clearly looking displeased.

Dr. Sovia gets confrontational, "That doctor would have killed that patient had I not intervened sir."

Major Goldstein covers his mouth to cough then recovers, "look Sovia, I don't care if you were some big shit surgeon back in Mexico. Not here you're not."

Dr. Sovia swallows his rage and takes a breath, "I know sir, I have been counseled."

Major Goldstein coughs furiously and again recovers, "listen Sovia, Doctors Chang and Jones are out with this goddamned virus. Use what medical knowledge you may have to assist us."

Dr. Sovia looks crestfallen, I got it sir. I'm only a medic. Major Goldstein leans heavily against the surgical table and looks at Dr. Sovia.

"Listen here Sovia, I recognize you care about patients but this is the Army."

"I'm just trying to save lives just like you sir," replies Dr. Sovia.

"But you're NOT just like me Sovia. You're not a doctor here. You're not even an officer. You're a Private." Dr. Sovia looks away uncomfortably, Major Goldstein puts a hand on his shoulder. You've got a good thing going here, Sovia. You joined the Army and got legal status for your family right?

Dr. Sovia looks away, "that's right Sir. That was the recruiter's slogan."

"So no worries about deporting your kids, right Sovia? A few more months to get your citizenship?" Dr. Sovia nods yes and Major Goldstein leans forward into him. "It'd be a shame if you screwed it up by doing something stupid Sovia. What would happen if your kids lost their legal status?"

Dr. Sovia's eyes narrow as he grits his teeth, "nothing good sir," he replies.

The Operating Room is shared by three patient gurneys, each with its own set of beeping electronic medical equipment. Captain/Dr. Mike Smith, thirty-four years old, is perspiring profusely while operating on his patient. The next gurney over, Maria is working on her patient when she looks up to see Mike Smith not looking so good.

"Dr. Smith, how are you holding up", she asks.

He does not look up to answer her, instead he focuses on his patient and looks to his surgical nurse. "Give him another…. Unit of… Sovia!... Ahh… One unit of O negative". Dr. Sovia is running items to every gurney and stops at Dr. Smith's patient to hook up the unit of blood.

Major Goldstein two table's away notices Dr. Smith's erratic behavior, "Doctor Smith, do you need assistance?"

"No. No I'm good sir." Replies Dr. Smith. "I just gotta…." Captain Smith steps back from his patient and says "can't stop shivering. My god, why is it so cold in here?" He wobbles and shivers.

Major Goldstein stops working on his patient and stares in amazement. "Dr. Smith, are you able to operate or not?"

Dr. Smith, still shivering, replies, "I don't know sir… I can't stop my hands from shaking. I'm gonna kill this kid if I cut wrong."

Major Goldstein points at him then the door, "leave the O.R. Captain. Now! Captain Smith staggers out of the O.R. Dr. Sovia is still standing over the patient on the table. He looks down at the patient then back at Doctor Paredo, "this guy here is hypovolemic from blood loss. If we don't transfuse now, he is going to crash."

Major Goldstein interrupts, "Private Sovia bring me two units of clotting agent right now. "

Maria looks to Captain Smith's patient, lying with his chest cracked wide open on the operating table. She looks to Dr. Sovia who confidently looks back at her. She turns to her assistant and says, "Sergeant Douglas monitor my patient." Maria runs to the abandoned patient whose blood pressure monitor is beeping crazily and begins working on him.

Major Goldstein injects himself into the process again, "Sorry I can't help you Captain Paredo, my guy here is Imminent Critical. Sovia! Bring me that clotting agent now!" Major Goldstein 's voice appears more slurred. He wobbles a bit on his feet then recovers while his patient's blood pressure monitor begins beeping faster.

Nurse Anesthetist Judy Tonas is monitoring Major Goldstein's patient, "Blood pressure dropping Doctor". Major Goldstein turns quickly back to his patient then spins back around, lifts his mask up and vomits violently on the floor.

Sergeant Douglas yells out, "Sovia! Get that cleaned up!" Major Goldstein keels over face first onto the floor. The patient's blood pressure monitor is screaming.

Dr. Paredo sees the unfolding catastrophe and attempts to take command. "Nurse Cruz", she yells out, "Get over there and look at the patient".

Lieutenant/Nurse Christina Cruz, twenty-six years old, leaves Dr. Paredo's patient and moves to Dr. Goldstein's patient to help. "Oh my god", Christina cries out, "It's a mess in here! I don't know what to do".

Dr. Paredo yells from across the O.R., "Nurse Cruz, I can't get there right now, do your best to stop the bleeding.

Christina Cruz screams over the beeping of the machines, "I've never done this!"

"Blood pressure is dropping", Nurse Anesthetist Judy announces, "we're losing him".

Dr. Sovia, now standing over the Dr. Goldstein's patient makes a frank yet loud assessment, "He is going into Cardiac Dysrhythmia, he'll be dead in thirty seconds. The other surgical teams gawk at Dr. Sovia as he rips his latex gloves off and puts on a fresh pair and moves in to the patient. "Nurse Cruz", he barks, "Get the Cardiac Stimulator! Nurse Tonas, administer 10 CCs of Epinephrine right now!"

"Sovia", Nurse Cruz exclaims, "What are you doing?"

"Somebody get me two units of plasma right now!" Dr. Sovia yells aloud to no one in particular. "Nurse Cruz, give me the forceps and number 2 clamp.

Sergeant Douglas chimes in from across the room, "Sovia back away from that patient!" Dr. Sovia ignores him and sticks his hands into the patient's chest cavity and begins working.

Without looking up, he speaks very loudly over the chaos, "Captain Paredo, we are down two surgeons. This man will die in seconds if I don't stem the bleeding. I've done this procedure fifty times. Are you ordering me to let him die? Dr. Sovia looks over his shoulder at Captain Paredo. "Captain Paredo shall I stop?"

Captain Paredo looks to her previous patient, "Sergeant Douglas, how's my guy doing?"

Across the room Sergeant Douglas checks the monitor on the patient, "Stable ma'am", he replies. "Sovia is you hearin the Captain?! Get the fuck away from-"

"Sergeant Douglas!" Maria cuts him off mid-sentence, shaking her head no at her assistant. Dr. Sovia keeps working on his patient.

"Sovia!" Sergeant Douglas calls out why slamming equipment, "yo ass in a lot a trouble boy!"

Without looking up from his patient, Dr. Sovia responds, "I'm sure you're right Sergeant. Suction here Nurse Cruz".

Sunlight illuminates the first 30 feet of the cave entrance buried underneath the compound. Beyond that the cave grows black. The Special Forces are searching for intelligence or equipment left behind by the Taliban. Lance is pacing back and forth waving his hands incredulously.

"What do you mean they're gone?" Lance questions his Chief Warrant Officer.

"I mean they are gone, vanished, beamed the fuck out of here", Chief M calmly replies.

"Yeah I get that Mike, but how the fuck did we lose them. This was supposed to be a cakewalk here. I mean this is a big score here, this is my ticket to Field Grade Officer." Lance replies.

"I know" says Chief M.

"And you…. Chief Warrant… Something or other.

"Chief Warrant Four", replies Chief M as he

rubs his head, "yes I know".

"Well we ain't gettin promoted if we can't fucking find them. Can't we pick them up on the drone Chief?"

Chief M shakes his head no, "No drone coverage today. Bad weather at Kandahar Airfield."

"You gotta be shittin me!" Lance kicks over a nearby box.

"Bad guys had trucks, you're standing on tire tracks right now."

"How about the Satellite?" quips Lance, "Is it raining in space?"

Standing among the American troops is a man wearing a native Afghan Turban and shirt along with military style pants and boots. Walid Noor, twenty-nine years old, with old man eyes and a long black beard steps forward. Walid was a teenager when the Russians finally left Afghanistan. Lucky enough to have been spared the horrors of the Russian invasion, he was not lucky enough to escape the terror of the Taliban. Those fundamentalist Muslims wanted to return to the sixth century and brutally punished anyone who did not subscribe to their interpretation of the Koran.

Walid was at teenager when he watched a group of the Taliban religious police publicly whip his mother for not covering her hair and being outside without a male relative. The same Taliban came back a week later and dragged his father outside and shot him for not paying the fine for his wife's crimes. His mother died a short time later and Walid joined the Northern Alliance's rebellion against the Taliban. When the American Special Forces showed up in early 2002 he leapt at the chance to work with them and never quit.

"I have my local militia searching, setting check points on the road", said Walid Noor.

"Thanks Walid, those guys work great on short notice."

"And my network of spies is calling everywhere. We will find them, I assure you," Walid proudly announces.

Lance turns back to Chief M. "Good work, Mike, Any word on Craig?"

"Medevac flew him to the hospital three hours ago. I'll check his status. Higher command really fucked us on this Lance."

Lance turns sharply at his Chief, "What are

you talking about?"

"No one up at headquarters even knows about the hostages." The Chief says, "Special Forces Group Command wants this kept quiet as possible."

Lance turns directly to his men, "does anybody here have any fucking suggestions of how to find these people?"

Chief M rubs his chin and looks towards Lance, "What was the name of the tribal elder who owns this place?"

When the girls were kidnapped two days earlier, the local Afghans who were honestly working with the American women, reported the abduction immediately to the village elders, who reported it to a relative of someone working in the new Afghan government. They were working high up in the Afghan government. So important was this matter that the new President of Afghanistan was briefed within hours while only a handful of government workers knew of the kidnapping. The President of Afghanistan wanted this handled quietly and as quickly as possible. If they, the Afghan government could get the girls back within a day or two, it could all be explained away as a cultural misunderstanding. No one need know the wiser. Especially since their American patrons were now sending billions of US dollars directly into Afghanistan. Giant stacks of US dollars, shrink wrapped in plastic and unloaded from giant cargo planes by forklifts were a daily occurrence at the Kabul airport. This was like a fairytale for the corrupt Afghan politicians and especially the Afghan President, who got to control it all. Well almost all of it. He had to dole out quite a bit to his closest aides and supporters who in turn doled it out to their closest aides and supporters and so on and so forth down the line. This is the way life had gone on in Afghanistan for the past three thousand years. Since before Alexander the Great, yet another conqueror, brought his country's culture to Afghanistan.

The President of Afghanistan new the right man to turn to. Imran Khan could be trusted to quietly handle the exchange of ransom for the hostages. He knew the right people to turn to. There was a problem though, this information could never be trusted with is security services or his Army. Not only were those cops and soldiers corrupt to the very last man, they were incompetent. And besides, intelligence leaked out of those organizations so fast, the kidnappers would know of any rescue plans before he, the President of Afghanistan would know. This was unacceptable. Not if he wanted this solved quickly and quietly.

"Now what was the name of that Special Forces Officer who I rode along with in the battles with the Taliban?" the President thought to himself. "McKenna," was the name President said again to himself. He would call McKenna and HE would have a team of soldiers quickly and quietly assembled. The President of Afghanistan picked up the phone to his secretary, "Get a message to Imran Khan I want him to call me, no, ask Imran Khan to please call me it is important. And put a call in to that Special Forces Officer in the American section, I need him quickly."

Inside the darkened interior of a cargo truck, a group of men in Afghan garb sit across from six blindfolded women with their hands and feet tied by rope. Other Afghan men hog tie their new captive Imran Khan. Kelly Roberts, twenty-three years old, tries to get her captors attention.

"Hello. HELLO! Can we get some water," yells Kelly. "We are thirsty. PLEASE!"

An Afghan man, sitting nearby, kicks her in the legs and mumbles something in Pashtun. Baraat Mansoor sitting a few feet away peaking out of the canvas cover of the truck, takes notice of the abuse.

"Abdul! Don't kick them!" Baraat says in Pashtun, "God willing, they are more valuable unharmed and at least… healthy looking." The young man who kicked them is Abdul Karzai, thirty-one years old, he shoots his boss Baraat a dirty look. Baraat is a man not to be trifled with.

"Mind your look!" screams Baraat, "You work for me! Give our guests some water. NOW!" Abdul pours some water from a bottle onto Kelly's face. Baraat has some sense of decorum and manners he learned from living in British society. He comes to her aid in English so his men will not know what he is saying.

"Please forgive my friend. He is in dire need of a lesson in manners," Baraat politely says to Kelly in gentile British accented English.

"Yours aren't so great yourself mister," Kelly barks out in her mid-western American dialect.

Baraat stares intently and silently at the captured girls.

The four heavily armed Humvee's of Operational Detachment Alpha (ODA 666) slowly drive with their headlights off. They come down the mountain road and take up tactical positions at a giant walled compound. Lance exits his vehicle and knocks on the solid metal gate.

"Hello. I need to speak to Mr. Masoud Mansoor!" shouts Captain Lance Erikson. No answer at the gate causes Lance to bang a steel Haligan bar, (a type of crowbar) over and over again against the gate. Lights begin to go on inside the massive stone home. The gate door opens and an Afghan man, Mansoor's Manservant, fifty years old, stands waiting.

"Good evening, my name is Captain Lance Erickson, US Army Special Forces. I'm here to see Masoud Mansoor. I don't have an appointment." Lance smiles as the Manservant stares back and then speaks Punjabi into a cell phone.

"Yes, sir, I will escort him in," says the Manservant into the phone. He smiles at Lance and switches back to English with a slight British accent, "right this way Captain."

The Manservant leads Lance down a long set of stone stairs and into a room resembling a modern western hospital with bright fluorescent lights that illuminate a sterile medical exam room. There is a young Afghan girl of about thirteen years old. Her mother is trying to comfort her, but the young girl's face registers pain. A tall broad shouldered bearded Afghan man dressed in a mix of Pashtun and western clothes stands up from a chair and looks directly into Lance's eyes. Masoud Mansoor, fifty years old, is a commanding presence.

Lance looks straight in his eyes, "Good evening sir." Lance instinctively stands straighter as if subconsciously coming to attention for a superior officer.

"What brings you to my humble abode at this late hour Captain?" Masoud asks.

"I watched your brother Baraat kidnap the future Vice President of Afghanistan today."

Masoud stares blankly at Lance and ponders

the question. "What a wonder democracy is, the US Government already knows who the winner of the next election will be."

"I am not interested in your internal political conflicts sir," Lance responds forcefully.

Masoud glares intensely at Lance and replies, "I am. I am very interested in our politics." Lance stares at Masoud for a beat trying to size him up. Lance knows this man not only controls crime, vice and smuggling but also local politicians.

"Mr. Mansoor," Lance continues taking a softer tone, "Imran Khan was on a mission of peace today, bringing a ransom to save six young women."

Masoud Mansoor looks at Lance suspiciously, "Go on," he replies.

"Six young women who came to your country to help Afghans," Lance continues, "as part of an international aid organization, who were kidnapped two days ago."

Masoud gestures to the young woman lying on the exam table, writhing in pain. "As you can see I am trying to save one young Afghan woman right now. My daughter Ameena, she is only thirteen years old."

Her mother, holding the girl's hands, rushes to cover the girls head with a burka.

"She looks like she needs a doctor sir," says Lance.

Masoud looks at his daughter, "she has been ill for days and our doctor was killed in one of your coalition bomb strikes while treating children in a village."

I am sorry for your loss Mr. Mansoor. Masoud turns and stares at Lance, seemingly looking for a lie in his eyes.

"Are you now?" Masoud asks sarcastically as he looks back at his daughter who has pulled the burka off her face and grimaces in pain.

"Sir, I have two of the greatest medics the US Army has ever produced," Lance proudly boasts. "Can I have my men examine your daughter?"

"One medic will do young Captain."

Lance looks at the Warlord silently for a moment, then squeezes and speaks into a small microphone on his chest. "Ritchie pick up."

The US Army is a big machine. In order for any hierarchal organization to remain operationally efficient, there must exist the strictest of standards. Those standards are drilled into young soldiers in their first thirteen weeks of basic training. After that and for the rest of their careers, the people that control the soldier's lives, the Non-Commissioned-Officers or NCOs as they are called, reinforce those values, daily if not hourly. This dedication to uniformity is reminiscent of McDonalds, where a Big Mac in New York City tastes the same as a Big Mac in Kansas City. In other words, the soldiers, like the burgers are all the same. This system of uniformity and lack of individuality at first seems an anathema to Americans including young American soldiers. The soldiers either adapt or they are out. After a long enough time, that system of conformity becomes like a security blanket to the majority of enlisted troops and NCOs. Highly intelligent or well educated soldiers typically have the hardest time adopting to Army uniformity.

The US Army Special Forces traditionally attracted those soldiers who despise conformity. Not merely conformity in their uniform standards but in the way that wars are fought. Special Forces, started in the 1960's were the best of the best soldiers who trained to do the jobs no one else could. Because of this exceptionalism, Special Forces units were afforded some measure of autonomy from the mainstream Army. This environment bred independent thinkers at all levels of the Special Forces community.

Each member of an Operational Detachment Alpha, or ODA, (formerly an "A-Team" in the Vietnam era), is a super highly trained specialist in their areas of expertise. An ODA consists of 12 men, One Captain to lead, one Chief Warrant officer as a second in command and ten Sergeants. Two Sergeants who were Weapons experts, two who were Engineer/Demolition experts, two Communications experts, two intelligence experts and two who were the Medical experts.

Sergeant First Class Ritchie Long, thirty years old, of Lance's ODA 666 is one of the Medical experts on the team. Special Forces Medical Sergeant, known as 18 Deltas, are the most highly skilled military medics in the known world. They are not Medical Doctors, but very close to it. They were required to have the highest of test scores of all the Army just to qualify for the school. Fort Sam Houston in Texas, was where they spent eighteen very long and hard months to complete the complex and rigorous course which ended in a several month stint working in the local trauma hospital to learn and treat real world gunshot wounds.

Ritchie is pointing his weapon out and away from the Fortress of Masoud Mansoor along with the other Special Forces soldiers of ODA 666 when he hears Lance's call for him in his helmet mounted radio. He squeezes his radio button and speaks into his helmet mounted microphone; "Yeah Lance, go for Ritchie."

A woman and two children sit on a couch with their arms tied behind their back screaming. A little girl cries out "Papa Papa". Shots ring out, the shots are suddenly replaced by the sound of banging on a door.

Dr. Sovia wakes up and sits up straight in his bunk in his trailer breathing and sweating heavily. The pounding on his door gets louder. He stumbles out of bed and opens his trailer door. Sergeant Douglas stands outside in the dimly lit compound.

"Sovia! Get yo cleanest uniform on an get yo

ass over to Major Goldstein's office at 0500 hours. Roger that?!"

"Roger that Sergeant," Dr. Sovia glumly replies "yes Sergeant. Sergeant Douglas looks contemptuously at Dr. Sovia and walks off into the darkness. Dr. Sovia closes his door and goes to his laptop computer, attempts to Skype his kids. There is no answer.

Back at Masoud Mansoor's stone fortress, Lance &Masoud stare at each other in uncomfortable silence facing away from the exam table. Sergeant Ritchie Long, one of ODA 666's medical experts is examining Ameena Mansoor with the help of her mother.

Masoud Mansoor had been suspicious of the American Army since before they invaded his country. He turns to Lance "And what does any of this kidnapping business have to do with me Captain?"

"Earlier today your brother Baraat, reneged on a deal to exchange the kidnapped girls for money. Instead, he and his men kidnapped Imran Khan and then he killed his own man who brokered the deal."

"I had heard he was your man," quips Masoud.

Lance pauses a minute to absorb what he just heard. Lance had met personally with Aasif Ahmad, the walk-in informant who was killed earlier today. "How had they uncovered Ahmad? Was Masoud Mansoor in on it?" Lance wondered. With Masoud's comment, Lance was certain the Warlord at least know about Ahmad's betrayal.

Lance takes a breath, hoping Masoud cannot see his nerves bursting at the seams Lance states, "Nothing happens in this area without your knowledge sir, if not at least your tacit approval."

"You think too much of me."

Lance smiles, "your brother works for you, no?"

"All Afghan tribes work together," Masoud replies coyly.

Lance begins acting annoyed. "So, perhaps you see why I am drawing a connection between your brother, you, a kidnapped Afghani Elder and our missing girls."

Masoud, ever the businessman smells an opportunity. He pauses to think then looks directly at Lance. "So I am hearing you were looking to acquire one hard to get item. And now you are looking to acquire two hard to get items. Is this correct?"

"Yes, Lance replies, well seven items actually."

Masoud smiles at the young Captain. "And you know I am a business man and sometimes can put together buyers and sellers of hard to obtain items."

"That a very diplomatic way of describing yourself Mister Mansoor." Masoud stares and does not answer. Lance breaks the silence. "Yes I would like very much to obtain these hard to get items, the six Americans and one Tribal Elder."

"I can assure you I do not have them. But I believe I could get them for you," said Masoud.

Lance takes on a serious look and retorts, "Like your brother got the six girls for Imran Khan?"

Masoud glares hard at the Captain. "I am not my brother Captain. Do not make the mistake of confusing us."

Ameena moans in the background and Ritchie interrupts. "Boss, Mr. Mansoor, you can turn around now. She has an acute appendicitis and it is aggravated."

Masoud looks puzzled. "This means?"

"She has got to get to a hospital," replies Ritchie, "she has to have surgery."

"This is something you can do?" asks Masoud.

"Sorry, above my pay grade sir," replies Ritchie.

Masoud raises an eyebrow questioningly, Lance looks to Masoud. "Special Forces Medics are trained for gunshot wounds and trauma, but this situation requires an actual surgeon at a hospital." Lance explains. "Sir we can have her on a Medevac helicopter in thirty minutes, and in surgery within an hour."

As powerful as a Warlord he was Masoud knew the lessons of history. Any leader only has his power because his subordinates keep him in power. Part of maintaining that was keeping up appearances and that meant, absolutely no visible cooperation with the occupiers. As much as he loved his daughter, he could not be seen bringing his daughter to the Americans. He shakes his head no and says, "no. I will not bring my daughter to a coalition hospital. We will drive her to Kandahar hospital."

Ritchie, ever the conscientious medic argues against this, "Mr. Masoud I strongly urge you NOT to do that. That appendicitis is ready to burst. Any long trip could cause it to rupture and she will die."

Masoud ponders for a moment and responds, "I will have a surgeon brought here. "

"Mr. Mansoor, with the recent kidnappings, increased coalition and Taliban activity, getting a surgeon through all the check points and Taliban ambushes, just won't work."

Masoud takes a minute to think. "I told you I cannot, I will not bring her to a Coalition hospital."

"What if I brought a surgeon to you?"

The girl on the exam table winces in pain and her mother, Mrs. Mansoor, forty-five years old, holds her tightly and speaks up in Pashtun, "you had better get my daughter help."

Masoud answers her in Pashtun, "can't you see I am doing that now."

"Do it faster, you and all your money and power!" Mrs. Mansoor berates her husband in Pashtun. "You had better-"

"Quiet woman!" Masoud yells back in Pashtun. Mrs. Masoud complies and is silent.

Masoud turns back to Lance, "you can get a surgeon here?"

"Yes sir I can."

Masoud Mansoor extends his hand to Lance's. "I will get you your hostages Captain, only if you save her. We have a deal?"

"We have a deal," Lance says as he shakes Masoud's hand. "We will save her."

Masoud's tone turns serious, "If she dies, we have no deal." Lance nods in agreement.

The sun has not yet risen over the mountains of Afghanistan. Dr. Sovia's boots crunch along the crushed concrete that makes up the ground of the medical base. He approaches the Command building and walks inside. He is greeted by the unit's senior enlisted man, First Sergeant Ron Hebblewaithe, forty-four years old. The First Sergeant or "Top" as most First Sergeants are called, is on his twenty seventh year in the Army. He knows Army regulations backwards and forwards and like most lifers, he earns his keep by advising his commander what they can and cannot get away with legally. Top Hebblewaithe has seen young punk soldiers come and go. Few, if any, measure up to his standards to make the Army a career. For Top, it is a calling where only warriors need apply. Top, like many senior enlisted men, has never been in combat. No, for lifers like Top, successfully navigating the maze of rules, regulations, deployments, inspections and promotion broads are the keys to a successful career and healthy retirement package. Three more years to retirement and no little Mexican wetback was going to rock the boat.

"Stand over here and wait for instructions," Top Hebblewaithe barks at Dr. Sovia. "NO! Over here! Do you not see where I am pointing soldier? Is it fucking impossible for you fucking people to follow fucking instructions?"

Dr. Sovia stands before the desk of Major Goldstein the Commanding Officer of the 313th

Forward Surgical Team. Top Hebblewaithe takes up his position standing to the side of the Major looking like an attack dog. Also in the room is Dr./Captain Maria Paredo and Sergeant Doug Douglas who is staring lovingly of an Army poster of the Green Berets. Major Goldstein sits behind his desk with a swollen lip and bruised face from last night's face-plant.

Major Goldstein barely looks at Dr. Sovia when he calls out his name and rank, "Private Roberto Sovia."Dr. Sovia stands a bit straighter when he hears the authority in Major Goldstein's voice as he reads off a sheet of paper. "You are hereby charged under the Uniform Code of Military Justice with willfully disobeying a direct order from a commissioned officer, dereliction of duty, and damage to government property.

Dr. Sovia attempts to speak, "Sir I-"

"Shut your fucking pie hole Private," barks Top.

Major Goldstein puts the paper down on his desk, "It's not you Sovia, it's your attitude."

Dr. Sovia tries again, "Sir I-

Top jumps in Dr. Sovia's face, "What part of

shut your fuckin pie hole do you not understand? Is it the language barrier Sovia? Should I get a spic interpreter in here?"

"I think I understand just fine Top."

Major Goldstein picks up the papers off his desk and commences his speech, "No Sovia, I don't think you do. Stop talking, you are charged with crimes. You have the right to remain silent."

Dr. Sovia puts his hands to his head crying out, "what? What? Oh this isn't happening!

"Shut the fuck up Sovia," Top barks.

Major Goldstein continues reading off his papers, "anything you say may be used against you at a Courts Martial. An attorney from the Judge Advocate General or JAG Corp. will be provided to defend you."

Dr. Sovia looks around the room for a friendly face or an ear to listen to his cries for help. "This can't be happening," he says to no one in particular.

Major Goldstein looks up to Dr. Sovia from his papers, "Oh it is happening Private Sovia. You are remanded to custody and confined to your housing unit."

"That doesn't sound too bad," says Dr. Sovia.

Major Goldstein continues, "a detail of Military Police will arrive later today to transport you to Kandahar Airfield where you will be held in a detention facility to await trial."

Dr. Sovia's mouth hangs open, his eyes begin to tear. "Oh that sounds bad."

Major Goldstein turns to his attack dog. "First Sergeant, he's all yours."

First Sergeant Hebblewaithe smiles as he produces a pair of shiny handcuffs and slaps them on Dr. Sovia's wrists. "Just in case you didn't believe this is happening," top gloats as he speaks. The First Sergeant pulls Dr. Sovia by the cuffs out of the office.

Dr. Sovia begins to resist and react, "I saved that man yester-"

Maria steps forward and pleads, "Major Goldstein, this is wrong. I was there, Sovia asked me if he should stop."

Sergeant Douglas jumps into the conversation. Ahh told him ta stop suh, he din listen.

Both Major Goldstein and Maria react, "Shut up Sergeant!

"That's right," Dr. Sovia adds, "I did ask Dr. Paredo if she wanted me to stop and let that man die."

Major Goldstein slams his hands and papers down on his desk. "All of you shut up! Captain Paredo, Sergeant Douglas you will accompany the Military Police to Kandahar later today where you will give your statements to the Judge Advocate General's office while your memories are still fresh."

"This is ridiculous! I saved that man last night. And now you are Court Martialing me?"

The First Sergeant tugs hard on Dr. Sovia's handcuffs, "Shut up Sovia! Let's go."

"I can't get thrown out of the Army," Dr. Sovia now yelling, "I can't go back to Mexico. I can't go back!"

The First Sergeant forcibly drags Dr. Sovia by his cuffs back to his housing trailer and roughly pushes him inside. "This is no way to treat a man," Dr. Sovia says to the First Sergeant.

Top looks at him with contempt. "I'm posting a guard outside your trailer. Do not even THINK about leaving."

Dr. Sovia stands in the door of his trailer, his hands still cuffed in front of him. He yells out to Top who is now walking away, "In a war zone?! You're leaving me hand cuffed in a fucking war zone?"

The First Sergeant walks away leaving Dr. Sovia standing alone. "Fuck you spic!"

Dr. Sovia, hands cuffed, stands alone in his trailer door. "Shit," he says as he closes his trailer door and opens his laptop. The face of an eight-year old girl we saw earlier in his dream, fills the computer screen.

"Hello my baby," Dr. Sovia puts on his best daddy voice, "I miss you.

Ariana Sovia, eight years old, looks at her father through the computer screen and kisses him. "Papa, Papa. I miss you too Papa. When are you coming home?" The little girl kisses her computer screen again.

"Nine more months pumpkin, I keep telling you daddy went to Afghanistan for one year."

"I miss you daddy!" she says, "come home."The face of an adolescent boy, Dr. Sovia's son Alberto, thirteen years old fills the computer screen.

"Hey pop."

Dr. Sovia replies, "why are you guys up this late?"

"It's Saturday Pop."

Dr. Sovia rubs his face, "Ahhh...I forget the days lately. Put Nana on. I've got grown up things to say."

On the computer screen, Alberto Sovia turns away and yells out, "Nana! Ven aqui por favor." The face of Dr. Sovia's mother in law, Valeria Torres, fifty-one years old, fills the computer screen.

"Donde? Donde", Alberto ayuda me! Young Alberto tries to help his grandmother use the computer to speak to Dr. Sovia.

"Here nana, no here. Look here," Alberto shows his grandmother where on the computer to look.

In Spanish Valeria speaks to her son-in-law,

"Roberto, there you are."

"Mama, everyone's paperwork is ok?" says Dr. Sovia over the Skype. "Everyone's got their permanent resident cards now?"

"Si, joining the Yankee Army was very smart."

"How are you holding up Mama?"

"I miss my daughter Roberto."

"I miss her too mama. I miss her everyday... Any word from Diego?"

Valeria's face takes a serious tone. "My husband says the hunt for you is hotter than ever, it's been more than a year now. I don't know what you did to make the Rosa family hate you so."

"You're being careful right Mama? No late night phone calls to Diego when you are lonely? Only call from the call center downtown."

"Yes I know all about it, they use the satellite system, bounce calls over the earth so they can't tell the calls are coming from Texas."

Dr. Sovia breaths a sigh of relief, "good," he says.

"I use the prepaid phone cards Roberto, we've been through this Roberto. I am not going to let them find us. I did not even tell Diego where we are."

"Eight more months and I get my US citizenship. After that we can never be deported back."

"I know, why are you telling me this?"

Dr. Sovia pauses, looks down, looks back up. "My pride... might have screwed things up... at work."

Valeria's face drops, "again? ...How bad this time?"

"I don't know right now... I'm so tired of screwing things up mama."

Valeria collects herself and glares straight into the camera. "Roberto... You know it was not your fault they killed her... You do know that... right?"

"I gotta go mama."Dr. Sovia closes the laptop, holds his head in his hands.

The four Humvees of Operational Detachment Alpha 666, (ODA 666) roll down an Afghan dirt road. Lance is in the front passenger seat, looking at two computer screens and talking into the radio handset.

"Don't give me that Bullshit! This is an A-1 priority operation. I need that surgeon standing by in twenty minutes."

A voice comes back over the radio, "that's a negative Red Rhino. Higher authority says no-go on your request."

"No, no, NO!" Lance yells into the radio handset, "this is flagged as A-1 priority. This has to be turned down by the Group Commander."

"Sorry Red Rhino," says the Radio Voice, "all I know is what data they put before me."

Lance rubs his face in frustration and tries again, "contact Group Commander McKenna. Colonel Kevin McKenna!"

"Sorry again," says the Radio Voice, "Group Commander is away for the next few days."

"Then get it to his god damned deputy!"

"Deputy is also away," says the Radio Voice, "cannot proceed with your request for surgical team without higher command's approval. Sorry."

Lance throws the radio handset across the Humvee and screams, "Fuuuuuukkk!!"Lance pulls the wire until he gets the handset back in his hand then changes the frequency on the radio. "Mike did you hear all that?"

Chief Mike Mastronardi in the passenger seat of his Humvee as it speeds along. He presses the radio handset to his head. "I heard it Lance. Just our good goddamn luck!"

"Fucking Army Bureaucracy," says Lance over the radio, "everything is so fucking classified no one can work together."

Chief M answers into his radio handset, "it's a wonder how we fight a war."

Lance takes a breath and speaks into his radio handset, "I mean this is an A1 Priority Mission. Where is our support?"

"It's all in Iraq, they've put all of our resources there for now. It's like Afghanistan is the red headed step child of war, no one wants to pay attention to us. Hey don't feel bad, it's also classified at the highest level Lance. If they ever got word of whose daughter it is they kidnapped, we'd never get her back."

Lance looks at the map on his laptop computer, "where in hell is that hospital Craig is at. We gotta get a surgeon fast."

In a sterile looking operating room, clearly not military, a team of doctors and nurses, all dressed in surgical scrubs and caps, work feverishly on a patient. A nurse wipes the sweat away from Dr. Sovia's brow. Suddenly automatic gunfire erupts in the operating room. Several of the surgical staff are instantly shredded from machine gun fire, blood sprays everywhere. The sound of staccato gunfire becomes a rapid knocking on a door.

Dr. Sovia wakes up into to a sitting position in his bed in his housing trailer. He is breathing hard and sweating profusely. He hears the sound of the knocking on his trailer door. He gets up, walks to the door and opens it to find Captain/Dr. Maria Paredo holding a white plastic bag.

"Hi.... I... ah, saw the First Sergeant drag you away. I thought you might be... hungry." Maria holds up the white plastic bag.

Dr. Sovia still breathing hard stares, rubs his face with his still cuffed hands and takes it. "Yes. I am hungry, thank you Ma'am."

Maria stands at his door in silence.

Dr. Sovia realizes her lingering presence, he asks awkwardly, "was there anything else Ma'am?"

"...Ah, yeah, can we talk?"

"Oh... Yeah, ahh. Yeah, of course. Please come in Ma'am."

Maria looks around at the Spartan settings as she enters the tiny housing trailer. "Wow, they don't give you a lot of room, do they?"

"I guess it's meant to prepare me for my jail cell."

Maria cracks a smile at his joke then asks, "May I sit?"

Lance's Humvee comes through the security

gate entrance to the base. A nervous young soldier is working the gate, checking IDs.

"Hey soldier, where can I find the commander of this outfit?"

The Nervous Soldier pauses for a second while staring at the bearded men and their strange clothing holding military IDs.

"Hey Joe!" Lance puts on his commander voice, "I asked you a question."

The nervous soldier points towards some trailers, "Ahh, Major Goldstein sir, you can find him back by those trailers." The Humvees drive through the checkpoint into the base.

Back in Dr. Sovia's trailer, Maria sits across from him eating his breakfast. "I am not used to being so familiar with commissioned officers... Ma'am," says Dr. Sovia.

"Sovia, I... I feel partly to blame for this... I fought with Major Goldstein not to charge you. Dr. Sovia eyes her up and down. "It's not decided yet,"

Maria says trying to raise his spirits, "a trial will-"

"No doubt convict me of some bull shit charge Doctor," Dr. Sovia interrupts Maria. "I saved that man's life last night." Dr. Sovia talks while swallowing his food.

"I know. But they are still charging you with a crime," Maria says woefully, "you were counseled more than once about exceeding your medical authority."

"And why do you think that is?" the anger growing in Dr. Sovia's voice, "because I'm Mexican? I am an illegal alien, a border jumper?"

"You're a Private. A lowly Army Private and you saved the day where commissioned officers could not. And they will crucify you for it."

Dr. Sovia hangs his head. Without looking up he speaks. "So I'm fucked. I went into the Medical Corps so I could help save people."

"Why not join as a Doctor?" asks Maria.

Dr. Sovia looks up sharply, "Your American Medical Association has a lock on who gets to be a Medical Doctor in the US. Have to graduate from an American Medical Association recognized school, mostly in the states."

"Yes I know."

"Protects their monopoly from those pesky low wage Mexican doctors coming to steal American jobs."

Maria looks away for a bit, and then turns to him, "so tell me, how is a surgeon from Mexico a Private in the US Army?" Dr. Sovia stares at Maria from across the desk.

CHAPTER 3

ONE YEAR EARLIER

Guatemala, 2003

The morning heat was nearly unbearable when combined with the humidity and lack of breeze in the thick Guatemalan jungle. The villagers were accustomed to the heat and bore it no mind and went about their lives. What they could not ignore were the aches and pains they accumulated along the way from years of hard labor, poor diet and non-existent medical care.

When rumor of a visiting team of doctors began floating around few of them believed it real. When the doctors finally arrived and started treating injured, sick and suffering villagers, the doctors were revered like gods.

Inside one of the portable surgical tents, the doctors brought with them, a team of masked and surgically dressed doctors and nurses are operating on a patient. Dr. Roberto Sovia, thirty-three, is the lead surgeon, "suction here please," Dr. Sovia points to something inside the patient. His colleague Dr. Kathy Deutche, thirty-one years old, applies the suction as the smashingly handsome Dr. Sovia ordered. "No, here to the left," he says as he moves the tube himself.

Dr. Sovia takes his time and is patient with his peer, though her face is masked, his gaze exceedingly falls on her amazing eyes. "Sorry," she says.

"No need to be sorry. Todos Buenos," Dr. Sovia says while making his eyes wide with a smile. "It's all good Kathy."

"I've never seen it done that way Doctor."

"Really?" Dr. Sovia smiles with pride

underneath his surgical mask.

"No, really," Kathy goes on, "that was amazing, how did you know that the bleeding was coming from that section of the Aorta?"

"I've seen it before doctor," Dr. Sovia says, "the Arterial bleeding was inconsistent with normative discharge. It could only have been the Ventricular Passage."

"Amazing," replies Kathy.

"Now just suture that up and then you can close Dr. Deutche." One of the monitoring machines starts making a beeping sound that grows faster and faster.

"I didn't touch anything," says Kathy.

Dr. Frank Hendenberg, forty-one years old, an anesthesiologist is monitoring the patient frantically looks at his devices. "I have not altered any mixtures on his sedation"

"What is his pressure?" asks Dr. Sovia while exploring the body cavity.

"Dropping fast Doctor," replies Frank.

"Give him 10cc of Epinephrine," says Dr.

Sovia, "we've got to get his pressure back up fast."

"Goin in now," says Frank Hendenberg as he begins administering the injection.

"What can I do Doctor?" asks Kathy. Dr. Sovia locks eyes with her for a beat. Before anyone can answer a massive explosion can be heard and suddenly sunlight flashes into the operating room as part of the tent is ripped away.

Dr. Sovia yells out to anyone that will obey, "Holy Christ! Get that flap back up, we have germs and dust coming in."

Kathy looks over her shoulder, clearly frightened asks, "what was that? Before anyone can answer the sound of gunshots ring out and additional rays of sun are cast into the operating room from bullet holes now in the tent's roof flaps.

Dr. Hendenberg quickly ducks behind his anesthesia gear and nervously yells out, "Holy shit. We are being shot at!"

Dr. Sovia remains calm and says, "Kathy keep exploring for where he is bleeding from, he's not losing pressure for nothing."

"On it," she replies and continues to explore

inside the patient's open body.

Dr. Sovia looks at one of the surgical nurses standing next to Dr. Deutche, "nurse, get a pint of blood and a pint of blood expander started on him right now." The gunfire outside grows.

Dr. Hendenberg looks up from behind the perceived safety of his anesthesia gear and asks, "what the Hell is going on out there? Anybody? Tell me something."

Dr. Bush, forty-nine years old and the oldest doctor on the team and not currently in surgery runs into the operating room from outside and announces, "It's the rebels. They are attacking the village."

"What fucking rebels?" yells out Dr. Hendenberg, "I thought the rebellion ended."

Dr. Bush looking back over his shoulder spins back to the doctors operating, "well maybe it's the gangs, who the Hell knows in this place." Outside commands can be heard from soldiers along with an increase in the volume of gunfire. A truck is heard racing by just as a whole half of the surgical tent's side flaps are ripped off as the truck speeds by. The whole Operating room is now cast in sunlight. Dust pours in.

Dr. Sovia takes command of the situation and yell out, "everybody get in here and lean over this patient! We have an open chest cavity. I'll be damned if we lose this guy to an infection."

Dr. Hendenberg steps back from his anesthesia equipment looking consumed with fear, "screw this," he says with contempt, "I did not sign up for this!"

Dr. Sovia ignores him and continues to compel his colleagues to help, "lean in here everybody," orders Dr. Sovia and the Doctors and Surgical nurses lean in their clean scrubs over the patient's body to protect him.

Still standing away from the operating table, Dr. Bush cries out, "I'm with Frank folks. We gotta get outta here."

A Guatemalan Army officer, Captain Moreno, steps in to the Operating Room through the now open tent and politely announces, "hello doctors. We love you for helping but you must go. NOW!"

Dr. Bush standing next to the Captain implores him for information, "what the hell is going on out there?"

Captain Moreno calmly answers, "shooting, lots of it."

"Shooting by who?" screams Dr. Bush.

Captain Moreno reacts with the calmness of a man who has done this before, "could be drug gangs," the Captain says, "could be leftovers from the civil war."

Dr. Hendenberg begins walking away from the Operating Table and is pulling off his surgical gloves and says, "hey folks, I volunteered to come down here and donate my time to help you people, not go into combat."

"Frank we could really use you over here right now," says Dr. Sovia. "We found the bleeding but it's going take some time to stop it." More gunfire is heard and Dr. Bush looks at Dr. Hendenberg and shakes his head no and begins to walk away. Soldiers outside the tent are now running the opposite direction they were running just a few minutes ago, they're running away.

Suddenly Captain Moreno sounds more serious, "Doctors, things are happening quickly. We must go. Now."

Gunfire nearby grows in frequency and Dr.

Sovia does not look up from the patient as he loudly announces to all, "go if you must. Dr. Deutche just hold that clamp for 30 more seconds while I suture."

"I hear you Doctor," Kathy bravely responds, "I've got it. And I'm not leaving."

Dr. Sovia glances with one eye up at Dr. Deutche. Dr. Hendenberg looks at them working on the patient. Another explosion can be heard to close for comfort. Dr. Hendenberg shakes from the explosion, looks outside and the action then looks back at the patient. "Son of a bitch I'm gonna regret this," says Dr. Hendenberg as he returns to the operating table and puts on a fresh set of surgical gloves, "All right where are we at?"

Captain Moreno shakes his head no and walks away out of the tent. Three other medical people chase after him with staccato machine gun fire in the air. Dr. Bush cries out, "Captain! Wait for me." What started out as a surgical team of eight is now reduced to four.

Dr. Sovia continues to work on the patient and without looking up speaks, "nurse, now is the time to go if you want." The nurse gives Dr. Sovia a dirty look and hands him an instrument.

Hours later the flames are reaching up into the night sky where they seem to touch the stars. The noise is loud, music is playing and voices are heard. It is not combat or the carnage of war. A large bonfire is roaring as a dozen doctors and nurses dressed in shorts and T-shirts suck down beer and smoke cigars. Dr. Sovia is the center of attention.

Dr. Bush who ran away earlier sheepishly approaches the team who stayed behind, beer in hand. "I can't believe you guys are alive," *he says*, "I can't believe it."

Dr. Hendenberg, with a few too many beers in him, has fun at is colleague's expense, "well believe it you yellow bellied Yankee boy. You ran away."

"Hey a bunch of us ran away," *says Dr. Bush*, "who the hell knew the Army or the Guatemalan Police or whatever you call them, who knew they were going to win so fast." *Dr. Deutche walks up to Dr. Sovia and hands him a beer.*

"Thanks Kathy. I might need more than one after today."

"They have more," Kathy replies while smiling.

"Some heroic stuff today Roberto," says Dr. Bush, "sticking with your patient while the bullets were flying by."

Dr. Sovia smiles and humbly tilts his head down. Dr. Hendenberg adds, "yeah, I'm sure my family will thank you for getting me killed."

"They can thank our lovely volunteer organization," yells out Dr. Bush while cracking open his beer, "and we can thank them for the lovely accommodations. Tents in a swamp. Here's to you."

Dr. Bush raises his beer and the whole surgical team follows his lead in raising their beers and shouting, "Doctors Without Frontiers!" The group quiets down and Dr. Bush steps forward, "but thank you Dr. Robert Sovia the bravest Surgeon."

Guatemala-Mexico border 2003

The jungle is thick enough to nearly block out the summer sun above yet the heat radiates off the ground like a dessert. Many men dressed in military camouflage garb can barely be seen while they nestle amongst the jungle foliage. Their faces painted multi-colored green to blend them in and are invisible while hidden. They wait patiently in silence. Jefe Hector Rosa, fifty-six years old is the leader of the Chiapas Cartel stands with a group of his henchmen around him, "any word yet?" he asks.

Pedro Garcia, twenty-two years old, a young Mexican of the right breeding but with little to no intelligence to speak of is squatting over an oversized two-way radio turning knobs while wearing headphones trying to pick up any communication. Many people in the region owed Jefe Rosa favors, and Pedro's parents were no different. Pedro Garcia served Jefe Rosa out of combination of gratitude, parental pressure and of course fear.

Jefe Rosa snaps his fingers angrily, "Garcia! Don't make me ask twice!"

"OK. Okay. Yeah, ahh... What again?"

"Any communication yet?" Jefe Rosa asks with growing anger in his voice.

"No Senor," Pedro snaps to obedience, "not yet. OK."

Jefe Rosa built a relatively large but stable organization over thirty years. He did not squander his drug proceeds on fancy cars or yachts, like the idiots in Columbia did. No Jefe Rosa took every opportunity to purchase land and buildings and legitimate businesses. Of course many people owed Jefe Rosa their livelihood as he needed them to staff and run his various operations. Jefe Rosa liked being King and he did not like surprises. That is why he personally oversaw new business deals with new players.

Jefe Rosa looks around at the jungle, "I don't like the feel of this," he says, "get my sub commanders up here, right now."

"OoohKaay," Pedro says as he reaches for the portable two-way radio, "oh wow. Here's the big man now Jefe." Silent as a professional soldier should be, Jose Canale, thirty-two years old, one of Jefe Rosa's top men, walks up to them out of the jungle darkness.

"Jefe," Jose calmly reports to his boss, "everyone is in place."

"Canale, Mi culebra," Jefe Rosa says to his man, "I do not like the feel of this. Is this government dog going to turn about and bite the

hand who feeds him?"

"Like the last 4 deliveries, they have been making timely communication Jefe," Jose reports.

"Oh yeah?" asks the boss.

"Yes Jefe, and my people have had them under surveillance since the first checkpoint."

Jefe Rosa ponders over what Jose has just told him. Jefe Rosa replies, "I have been in the game for too many years to trust a delivery this important to anyone but myself. Especially in this time of uncertain loyalties."

"Understood Jefe," says Jose.

"But this time, Jefe Rosa adds, "I want to look in the eye of our new government pet."

Only god knows why the seemingly mentally challenged Pedro decides to add to the conversation by saying, "Oh, come on Jefe. We've got this. OK? We've done this before."

Jefe Rosa stares icily at Pedro Garcia as Jose smirks incredulously at Pedro. "Did you call the other sub commanders like I ordered you to?" Jefe Rosa says while barely concealing his rage.

"Ok ok, I'm getting on it now. OK Jefe?" Pedro whose place next to the boss is tentative at best, slinks off a few feet away and goes back to his radio.

Jose begins to brief the Jefe, "we've got security posted with radios on all roads coming in plus any possible routes off road in here. If something goes wrong, they're not making it out of here."

Jefe Rosa gives the approving grin of a grandfather and pats Jose's shoulder, "and that's why I keep you around Canale, you're an expensive asset, but worth it."

"Si Senor," replies Jose, "thank you." Jose Canale was a relatively new hire for the Rosa family, only nine months out of the Army and the drug gang wars were getting so out of control, the cartels and families needed to hire professional soldiers to lead and train their men.

Pedro interrupts the conversation again, "OK, Jefe Rosa, Look!"

A convoy of 6 Guatemalan border police Suburbans and pickup trucks pulls around the jungle road. Jose's radio crackles to life, "Canale?

This is security OP 1. They are arriving now."

Jose keeps his eyes on the trucks and brings his hand held radio to his mouth and speaks, "copy that OP 1." The convoy of trucks begin to appear as they come around a curve in the jungle road. They slowly roll to a stop. Jose leaves the anonymity of the jungle leaves and walks to the lead truck. The trucks occupants get out. They are all Guatemalan Border Police. The Rosa man gives a thumbs up and then Jose approaches the Police truck and extends his hand to the senior man, "Colonel Escalera, a pleasure to see you again senor."

Sitting in the passenger seat of one of the trucks with the window rolled down is Colonel Luis Escalera, forty-four years old. He weakly shakes Jose's hand and replies, "yes, yes. A pleasure. Would you like to count it young man?"

Jose whispers something into his radio and waves. Two dozen men dressed in total camouflage leave the jungle and walk towards the trucks. The border police exit the vehicles and begin to help unload bales of something wrapped in white plastic. Colonel Escalera questions Jose, "where is Jefe Rosa?"

Jose puts his radio to his mouth and speaks,

"Jefe?" Jefe Hector Rosa walks out of the jungle and approaches the Colonel by the truck.

Colonel Escalera extends his hand, "I am sure you wouldn't remember a lowly civil servant such as Me Jefe Rosa."

"You are too humble Colonel," The Jefe replies, "any problems with your friends South of the border?"

"They can all go and fornicate with themselves," Colonel Escalera replies sharply, "always with their hands out looking for something they did not earn."

"Guatemalan Police looking to skim money," the Jefe says sarcastically, "what a shock."

They both laugh at the obvious irony then the Colonel gets serious, "ahh, it is the same everywhere. Government dogs roaming the street, all they want is a free meal."

Jefe Rosa takes a serious tone, "I assume you have everything we were promised."

"Yes."

"Good," Jefe Rosa replies, "my man here will

check the details."

Just as they shake hands the whistling sound of incoming artillery or mortar rounds fill the sky. All the men look up in wonderment for the 1-2 seconds they have left. Pedro Garcia still on a knee listening for radio reports hears it first, "OK, what the fuck?!?!" The quick whine of incoming artillery shells pierces the sky. The sound grows from a small scream to a huge scream in a matter of seconds,. A puff of red colored smoke rises from the jungle a few meters away from one of the trucks.

Jose, a well-trained military man knows exactly what is happening. He yells a warning for everyone around, "Incoming! Get down, get down!"

The next scream of artillery shells is followed by a massive explosion near the truck in the middle of the convoy. The piercing shriek becomes multiplied as a dozen incoming artillery rounds land and explode one after another after another. Half the convoy is obliterated. Along with the flying shrapnel and smoke, screams fill the air.

Experienced soldier that he is Colonel Escalera dives to the ground and takes Jefe Rosa with him. Jefe Rosa is not a man who is accustomed to losing his cool spits at the dirty cop, "this is your doing you cop rat!"

Colonel Escalera reacts with legitimate shock, *"no! Are you crazy? Get down! Crawl! Get to the trees, stay down!*

The whistles and explosions of incoming mortar rounds go on for almost 30 seconds. Some men run and are cut to ribbons, others crawl to the relative safety of the jungle trees. Some make it to safety, most do not. Jose rolls on top of Jefe Rosa to protect him. The explosions stop.

"There's our break," snaps Jose, *"they're recalibrating. Let's Go."*

Colonel Escalera jumps to his feet and begins looking furiously for his men. Jefe Hector Rosa does not move. Jose is the first to notice the Jefe and screams/pleads with the unconscious Jefe, "Jefe Rosa! JEFE! Please get up. We have to move!" Jose grabs Jefe Rosa's shoulders and rolls him over only to find Jefe Rosa bleeding badly yet still alive. Jose begins to shout orders for whoever of his men are left. "You! You There! All of you, get over here!" The men obey Jose fearfully. Jose grabs a piece of Jefe Rosa and waves more men over to help.

"Grab him," orders Jose, *"come on, move*

your asses back to the secondary position. Glad to see you alive Garcia. Radio ahead that Jefe is hit. We need that doctor and his clinic."

"I can't," cries Pedro Garcia, "the radio is blown to shit OK!"

"Your cell phone," snaps Jose.

"No signal out here in the mountains!" screams Pedro. Just then, two hundred yards away sudden burst of automatic weapons fire pierce the sudden lull in violence.

"Your Boys Colonel?" yells Jose.

"No," replies the Colonel, "wrong Caliber Weapon. I know the sound." Men dressed in a mixture of civilian clothes and army gear, all heavily armed with AK-47s and Uzis, still some distance from the Colonel and Jefe, begin running and spraying machine gun fire towards the survivors of the artillery attack.

Pedro is terrified beyond measure and accidentally relieves himself in his pants and screams, "OK! What the fuck is this?"

The group struggles to run and carry the unconscious Jefe with them. Jose, breathing heavily from all the exertion yells out, "they must be from your side of the border Colonel."

Colonel Escalera, still carrying part of Jefe Rosa by his clothes, pants and answers, "no, it can't be. They could not mount this type of operation."

Jose grabs the Colonel violently by his shirt collar, "who? Who couldn't mount this?" Mortar rounds begin landing and exploding again, this time closer to the group. Jose lets go of the Colonel, "ah fuck it! Let's go amigos! Vayate! Vayate! The motley crew of survivors and the Colonel head out all holding a piece of Jefe Rosa.

MEXICO CITY, MEXICO

The giant concrete building looms over Mexico City as a towering representation of Mexican Federal Government power. For so many Mexicans who already live in fear of the corrupt power of corrupt Federal cops, the building remains a constant reminder of their place in society, forever below government power. As imposing as it is on the outside, the public saw only the first three floors, all were an example of Spartan working environment. That ended where the fourth floor started, the posh and comfortable workspace the Feds made for themselves remained secret from the citizenry. No need to provoke a revolution.

On one of the higher floors of the Federal building, sits the office of an important man in an expensive suit. Chief Inspector Hugo Rivera, forty-two years old, stands staring out the floor to ceiling window of his high rise office. "Long is the road that up from Hell, leads into the light" was the John Milton quote he had hanging on his wall. Hugo loved to look at that sign as he peered over all of Mexico City. It certainly had been a long and hard road from the Hell that Hugo grew up in. He was raised in the barrios of Mexico City, his mother and two other brothers alone since Hugo's dad had abandoned the family when the kids were young.

Saved from a life of crime when a police man caught him stealing when he was ten years old. The police man sent him to live in a boys home where he learned the discipline of boxing coupled with hard study in school. Both efforts served Hugo well when he entered the local Mexico City Police force. A few years of college at night while patrolling the streets by day earned him his college degree, not to mention a nice nest egg from all the bribes and graft he collected along the way. But more important than the money he saved were the connections he made along the way. Smart cartel leaders took notice of him and the intelligent way he handled problems for them. It was not long before the powerful crime lords of Mexico City got him a spot in the Mexican Federal Police. Mexico's version of the FBI, a place where a smart and ambitious Hugo Rivera would do more for the drug cartels than he could do as a beat cop in the city. Now he was Chief Inspector Rivera, a man of power and influence in Mexican law enforcement.

He is speaking on the land line telephone when his cell phone rings. "Gracias senor Inspector General, I will have to call you back in a second" says Chief Rivera as he hangs up the phone and answers his cell. "Yeah?... What do you mean he got away?... You had him alone, dead to rights. How the FUCK do you miss him?" Some mumbling is heard on the other end of the line. "I don't give a shit how good his guys were. How many of them did you get?... That many huh? Well I'm very fuckin proud of you." Some more mumbling on the other end of the line. "FUCK YOU!!!" screams Chief Rivera, "I was being sarcastic." Even more mumbling on the other end of the line. "FUCK YOU AND YOUR MOTHER!! Now listen to me you ignorant piece of horse manure, track them down, they can't get far on foot, they will be trying to make it to a car or a truck already parked somewhere. I mean you guys ARE former Special Forces aren't you?" More mumbling on the other end of the line. "I need them captured or dead before they have a chance to get back. Do you read me soldier?" Chief Rivera hangs up and puts his cell phone back into his pocket.

He picks up his office phone and dials, "Judge Ortega, thank you for picking up. I was just speaking with Deputy Inspector General Hernandez and he told me the most interesting development." Hugo smiles and looks out the window.

GUATEMALA

The morning was strangely cool for a morning in the Guatemalan jungle. The coolness made Kathy snuggle her naked body closer to Dr. Robert Sovia's naked body. Both, lying together on a twin sized blowup mattress covered in a sleeping bag. Dr. Sovia is awake and appears anxiety ridden while Kathy Deutche slowly opens one eye and sees him. She gently kisses his hand. Dr. Sovia props himself up on one elbow looking perplexed. "Kathy... I ah..." starts Dr. Sovia.

Kathy puts a finger over his lips, "It's OK. I'm not expecting anything more than last night."

"I'm not trying to treat you like a whore," says Dr. Sovia.

Kathy smiles at his old fashioned sentiment, "Nice girls like sex too Doctor."

"I'm sorry. I did not mean to imply-"

"I know. It's OK." She says while gazing into his dark eyes. She plays with the thick black hair on his chest. "I like you. I admire you. I'm attracted to you."

"Yeah, I kind of got that," he says.

Kathy kisses him passionately, grabs his chin and stare straight into his eyes, "Go home Robert. It's our secret." He sweeps his strong arms over her soft shoulder and presses his lips to hers. She melts inside and returns his kisses passionately. They sink back under the sleeping bag.

CHIAPAS MEDICAL CENTER, CHIAPAS MEXICO

The Medical Center is fairly modern, clean, well lit, well-staffed, computers, EKG, X-ray, everything a modern Trauma Hospital would have in any metropolitan city in the US. Strangely the Medical Center did not have much in the way of preventative medicine. They could handle, car accidents, broken bones, heart attacks but best of all, they were aces at gunshot wounds. No wonder that Jefe Rosa had bank rolled investment in the Medical Center. Dressed in medical scrubs, the staff are working behind the counter. Patients wait to be seen on seats across from the reception desk.

A group of dirty, bloody camouflaged men burst through the front door carrying a bloody Jefe Hector Rosa. Pedro Garcia leads the way, out of breath and the dirtiest he has ever been. He yells for attention, "Ooooh Kaaayyyy! We need a doctor!"

The whole staff jumps out of their seats with fear on their faces, they stare at the bloody, dirty men dressed as soldiers carrying the wounded Jefe. Jose Canale steps to the front desk while pointing his two men towards a nearby door, "carry him back there."

A beautiful young clinic staffer dressed in pink scrubs, Isabella Perez, twenty-eight years old, steps forward from behind the reception desk, waving frantically, "Wait! You can't-"

Jose pushes past her and growls, "shut up! Look at me! We are friends of Dr. Sovia. We need him here now!"

"He's not here!" screams back Isabella. Jose is helping to lift Jefe Rosa onto the exam table and he spins back at Isabella.

"What?! Where is he? Do you know who this is?" Jose fires off questions rapidly.

One of the clinic's surgical staff, Dr. Sebastian Cruz, Thirty-one years old, steps around the reception desk and rushes to the exam room snapping orders at his staff along the way, "get him prepped for surgery now. Isabella call ER Trauma Team to scrub up for Operating Room one."

Isabella grabs a Public Address microphone and calls out over the speakers, "Trauma team to Operating Room one."

Jose grabs Dr. Cruz by his white medical jacket, "what is going on? Where is Dr. Sovia?"

Dr. Cruz is busy examining Jefe Rosa, he does not look at Jose when he answers, "Dr. Sovia is in Guatemala."

"What!? When, when is he coming back?" barks Jose.

Dr. Cruz looks to Isabella. "He is arriving this afternoon. 3:30 I think," says Isabella.

"This is Jefe Hector Rosa!" says Jose. "You know who that is right, you know who we are?"

Isabella hears the name, shrieks and drops clipboard she was carrying on the floor. Dr. Cruz answers for her, "yes, we know." Dr. Cruz is grabbing medical gear and orderlies arrive with a wheeled gurney. Dr. Cruz issues his orders, "get him to the operating room."

"Fix him doc!" Jose half orders and half pleads, "we can't lose him."

Dr. Cruz ignores Jose while directing his staff, "let's get to workpeople." The Doctor goes to walk around Jose and Jose grabs him by the arm and looks into his eyes.

"This is important doctor," Jose implores, "no one can know he is here. NO ONE! Tell your staff to

keep quiet. No phone calls! NO ONE KNOWS! Understand?!"

"Yes, of course. Let me go now so I can save him." Dr. Cruz turns to Isabella, "Isabella, spread the word, everybody shuts up." Isabella nods before running towards the Operating Room one. Jose rubs his head as he walks out into the waiting room. He looks up to see through the window outside the clinic, Pedro Garcia is on his cell phone again speaking frantically.

The Twin Engine, 10 seater Cessna airplane lands on the narrow runway surrounded by thick Mexican jungle of the Chiapas airport. Chiapas, the Southernmost state in Mexico and perhaps the poorest, never had a functioning airport. Not before Jefe Rosa's investment who made it possible. Dr. Sovia steps off the plane after it stops and is walking back to the small airport terminal carrying his carry-on bag and a giant 5 foot Snoopy stuffed animal for his daughter. A dark, four seater Mercedes Benz races onto the tarmac and stops alongside the walking air travelers. A young man dressed in the expensive clothes of Jefe Rosa's

Chiapas Security Thugs steps out of the front passenger door and grabs Dr. Sovia's bag, "Dr. Sovia, please come with us now. It is an emergency."

"What?" says Dr. Sovia as he protests still holding on to his bag. The Chiapas Thug pushes Dr. Sovia in the back seat next to him squeezed up against the giant stuffed Snoopy doll. "Guys, can this wait? I just flew three hours, my wife misses me. I would like to go home first."

The Mercedes speeds away and the Chiapas Thug continues scanning the airport when he answers, "no it can't wait doc."

"What is going on?"

The Chiapas Thug is dialing his phone, "Nobody told you?"

"No," answers a suddenly concerned Dr. Sovia, "told me what?"

"It's bad doc," replies the Thug, "this morning..."

The Sovia family home was not lavish or overly large but rather, clean, well lit, well apportioned home befitting a successful Doctor. The tempting smell of roast goat wafts through the air. The Sovia children, Alberto Sovia eleven years old and Ariana Sovia eight years old, are running across the tiled floors. Mrs. Sofia Sovia, thirty-three years old, is cleaning and chasing the children, "Alberto! Ariana! Stop this silliness," *Sofia yells at the kids,* "your father will be home any minute. Do your homework!"

Little Alberto tries to plead, "moooooom! Ariana wont' give me back my hair brush."

The little girl taunts her brother, holding up the brush as she runs behind a couch, "haha, he only wants to look good for Valentina next door."

"Shut up! I'm gonna kill you!" *Alberto screeches as he lunges at his sister but she is quicker and sidesteps him and he crashes into some furniture.*

"ENOUGH!!" *barks Sofia,* "Ariana, give him back his brush, both of you stop horsing around and get ready, I want you to look your best for when your father arrives. Abeula!!" *Sofia's mother Valeria Torres, fifty-one years old, who lives with them, comes into the room.*

"What are these little monsters doing this time?" the grizzled old woman asks.

"Mama, help me get them ready for their father's arrival."

"Vayate!" the grandmother barks at the kids in Spanish, "go to your room and clean up." Valeria ushers the children down the hall and as the children are walking to their bedrooms the home phone rings and Sofia runs to answer it.

"Hello... Oh hello my love... What? When?... NOW? No, tell them you can't! The kids have not seen you in a week. I have not seen you." Sofia's face turns from joy to near despair in seconds as she listens to her husband on the phone. Her tone changes to a serious one, "yes, I know they fund the clinic but you haven't seen your children in a week. Not to mention me...... GO THEN! Go to your masters. I'll be here as always." There is some mumbling coming from the phone. "yes the kids are fine. Aren't you getting tired of asking that from the phone all the time?" Sofia hangs up the phone and walks down the hall.

MEXICO CITY – FEDERAL POLICE BUILDING

In the lavish office suite we saw earlier, a now nervous Chief Rivera is frantically placing calls between two cell phones and his office line. He is juggling the phones trying to keep track of with whom he is speaking, "hold on! Yes you Raul." Chief Rivera switches to the other phone, "Judge Ortega sir, thank you so much for calling me back. Would you hold on for just a second please?" Juggling back to his other cell phone while shielding the mouthpiece of Judge Ortega's call. "RAUL! Get that mother fucker now. I don't care where he is.......... NO you fucking imbecile, you cannot have cops on this hit. It has to Look like the rival people!!!" Hugo closes shut the flip phone from Raul and picks up the Judge. "Judge Ortega sir, thank you so much for waiting. I have a bit of an emergency and need an arrest warrant... Right now sir... How much?... OK. Cash? Right now or can I owe it to you?" The Judge hangs up the call. "Hello? Helloooo? Sir?" Chief Rivera says to the dead phone.

CHIAPAS, MEXICO

The Medical Clinic's operating room is ceramic tiled with mix of blue and white tiles. Expensive medical monitoring devices are chirping near an operating table while the clinic staff attempts to save Jefe Rosa. Dr. Cruz has his gloved hands inside Jefe Rosa's open body cavity. "Suction" he says.

"Where Doctor?" replies Isabella who is assisting him.

"To the left of the Aorta," Dr. Cruz says sounding annoyed, "where I have been suturing for the past 10 minutes!"

"I'm sorry doctor. It's been hours now," Isabella replies, "I'm starting to get tired."

From the side of the operating room a voice booms out loud, "wake the fuck up! If he dies because you fuck up…" Jose Canale, now masked and dressed in surgical scrubs like the clinic staff, approaches the operating table barking his warnings, "Just save the Jefe."

Dr. Cruz turns to another clinic worker on the operating team, "you! Get over here, hold the suction where the fluid covers the sutures so I can see.

Isabella tries to defend herself, "No. I'm fine, I'm fine, I can work.

"Isabella," Dr. Cruz chastises her, "go take a break! Go wash your face, have some coffee, come back in 10 minutes."

Jose starts to object, "whoa! Wait one sec-"

"Isabella GO NOW!" Dr. Cruz orders her. Isabella hands the suction tool to the other clinic worker and walks away out of the Operating Room.

She passes Jose on the way out the door, "Jefe Rosa's my uncle asshole!" Isabella says as she exits the room.

Dr. Cruz, still working speaks to Jose without taking his eyes off of Jefe Rosa, "Senor Canale. I can appreciate the severity of your situation, our situation actually. No one here will let the Jefe die. But my staff are only human, they need rest."

Jose smiles behind his mask admiring the Doctor's professionalism responds, "and you doctor? Are you a human who needs rest?"

"You already know the answer to that Senor

Canale, I am more than human. I am a Doctor."

Jose smiles at the bravado of the doctor when he hears cars screech to a stop outside the clinic and immediately speaks into his radio, "what's going on out there?"

Pedro's voice comes back over the radio, "OK. Dr. Sovia is finally here. OK."

The dark Mercedes Sedan races up to the Medical Clinic and slams to a halt. The Chiapas Thug exits the vehicle along with Dr. Sovia. Almost simultaneously a black suburban with tinted windows roars up to the clinic, parking at a diagonal in 3 car spaces. More Chiapas Thugs exit the suburban but one opens the rear passenger door. Out steps Francisco Rosa, twenty-four years old and son of Jefe Hector Rosa. He looks around to ascertain the situation and moves to intercept Dr. Sovia who is now rapidly walking into the clinic.

"Hey pretty boy," says Francisco snidely, "what the fuck is going on? How is my father?"

Dr. Sovia continues walking briskly towards the clinic and barely looks at Francisco as he answers, "shot I hear, but beyond that I don't know yet. Let me get in here." Dr. Sovia bursts through *the doors and is met by a clinic staff member who hands him a chart and begins frantically relaying medical updates to him.*

"Multiple ballistic trauma doctor," says the Staff Member.

"How long has he been under?" asks Dr. Sovia

"Two hours, Dr. Cruz and the rest of the trauma team have been working on him since he arrived." *Dr. Sovia and staff walk and talk all the way to the Operating Prep-Room where Dr. Sovia begins to scrub up for surgery.*

Francisco Rosa, still standing in the hallway feels the need to be heard and respected calls out very loud, "CANALE!! Donde Estas?!" *Francisco knows wherever his dad is, Jose, the ex-Special Forces soldier is bound to be nearby. Jose immediately exits the Operating Room dressed in blue scrubs and surgical mask and cap. Francisco laughs and mocks him,* "what the fuck are you? You a surgeon now?"

"Your father's safety is my responsibility," replies Jose very seriously, "I am standing by to help."

"Fine fucking job on his safety so far Canale. How the fuck did you let him get shot?"

Jose points his finger in Francisco's face and angrily snaps back, "hey, I did NOT let him get shot! This was a professional military ambush. They had Mortars. Real artillery! The kind from the movies that drops out the sky and explodes before you even know it's coming."

"Who the fuck has that stuff?" asks Francisco.

"The Army, only Armies have that kind of firepower and they knew how to use it. They had our position zeroed in."

"Holy shit!" replies Francisco, now beginning to grasp the seriousness of the situation.

"Then after they nearly wiped us out with the mortar barrage they ceased fire and ground troops poured in killing everything in their path. Classic military tactics. They were pros.

"Mexican Army?" asks Francisco, "You think the Army is coming after us?"

"I don't know right now, could be," replies Jose, "we brought that piece of shit Colonel from the Guatemalan Border Police back with us."

"What Colonel? Who the fuck-"

"The Colonel from Guatemalan border police we deal with. We have him secured back at your father's house. He seems to think it was MS-13."

"FUCK THEM!!" screams Francisco with his usual hot headedness, "what are you afraid of them?! Let's go kill these fuckers! NOW!! Call the boys up, let's get moving, I say we attack! RIGHT NOW!"

"I am your father's second in command, Jose says in a calm measured voice, "In your father's absence I am in command. You know that."

"FUCK YOU CANALE! Are you really gonna try and pull that ex-Army chain of command bullshit! You ain't a soldier no more."

"I will always be a soldier Francisco, I simply serve a different Army now."

"We are wasting time here," says Francisco.

"We don't even know who to hit just yet," says Jose, "I've put the calls out already. All of our groups are on alert and have been mobilized, in the meantime we are making inquiries everywhere. We lost 16 of our men out there today, not to mention a ton of cash."

"How much cash?" asks Francisco.

Jose stares at Francisco in silence, then answers, "I'll let your father tell you when he wakes up. In the meantime, position your guys around the outside of the clinic. We need to protect the Jefe."

Francisco stares hard at Jose before replying, "the fuckin balls on you! OK. We do it your way... for now."

Francisco looks both ways down the hallway. "The money my father sunk into this medical clinic!" says Francisco. "All for that little shit Sovia. I don't understand why he adores that pretty boy so much."

Jose finally smiles again, "am I detecting some jealousy here from the anointed one?

"Fuck you Canale!" snaps Francisco, "I could have been a doctor."

Jose tries not to laugh at Francisco and quickly changes the subject, "Frankie, how did you know we were here at the clinic anyway?"

"Pedro Garcia called me to let me know,"

answers Francisco. Jose looks suspiciously out the clinic window into the parking lot where Pedro is talking on his phone.

OUTSIDE CHIAPAS, MEXICO

The jungle in Southern Mexico is so thick and dark that it looks completely black at night. Several dark pickup trucks are parked along the side of the dirt road on the edge of the trees, no headlights are on. Between the jungle and the trucks more than a dozen men were cleaning their guns, loading magazines and otherwise prepping for a military raid. Their leader, Raul Benitez, thirty-four years old, formerly a Captain in the Guatemalan Special Forces, is clearly in command. The Kabilis as they are known, are killers to the last man. He speaks commandingly to his men. "Finish up people, we are on the move in 10 minutes."

The tight group of former Guatemalan Army Special Forces soldiers called Kabilis, now soldiers for hire, in solidarity cry out in solidarity, "Hoooyah!"

The Captain yells out to one of the Kabilis, "Martinez!"

A slender soldier, Martinez, twenty four years old, jumps up from what he is doing and stands at attention, "Si Capitan," shouts Martinez.

"Bring the map and the blue print of the Medical Clinic over here," orders the Captain. Martinez grabs his bag and trots over to the hood of the pickup truck and lays out the map and clicks on a little flashlight attached to his hat.

"Capitan, I have marked out in orange the route to get us from our current location to the Clinic."

"And the Clinic itself?" questions the Captain, "I want floor plans before we go in there." Martinez begins to lay out several 8x10 sheets of office paper with drawings on them. "This is the best you can do?" asks the Captain.

"Capitan, on short notice yes," replies Martinez sheepishly, "we just got these faxed to us inside the truck over the cellular system. Modern technology is wonderful is it not? The Captain looks at Martinez with contempt and stays silent for an uncomfortable amount of time. "We are a long way from the Staples store in Guatemala city," says Martinez, "I could run back there if you like and turn this into a full size blue print."

"Shut up Martinez. Give me the layouts for Christ's sake." Martinez smirks as he and the Captain Look over the plans. "OK, go get the team leaders over here to go over this." Martinez obeys and trots off.

MEDICAL CLINIC, CHIAPAS MEXICO

The Operating table is surrounded by blue clad surgical personnel. Dr. Sovia, now leading the surgical team is focused like a laser beam on his patient. "Now, slide the wide end of the probe under the tissue," advises Dr. Sovia, "if you feel a scratch or a bump go back as we have some more shrapnel."

Dr. Cruz obeys and follows the procedure. "Nothing in there," says Dr. Cruz, "smooth as silk."

"Then we are shrapnel free Doctor Cruz. You can start closing up."

Dr. Cruz is visibly impressed, "I can't believe it. You cut the time in half." Dr. Cruz begins to close the patient's chest as Dr. Sovia stands back and takes his gloves off. "That was really something else Dr. Sovia. I never would have taken that approach. I would have been here forever. You are really good."

Dr. Sovia tries to act humble but inside he is bursting with pride and joy. He lives for the adoration of his peers. "Thank you Doctor." Dr. Sovia says as he walks away into the scrub room, the surgical team claps a round of applause for him. He holds his head high but does not acknowledge them.

Outside the clinic in the parking lot, Francisco Rosa is skulking around the parking lot walking from corner to corner to check in with his men. In their haste they did not bring radios and most of their cell phones have dead batteries. He walks up to one of his men on guard duty with him. "This is fucking bull shit," he gripes, "we can't coordinate shit!" Francisco walks to one of his Chiapas Thugs is and yells. "Hey! Get the others, we're going inside." He turns back to the Chiapas Thug, "Let's go." They walk back towards the entrance to the Clinic. Francisco Rosa waits until he and the other four Chiapas Thugs are at the entrance.

Back inside the Medical Clinic, Dr. Sovia

walks in the laundry room and strips off his operating scrubs and kicks them into the pile of other dirty laundry. They sail through the air just as Isabella Perez opens and walks through the door. "Oh is that how you feel about me? Kick me to the curb and kick your dirty laundry at me."

"Sorry, long day."

Isabella stands by the door, Dr. Sovia doesn't move just stares back at her. "I missed you while you were away *says Isabella in a soft voice.*

"Izzie it's been a long day, I real-" *Isabella does not give him time to finish his sentence or formulate a defense, rushes to him and kisses him passionately*

"No," *says Dr. Sovia while pushing her off.*

Isabella wraps her arms around his head and kisses him harder. "Shut up. Kiss me!"

Dr. Sovia pulls away from her, "I said no." *He exits the other door to the back hallway and proceeds down the back hall and crosses through an examination room to the front side of the clinic and into his office. Isabella follows him into the office and gets up in his face.*

"Do you think I am a play toy you can just toss away when you lose interest?"

"Izzie, I can't. I don't want to go through this again."

Isabella reaches for him again and kisses him passionately. "I missed you. I want you." Isabella continues to kiss him and his will melts to hers. He returns her passion and she proceeds to heatedly pull his shirt off.

"Isabella."

"Tell me you love me," she says as she kisses his now bare chest.

"I love you…I love you," he says as he gives in to her passion and returns her kisses while caressing her soft skin. His hands gently pull off her clothes to reveal her tight, voluptuous body. He closes the office door with his foot. They stumble over each other to make it to the office couch. They fall into the soft cushions and make passionate love to each other.

Back outside in the parking lot, Francisco Rosa has his men gathered just outside the front entrance of the Medical Clinic. "All right compadres, we are going inside and staying inside, this wandering around in the dark is bull shit."

A collective yeah goes through the group.

"Anybody gives you shit, tell em to talk to me," Francisco boasts, "I'm runnin shit around here now." All five men walk through the front door of the clinic. No sooner than when the last man walks through the door, the roar of a truck engine fills the air. Francisco turns around at the sound, "what the fuck?!" The glass doors and walls explode as a dark pickup truck smashes through it and plows over the men into the lobby of the clinic. Screams fill the waiting room/front desk area of the clinic as glass and steel fly through the air as two tons of pickup truck comes crashing through, running over people, destroying furniture and structure. Automatic weapons open fire and more screams are heard. Captain Raul Benitez leads the charge of soldiers into the medical clinic.

"Move! Move! Keep moving and shooting!" yells Captain Raul Benitez as he runs through the open wall with several Kabilis alongside him. Spraying everything they see with short disciplined bursts of automatic weapons fire.

The Chiapas Thugs that are still alive quickly return fire in gangster fashion, sub-machine guns and shotguns down by their hip. Around the corner down the hallway Pedro dives through the Operating Room swinging doors and almost collides into Jose. The two Chiapas Thugs that have been with Dr. Sovia since the airport get on their knees, at the door, pointing their sub-machine Guns down the hall. They are trained and ready to fight.

"We've got company OK!" yells Pedro.

Jose, gun in hand and peering out the glass window in the operating room door questions him, "how many Pedro?... HOW MANY ARE THERE?"

"I don't know OK, I heard a crash, I jumped, I heard gunshots, I came in here OK."

Jose points to Pedro and then at a door, "get your gun out and get by that other door." *He points to the two Chiapas Thugs,* "Hombres! Anything comes down that hall, kill it. We need time." *The two Chiapas Thugs and Pedro Garcia take up defensive positions by their respective doors from into the operating room. Jose turns his attention to the boss,* "Dr. Cruz how is Jefe? Can he be moved?"

"Yes but slowly," replies Dr. Cruz, "we just finished closing him up. Don't-"A long burst of machine gun fire rips through the air. Chiapas Thug 1 shrieks out in pain.

Pedro screams out in terror, "Oh shit! Not OK! NOT OK!!"

Jose grabs Dr. Cruz to get his attention, "slowly is not a word we have right now doc! Where does that door lead to?"

"That's the scrub room, then there is a back hallway and then down that hall a back exit."

Jose points to the Operating Room door. His last Chiapas Thug is lying down looking down the barrel of his sub-machine gun, pointed down the hallway, Jose barks his orders, "Pedro! Get off that door and get on THAT door with my guy! Cover our asses! Surgical staff!" The surgical staff shriek with fright, Jose ignores this and commands again, "everybody grab a piece of Jefe and put him on the stretcher there with wheels."Pedro moves to the other door.

More machine gun fire rakes the main hallway outside the O.R., chunks of wall material hits Pedro in the face, he screams in anger and pain. "Aaahh!

What the fuck OK!?"

"Pedro, cover that door! And keep us alive long enough to get out the door, then come join us. I'll get the car and you cover Jefe once we're outside! Clear?!?" No response from Pedro who is hurriedly rubbing debris out of his eyes. Jose yells louder, "Pedro are we clear?!"

"Ok! OKAY!! Yes, I got it. Go GO! OK!" Pedro says while still rubbing his eyes.

Jose, trained soldier that he is, kicks open the swinging doors to the scrub room while pointing his weapon but not firing away his limited ammunition. He kicks over a heavy equipment rack to keep open the swinging doors for the surgical team and it lodges the swinging door against the laundry room door.

Dr. Robert Sovia and Isabella Perez lie naked together on the couch in the afterglow of passionate love making. She is looking in his eyes while looks in hers and strokes her hair. "You captivate me," he says.

"I'm in love with you," Isabella says while running her fingers through his thick black hair.

"No," Dr. Sovia says, *"you promised you wouldn't."*

"I don't care what I said. I can't stop loving you."

"I knew this was a mistake," says Dr. Sovia, *"I knew it. I told you I-"*

"I know what you said Robert."

"I ended it," Isabella," Dr. Sovia calmly says, *"I let you continue working here-"*

"YOU!? You don't let me continue working here," Isabella says incredulously, *"my uncle pays for this place to stay open, he decides who works here."*

"Yes, the uncle whose life I just saved. Actually WE just saved."

"Don't patronize me Robert. I am not a dumb little peasant like your wife."

"Enough already!" Snaps Dr. Sovia, *"don't blame me for your jealousy. You knew I was married when you started this between us."*

"When I started this between us? You were the one who-"

A thunderous crash is heard and felt through the walls of the clinic. Almost instantaneously machine gun fire from multiple guns blast throughout the building followed by screams. Isabella suddenly clutches Dr. Sovia in fear. "Oh my god! What was that?" she asks franticly

Dr. Sovia starts grabbing his clothes, "get dressed, quickly!"
They are up on their feet pulling on their clothes. The sound of gunfire is deafening.

"Oh my god! What is happening Robert?"

Dr. Sovia leans towards the front window. He is hidden by the heavy blinds but manages a peak outside where he sees many armed men dressed in camouflage running and carrying weapons.

"Oh no. no no. We have to get out Izzie." Dr. Sovia, still holding Isabella's hand moves to the door, slowly cracks it open and peaks out the door, down the hallway, then sprints across the hallway to the other examination room, dragging Isabella all the way. The sound of gunfire and shattering glass and screams intensifies.

Isabella is not built for this, "No! No Robert, Isabella pleads, I want to go back."

Dr. Sovia drags her into a different exam room, pulls her close and whispers in her ear, "Listen to me, if they search the clinic, which they are bound to do, we are dead Izzie." *More gunfire and screams punctuate the tension. Isabella is shaking with fear now, she makes her own choice and rather than wait, she bolts out the back entrance of the exam room they are in and into the back hallway of the clinic.*

Dr. Sovia is caught off guard when Isabella disappears out the back door of the exam room. He tries not to yell, but whispers loudly, "Izzie. Where are you going?" *Isabella runs frantically down the hallway and almost straight into an armed Kabili turning the corner. The soldier is fearsome looking with all his gear strapped to him. He sees her and begins to aim his sub machine gun at her.*

Isabella, always in shape from playing tennis on Uncle Hector's estate is faster in her reaction. "Oh shit!" *she says out loud as she dives into a side room and locks the door and continues to the back of the room. She crouches down on the floor behind the exam table, shaking with fear. The Kabili quickly aims his submachine gun and begins spraying the now locked door. These are metal medical doors and do not splinter apart right away. The Kabili walks to the door to try and turn the knob but it is still locked shut. He aims his submachine gun the door knob shredding it with bullets until he runs out of bullets. The door is now ajar and the Kabili stops to change magazines on his sub machine gun.*

Dr. Sovia, still looking through the narrow exam room door window, sees his opportunity and sprints out the door he was hiding behind, runs full speed for eight feet and slams all of his body weight smashing the head of the Kabili into the metal door frame. The Kabili goes down and Dr. Sovia charges into the room. Isabella is crouching behind a medical table.

"Let's go. Izzie, let's go!" he screams but she does not move, Isabella is frozen in shock and Dr. Sovia runs to her, grabs her and pulls her up and back to the bullet riddled door. "Listen to me Iz, we don't have a lot of time. There is an exit door at the end of the hallway. That's our chance."

Isabella begins crying, she clutches Dr. Sovia's strong arms, "I can't. Robert I can't anymore I can't!"

Dr. Sovia grabs her chin and looks into her eyes, "I'll protect you baby." He grabs Isabella's face and kisses her deeply. Grabs her hand and drags her down the hallway. A long burst of gunfire forces Dr. Sovia pull Isabella into a nearby door.

Dr. Sovia, inadvertently drags Isabella into the Laundry room where they were earlier. He protectively pulls Isabella Perez down to the floor and switches off the light in the laundry room on the way down to make it dark so they can hide. "What is going on?" Isabella asks.

Dr. Sovia switches to whispers, "Be quiet. I don't know." More gunshots are heard then crashing and yelling, a door right outside the door of the laundry room that connects to the scrub room we saw earlier, crashes open and a piece of equipment is knocked over to keep it that door open but blocks any escape from the Laundry room.

Jose Canale is attempting to make an exit with his helpless patron, Jefe Rosa. He runs away from the now opened door to the scrub-room, back into the operating room. He clears the rooms and goes back to drag the surgical team who are now pushing Jefe Rosa on a stretcher. "C'mon people," Jose pushes the staff, "let's go! Get through this room, get down the hallway and wait by the exit door." Jose barks out as he forces the surgical team to push the stretcher through the Scrub Room then dashes back to the Operating Room where Pedro is covering the door, "Pedro," Jose calls out, "in two minutes run through this door, down the rear hallway and get these people out the back exit door with Jefe. Clear?"

Pedro looks petrified but sounds off as bravely as he can, "OK! Clear! OK!"

Jose dashes down the rear hallway and motions the surgical team to join him at the exit door. "Ok folks, we are almost out of here," Jose tries to reassure the surgical team, "Wait here till I come back for you with the car. I'll flash the lights, Doc you pull the stretcher out and load Jefe Rosa into the back seat. Understand?"

Dr. Cruz looking very weary and scared weakly answers, "yes, but what if-"

"Shut up! Don't question," Jose snaps his orders at them. "Just do! Are we clear?"

"Yes," answers Dr. Cruz sheepishly.

Jose exits the building out the back exit and

runs off into the dark parking lot behind the Medical Clinic. As he exits the building he switches to his Berretta 9 MM pistol with an attached silencer with a small American made night vision tube pressed up to his eye. He sees his enemy before they see him and he ends their lives silently and swiftly while continuing to move towards the car.

Back in the Clinic Laundry room, Isabella Perez is frantic and barely able to stop herself from screaming out. She begins pushing on the door to get out of the laundry room but to no avail. The heavy medical cart Jose overturned to keep one door open now prevents her from opening the door from the laundry room. "Oh my God! We are trapped! Let me out!" Isabella begins pounding on the door, fortunately machine gun fire is going back and forth and no one hears it except Dr. Sovia.

He jumps up from the floor to grab her, "No! Izzie NO! He says to her while trying to subdue her. He pulls her back down to the floor and covers her mouth just in time to hear someone run through the Scrub Room and out down rear hallway. More machine gun fire from the hallway then a scream. Dr. Sovia slowly stands up to peek out the laundry room door's window. He peers into the rear hallway by the exit door and sees his entire surgical team is pushing the gurney with Jefe Rosa strapped to it.

Pedro Garcia runs down the rear hallway to the waiting surgical team as he was instructed to. The entire surgical team is waiting with Jefe Rosa strapped to the stretcher, next to the now open exit door to the parking lot. Pedro speaks to the surgical team, "OK how we doin folks? Ready to leave yet?"

A terrified looking Dr. Cruz, standing nearby is exasperated and answers for them all, "yes for God's sake! Where is your boss?"

Pedro sneaks a peak out the open back door. "He's pulling up the car. Close that door to the outside. OK doc?" Dr. Cruz obeys the young man with the gun without questioning. Pedro Garcia watches as the door is closed and then looks back to check down the rear hallway for witnesses. "OKAY... No hard feelings, OK folks." Pedro Garcia calmly opens fire at close range cutting down all six members of the surgical team. Bullets from the automatic weapon rip through flesh, blood sprays all over the walls in the rear hallway. Screams and pleas for life can be heard briefly over the machine gun fire.

Dr. Sovia, fifteen feet away, is still looking out the laundry room door's little window when Pedro opens fire. He is aghast with horror, his entire staff and Jefe Rosa have just been slaughtered before his eyes. He ducks down beneath the door's window again.

"Mother of God," he whispers.

Isabella crawls over to him and whispers, "What? Robert what?!"

Dr. Sovia rubs his face trying to hold back the tears. He maintains his composure and quietly says, "Isabella, please be quiet." Dr. Sovia slowly stands and peaks out the tiny glass window built into the door. He sees the murderer again, one of Jefe Rosa's own men, the young one who was there when he arrived. There he was, standing over the entire surgical team, including Dr. Cruz, now slaughtered and bloodied.

Pedro Garcia quickly tosses his sub-machine, smears a handful of the victim's blood onto himself then takes out his pistol and shoots himself in the shoulder and falls to the floor. Looking up now, from this angle down the hall, in the laundry room's door window he catches a glimpse of the face of Dr. Sovia before he blacks out.

Outside in the parking lot, Jose Rivera pulls

the Rosa Mercedes up on the grass of the clinic with the lights off to get closer to the exit door. He parks the Mercedes, gets out, leaving the car door open. He can hear the firefight inside the building come to a stop. Jose sprints past the bushes and yanks open the exit door expecting to grab the doctor and the surgical team and pull Jefe Rosa to the car. What he finds instead is a blood bath of human flesh and guts splattered and smeared up the walls and floors of the hallway. The entire surgical staff lies in pools of blood, some with their brain matter pouring onto the floor Pedro Garcia lies on top of one of the nurses, bleeding, with his gun in his hand pointed in the direction of the attackers. He turns his head and looks right at Jose.

"Ok help me.... HELP ME," whispers Pedro.

Jose makes a tactical entry into the building with his sub-machine gun once again in his hands and pointing in the direction of the danger down the hallway. He scoops up Pedro and stops for a second to see the bullet riddled corpse of Jefe Hector Rosa still strapped to the stretcher. "C'mon kid. Let's go!" Jose scoops up Pedro under his armpit with his left hand and begins firing the sub-machine gun down the back hallway with his other hand. The Kabilis are right on top of him, no more than fifteen feet away. A hail of fire is exchanged. Jose is able to get Pedro to the Mercedes and speeds away into the night. The last thing Jose sees of the clinic is the Kabilis celebrating over the body of Jefe Hector Rosa in the exit doorway.

Back in Mexico City, in the ominous Federal Police building, in the office suite we saw earlier, Chief Rivera is sitting at his giant desk, tie loosened enjoying a drink and a cigar. His cell phone rings. "Yeah?" he answers the phone. Raul, Captain of the Guatemalan Kabilis voice comes out of the phone, "It's done." Chief Hugo Rivera hangs up, smiles and sips his drink.

CHAPTER 4

AFGHANISTAN, 2004

Afghanistan has been plagued by war and violence for as long as the history books can remember. A country made up of different ethnicities and languages, Afghanistan has been a crossroads for traders and travelers from many different parts of the world. Most of the time the various tribes are killing each other over petty disputes. Historically the tribes only seem to unite when they are fighting a foreign invader. After the Russians left in 1989, the tribes fought against the Russian backed Afghan government; they slaughtered each other to the point where Afghans at least tacitly welcomed the calm that the repressive Taliban regime brought to Afghanistan.

However there were unspeakable cruelties committed by the Taliban against the common Afghan people. Stoning, beheading, flogging, rape, murder, all in the name of a purified strain of Islam. His Warlord brother barely cared that Baraat Mansoor was one of mid-level leaders of this extreme version of Islam. His stature in the Taliban helped facilitate his family's crime business. Baraat was a leader of enough renown, that the Americans and Coalition forces put a price on his head and hunted for him. Baraat could not and did not trust anyone outside his tight clan. Baraat used the techniques he learned from the Taliban to keep the villagers terrified of him. So terrified was he that when Baraat rolled into a village, even hardened Afghan fighters cowered.

The village of Marjan, with its stone houses,

built into the sides of a mountain, had stood for nearly three thousand years. Legend has it that Alexander the Great and his army passed through Marjan as they conquered the world before Christ arrived. The village of Marjan had a reputation as friendly hospitable folk. They were spared violence from both the Russian invasion, the Taliban. The American invasion had brought some inconvenient night raids, searching for Taliban but that was it. The village's dirt streets and homes have always known peace and quiet, until today. Until Baraat Mansoor, brother of the Warlord, Masoud Mansoor arrived.

Baraat Mansoor is shaking a man Akhtar Sherzai, forty-one years old, by his neck over a pit with flames coming up from it. Two of Baraat's men have Akhtar by his bound feet and hands. Baraat screams out in Pashtun, "you want to work for the Americans?" as he slaps the helpless man across the face.

Shaking in terror, Akhtar pleads, "No. No I only asked for help for the village, for the school-"

"You must only ask God for help." Baraat screams, "and you must ask only through me!" Baraat pushes Akhtar into the flaming pit with the help of two of his two goons. We hear endless screaming. Baraat turns to the nearby villagers who have gathered to witness. "You worthless Hazaras, you only live in this shitty village because my family and I let you." Baraat signals his men to leave and they quickly board the truck, keeping its contents in the rear hidden. Baraat leans out the back waving his gun, "talk to the Americans again, and I will come back kill all of you. Some of my men will stay here to help you." The truck pulls away and Baraat smiles and shoots his pistol. Four of his men stand stay behind holding rifles.

Dr. Sovia is being walked away from his trailer with Sergeant Douglas holding his cuffs. He is spotted by some tough looking soldiers with full beards wearing a mix of Army uniforms and civilian clothes. Chief M is the first to point him out, "Hey Lance. That's him there." Chief M waves over his Captain towards Dr. Sovia.

"Hey! Hey soldier," Lance calls out and Dr. Sovia looks up at him, "yeah you. Sergeant Douglas keeps dragging him by the cuffs. The two ODA soldiers run up to Dr. Sovia, "hey can we talk to you a minute?"

Sergeant Douglas, still dragging Dr. Sovia, turns to address the voice, "this here's mah Private an NO ONE-" Sergeant Douglas stops speaking mid-sentence and squints to see the silver bars of a Captain nearly hidden by all the gear on Lance's body armor. He comes to attention and salutes. "Oh ahm sorry suh. I din see yo rank," he says apologetically.

Lance waves over to Staff Sergeants Bob White and Chris Langan, both muscular, bearded and strapped with cool gear and weapons on their body armor. Sergeant Douglas looks like a young man in love and is captivated by their presence. "Holy shit, yous is Green Berets," he says lovingly.

"God damn right we are Sergeant, Bob says while cracking a big smile. Chris looks Sergeant Douglas up and down approvingly. "You're in good shape. You ever think about trying out for the teams?" asks Chris trying to patronize him.

Sergeant Douglas looks mystified by the unique weaponry and gear of the Special Forces soldiers. "What kind a weapon n scope is at?"

Lance leans forward, "Sergeant you mind if we chat with your soldier?"

Without looking away Sergeant Douglas waves them off., "yeah, yeah... sho, chat all ya want," as he admires the Special Forces soldiers.

Lance and Chief M move close to Dr. Sovia while the Special Forces keep Sergeant Douglas occupied. "Hey I just wanna shake your hand. You saved my friend Craig yesterday," Chief M says as he reaches out and shakes Dr. Sovia's cuffed hand.

"Was that your guy?" replies Dr. Sovia, "glad I could help. But I think my ass is grass now because of it."

Lance looks puzzled, "whadaya mean? You in trouble or something?"

Dr. Sovia smirks and holds up his cuffed hands.

Outside an outdoor double row of blue Port-a-Pottys stands Lance and First Sergeant Hebblewaithe speaking to Major Harvey Goldstein who is sitting on the toilet with his pants down at his ankles with the door cracked open.

"Sir my name is Captain Erickson, 7th Special Forces group and I have an A-1 Priority Operation that requires your assistance."

We hear a burst of diarrhea from inside the Port-a-Potty and then Major Goldstein's empty hand juts out from the door, "Orders Captain? Need to see them."

Lance rubs his chin, "highly classified operation sir. We don't have anything in writing as of yet sir. But don't worry everything is legal."

"Oh god. Captain I don't need any more headaches this week." Another burst of diarrhea can be heard. Major Goldstein weakly says, "my health isn't so good. What do you need Captain?"

"Well," Lance begins... "sir I need-"

Cut back to conversation between Lance and Dr. Sovia

"Tell me Doc, you ever hear of the Special Forces?" Dr. Sovia looks strangely at Lance.

Cut back to conversation between Lance and Major Goldstein

"I don't care if you are Special Forces," Major

Goldstein chastises Lance, "this is United States Army and you will follow procedures Captain."

"But sir this is op is an A-1 Priority."

"I have not been informed of any such Operation Captain."

<u>Cut back to conversation between Lance and Dr. Sovia</u>

"Ya know, we could really use a guy with your skill set Doc," Chief M tries to stroke Dr. Sovia's ego.

"Wow, that sounds great, I'm honored but no," Dr. Sovia replies, "I'm no hero, just want to complete my contract and get my citizenship."

"We need you Doctor Sovia," Lance goes on, "the United States of America needs you."

"My kids need me Captain. They don't need to grow up with a memory of a dead dad who tried to be a hero."

"No need to be a hero Doc. Can you do an appendectomy?"

"In my sleep I can do an appendectomy Captain."

Cut back to conversation between Lance and Major Goldstein

"Who is this kidnap victim that has half the United States Security Council pulling strings for her?" Major Goldstein demands.

"I can't tell you that sir. But what I can tell you is, after we save her your participation will be noted."

Cut back to conversation between Lance and Dr. Sovia

Lance puts on his most sympathetic voice to Dr. Sovia, "Lemmee tell you about this girl who was kidnapped."

Cut back to conversation between Lance and Major Goldstein

Major Goldstein lets loose a blast of diarrhea and moans, "Captain. I do not have any surgeons to loan you. Most are out with this god damned virus." Another blast of diarrhea echoes from the port-a-potty, "including me." Lance winces and looks away holding his nose. Major Goldstein continues, "the 313th Forward Surgical Team is officially off line right now. Patients are being directed to other facilities."

"Sir, can you refer me to another hospital or Forward Surgical Team, we really need-"

"Are you hearing me Captain?" Major Goldstein yells as another blast of Diarrhea makes Lance start gagging, "with our hospital offline, the other medical units have to pick up the slack. I highly doubt anyone will loan you a doctor." Lance bangs his head against the Port-a-Potty.

<u>Cut back to conversation between Lance and Dr. Sovia</u>

Dr. Sovia looks incredulously at Lance, "you're telling me one of these girls, one the hostages, is the daughter a congressman?"

"Not just any congressman Doc," Lance replies, "her father is Roger Roberts, Chairman of the House Armed Services Committee, a very powerful dude."

"You're telling me if we save her, you're confident this Congressman can squash my Court Martial?"

"Doc, this guy decides how much money the Army gets to buy weapons," said Lance, "he can make anything happen."

Chief M adds to the conversation, "Doc, personally I hate the guy but he is one powerful SOB. Might runnin for President next election."

Lance takes a serious tone, "this is of course dependent on us rescuing his daughter, which we will do without firing a shot. But you have to save the warlord's daughter from an appendicitis."

Dr. Sovia holds up his cuffed hands to the ODA soldiers and says, "well it seems, the Army has different plans for me today, unless you can get me out of this."

Chief M liens in quietly to the Doctor, "all right doc, here's the plan."

Cut back to conversation between Lance and Major Goldstein

Lance continues to plead with the toilet ridden Major, "you said most sir, most of your surgeons are out with this virus, can I have-"

"I'm not giving you my last surgeon Captain!"

"How about this Mexican Private? The one who operated on one of my men last night? We need him just for a day."

"What? Hell no!" responds Major Goldstein forcefully. "He's being transported shortly to Kandahar for Court Martial."

Lance sighs in frustration. "Can your unit at least set up my Medics with the equipment to do an appendectomy?"

Major Goldstein is silent for a moment, and then yells loudly for the First Sergeant to hear him, "First Sergeant!"

"Right here Sir," says Top Hebblewaithe.

"Top, make sure the Captain's medics get every piece of equipment they need."

"Got it Sir," Top says as he looks disapprovingly at Lance.

"Get Dr. Paredo to make a list of the equipment they will be taking. And make god damned sure they sign for everything."

"I'm on it sir," replies Top.

"Now let me shit my brains out in peace, the both of you!" Major Goldstein lets the Port-a-Potty door slap shut as another blast of diarrhea echoes inside. Lance fights not to smirk while the First

Sergeant looks angrily at him.

Cut back to conversation between Lance and Dr. Sovia

Dr. Sovia gives a confident nod yes. "OK, I'll do it."

Lance & Chief M smile and Sergeant Douglas appears looking angry. He yanks Dr. Sovia away by his handcuffs. "C'mon taco boy, we gotta skedaddle."

VILLAGE OF MARJAN, AFGHANISTAN

The hanging man, hands tied together is hanging from the ceiling by a chain. The slow repetitive sound of a whip cracking on flesh is heard each time he winces. Baraat Mansoor presses is face up to the face of the tortured man. "Where is the money?" Baraat sadistically smiles while asking in Pashtun. Baraat presses his eye closer to the Hanging Man.

The hanging man coughs, breaths heavily and cries out, "I don't know! I swear!"

Baraat steps back and grabs a battery powered hand drill, holds it up, presses the trigger and the drill bit whirs. Baraat grabs the hanging man's legs and begins pressing the drill through his knees. The hanging man screams. This triggers the six female hostages tied up on the floor and sitting against the wall. They scream through their gags. Baraat smiles at the girls then back at the hanging man and in his quirky British/Paki accented English says, "TALK!"

The Hanging Man whimpers, "uuughhh!" Baraat stares at him for a second, pulls out his pistol and casually shoots a round into the hanging man through the head. The female hostages scream more. Abdul mumbles something in Pashtun and hands Baraat a phone Baraat switches to English.

"Brother dear, how nice to hear from you, wait one moment." Baraat covers the phone and glares with rage at the hostages. "Shut uuuuup!" Baraat growls and the girls fall silent. Baraat puts the phone back to his ear. "Of course…I'll have them ready in minutes… You got a good price I'm sure?" Baraat waits for confirmation silently. "Brother….? Shall we shall deliver them to you same as last time, hidden tunnel? Tata then." Baraat drags another

Afghan man bound and gagged towards the girls, hooks the man's hands and hoists him up to eye level, grabs Afghan man's hair while looking at the girls. "OK then, who wants' to go home?" Baraat produces a knife and slowly slices the flesh of the Hanging man and the female hostages scream through their gags.

Inside the rear area of a US Army cargo truck, on bench seats, sits Dr. Sovia, his hands still cuffed in front of him. He twitches and looks around nervously. A Military Police Soldier, MP Private First Class Boris Terry, twenty years old, sits next to him.

Boris Terry grew up in the bad ass streets of Baltimore as the youngest of three brothers. His oldest brother, Charlie Terry, shot dead in the streets when Boris was ten years old. The second brother, Marcus Terry, well he took on the role of avenging tough guy partly to impress his little brother Boris,

Marcus was shot down three years later when Marcus was only seventeen years old. Suspected of being a Police informant by the gangs, they exacted their own version of justice. Originally everyone not in a gang thought it was a drug related murder. Later reports from a larger narcotics conspiracy, it was disclosed, Marcus was indeed a police informant and his desire to avenge his dead brother, caused him to volunteer to go after the drug gangs. Marcus's undercover work, spearheaded the case against the gangs. Boris Terry felt driven to honor if not avenge his brothers by becoming a cop and beating the bad guys. Graduating High School at seventeen, Boris refused to wait four years to become a cop at the minimum age of twenty-one, Boris would gain real world experience by joining the US Army as a Military Police Soldier. He would get out of the Army at twenty-one years old, just in time to become a real cop.

On bench seats on the other side of the truck sits Dr. Maria Paredo, Nurse, Christina Cruz, Sergeant Douglas and the Nurse Anesthetist Judy Tonas from the operating room. They sway as the truck navigates the twisting mountain roads. Sergeant Douglas tosses his gum wrapper and hits Dr. Sovia with it to get his attention.

"I told you yo ass was gonna be in a lot a trouble Sovia!"

The Military Police soldier quickly shuts him

down with an authoritative voice, "I warned you earlier Sergeant! Witness will NOT speak to the accused in transit. Are we clear?"

Sergeant Douglas puffs out his chest to look more powerful. "And I outrank you Private, you don't tell me what ta do!"

The MP gives a steely look directly into Sergeant Douglas, "do not confuse your rank!... With my authority here... Sergeant."

Sergeant Douglas chest deflates as he bows his head and looks away. Maria picks up the conversation, "Don't worry Sovia, we'll be giving our statements right next to yours."

MP Private Terry sounds off in an authoritative voice, "Ma'am."

"We will get you out of this," Maria continues. Dr. Sovia gives her a cocky smile. Maria looks towards the MP, "I am a commissioned officer and I will speak to one of my soldiers."

MP Private Terry rolls his eyes and looks away. Dr. Sovia looks to Maria and calmly puts his finger to his lips, "It's going to be OK Doctor Paredo." Maria looks questioningly at Sovia's calmness but she is somehow reassured by him. "Is it wrong to have feelings for this man?" she wonders to herself. "He's an enlisted man, and a Private at that, the lowest military rank….yet he is a Doctor. What am I doing?" Maria questions herself.

How long has it been since she felt love, or the touch of a man. With her and her husband's, now ex-husband's divorce finalized, she knew she was free to love again. The pain of Roger's betrayal still stung her bitterly. Roger's deployment to Afghanistan started two years ago, just as US troops were starting to rebuild the country. She was faithful to Roger the whole year he was gone but she could not say the same for him. At first it was a missed phone call here and there and then after enough months it became obvious he did not care about her anymore.

Even when Roger came back to the states, she was willing let it go and forgive him. Maria understood the loneliness of long deployments, she was an Army officer also. It was two weeks after Roger's return that he served her with papers for divorce. She felt blindsided by his rapid abandonment and he did not even hide his affair. Instead he moved in with that nurse he was banging. Such a shit, she still hurt inside to think about it. She had not felt anything for any man except Roger and that had been only pain and sorrow for nearly a year now. She only met Private Roberto Sovia less than twenty-four hours ago but she could not stop this sudden infatuation. She hoped it did not show to the other officers.

Meanwhile on the other side of the mountain on a parallel road, Johnny Spann, our faithful Special Forces sniper is furiously spinning the steering wheel as the Humvee he's driving races along the, what would be called a goat trail anywhere else, but in Afghanistan passes for a road. The mounted radio cables hanging above his head, swing with each turn. "How we makin out Sir?" Johnny questions the boss.

Lance flips Johnny the middle finger from the passenger seat without looking up from the computer screen map. His cell phone pressed up against his ear as the engine roars. "Walid, pick up. C'mon, c'mon. Where the fuck is he?"

In the hills surrounding the road, a few miles away, dozens of Afghan men in military garb, scramble amongst the trees setting themselves up in tactical positions, lying down and positioning their machine guns towards the road. Walid Noor is barking commands in Pashtun when his cell phone chirps. He answers. "Hello, this is Walid Noor. How may I help you?

Walid hears Lance's voice on the phone, "Walid, you're not working in that Indian call center anymore, try and sound professional."

"Yes, that is very funny Red Rhino," Walid quips back at him, "I will always sound professional."Walid beats one of his soldiers with a riding crop forcing the soldier to move faster.

Lance, still tracing the map on his laptop reassures Walid, "And professional you are sir. Are you almost set up?"

"Yes we are in position and ready to go!" Walid beats more of his soldiers who are not ready or in place with his riding crop. "Sir, are you sure you want us only to use pyrotechnics? We have the explosives to really blow the snot out any vehicles we ambush."

Back in the racing Humvee, Lance looks concerned and raises his voice into the radio handset, "hey Walid It's an American truck. No casualties. Just blow the tree, block the road, and shoot the tires."

Walid responds over the radio, "Yes, yes sir! I understand, all gun fire goes over their heads."

"Don't fucking shoot anybody!" Lance tries to calm down, "we are moving into position now, the truck should be there in a few minutes. Be ready." Lance hangs up the phone and looks to Johnny at the wheel, "if anything goes wrong we are so fucked!

Johnny cracks a smile and looks over, "what could go wrong? It's Walid and a bunch of armed Afghan militia who can't read or write or seem to follow orders. I'm sure everything will be ok." Lance and Johnny look at each other with dismay but then they both break into laughter.

Back on Walid's side of the mountain, his militiamen are lying on their bellies, rifles and machine guns at the ready. They are mostly dressed in woodland camouflage so they blend in with the pine trees and sticks. Walid Noor peers through his binoculars at the road. He raises the walkie-talkie to his mouth, and squeezes the talk button, "open fire when you see the explosion. Remember men, shoot the tires then over their heads. Keep them pinned down. NO CASUALTIES!"

The US Army cargo truck, winds its way through the twisting, mountainous roads and slows as it approaches a hair pin turn. Walid watches then squeezes the detonator repeatedly. "Oooh wow," he marvels as giant multiple bursts of firework type pyrotechnics explode in the trees as the vehicle passes under them. One thick tree falls across the roadway. A hellish burst of automatic weapons fire shreds the vehicles tires and it careens off the road into the trees. A few stray rounds of heavy machine gun fire pierce the passenger window of the truck and explode the radio mounted in the vehicle. All the soldiers in the vehicle are screaming at the sound of the gunfire from outside as they sway to and fro. They suddenly crash to a halt.

MP Private Terry tries to take charge, everybody calm the fuck DOWN!" He bangs on the rear window of the truck to communicate with the driver, "what da fuck is going on out there?" The rear tarp of the cargo truck is tossed open and masked men in military gear dive into the rear area of the truck.

"What the fuck!?"Screams out MP Terry, the other MP soldier in the truck is jumped and zip tied as MP Private Terry fumbles for his M-4 rifle but he is kicked in the head and goes down. Dr. Sovia is quickly carried under each arm and then thrown from the truck into the arms of other masked men who carry him down the mountain through the woods and into a vehicle which quickly speeds away.

As the Humvee races away from the ambush on a side road, the soldiers of ODA 666 are hooting and hollering. Lance tries get in touch with Walid on the cell phone while yelling to his soldiers, "hold it down, I can't hear."

Dr. Sovia, lying in the back of the Humvee is breathing hard and crosses himself. "Holy Christ. I thought we were dead."

Lance yells into his cell phone, "Walid! Break contact. Do you copy?"

Back on the other side of the mountain, the group of Afghan Militia is on the move, hurrying away from the ambush site. The MP truck can be seen burning in the background. Walid presses the phone to his ear. "Yes, yes. We are already away."

Lance's voice comes through the cell phone loud and clear, "everyone is OK right? No casualties?"

Walid looks back to the burning cargo truck and two Military Police soldiers trying to stop the flames with a little extinguisher. "Not unless you count their truck," he replies.

Back inside Lance's cramped Humvee, the soldiers are calming down, "good work Walid, I'll see you on the next one." Lance ends the call, turns to the backseat and looks with godlike confidence at Dr. Sovia in the back seat of the Humvee, still breathing heavily and wiping his face.

"Well Doc", Lance exclaims, "you are about to be declared officially Missing in Action."

Dr. Sovia is still huffing, "everybody is OK... Yes?" Lance smiles recklessly and scrolls through the numbers in his cell phone while not even looking up at Dr. Sovia

"Everybody is OK doc. I'm sure they'll be calling for help on the radio. They'll be picked up by friendlies."

"You're sure?" Dr. Sovia questions him, "I don't want to see anyone get in trouble for my sake."

Snapping his phone shut and turning back to the windshield Lance calmly says, "Of course, don't worry so much."

"I don't know what the hell I was thinking agreeing to this crazy mission," Dr. Sovia starts to whine. "I better not get screwed."

Johnny, still driving, looks in the rearview mirror, "welcome to the Green Berets doc. We do crazy every day."

Dr. Sovia leans from the rear and juts his still cuffed hands in Lance's field of view. Lance sees the hand cuffs and while laughing gets on the radio, "all right, which one of you degenerates has the handcuff keys?" Bob White up in the gun turret laughs and passes down his set of keys which Lance then uses to un-cuff the doctor.

Dr. Sovia rubs his wrists still looking angrily at Lance, "you wanna tell me how in the hell am I supposed to operate on someone, I have no surgical gear."

Johnny, while steering the Humvee, looks in the rear view mirror, "gotchya covered doc. Your C.O. got us a lady doctor to put together everything we need for surgery."

"Lady Doctor? You mean Doctor Paredo. Maria?"

Johnny smiles playfully in the rearview mirror again, "she's pretty hot huh?"Dr. Sovia seems stiff and uncomfortable with this topic. Johnny won't let it go, "lighten up doc. You with the teams now son, we have fun at work." Dr. Sovia's face looks astonished and turns to Lance.

"I'm taking a big risk here on Congressman, I don't even know his name, Robert's, gratitude. I mean… What are we doing?"

Lance raises an eyebrow while looking at the map, "hey doc, do the appendectomy, the Warlord gets us the hostages back and we're all heroes. The congressman will be obligated to help his daughter's rescuers."

"And you have this in writing Captain? I joined the Army to protect my kids. If I'm thrown out of the Army or worse in an Army jail, I can't help my kids."

Lance turns around to look at Dr. Sovia, "lighten up Doc. This is the Special Forces, we operate quite differently than the mainstream Army you are used to." Lance returns to his laptop.

"You not kidding it's different."

Lance looks him over then goes back to the map, "are you ready for an appendectomy doctor?"

"I invented them Captain," Dr. Sovia responds.

Lance turns back to Dr. Sovia, "there! That's the kind of confidence we need in this outfit. Oh shit! One more thing," Lance pulls out his knife, leans over and cuts the Private rank insignia off of Dr. Sovia's uniform. "Under NO CIRCUMSTANCES Doctor, are you to tell ANYONE here, you are a Private. You will introduce yourself ONLY as Dr. Sovia. Clear?"

Dr. Sovia beams with confidence. "With pleasure Captain," he replies.

"And no Sirs or Captain either," Lance adds, "just be a confident, arrogant dick. Can you do that?"

Dr. Sovia smiles, "another one of my inventions."

All the Special Forces soldiers laugh at his

bravado. Someone throws Dr. Sovia a cold drink, he cracks the bottle and chugs it down. "What's a Congressman's daughter doing in Afghanistan anyway?" Dr. Sovia asks, "isn't that against the rules?"

"Saving the world I'm sure," Lance replies, "good for public relations I guess."

Johnny chimes in and adds, "hey, Senator McCain's son is an Infantry Marine in Iraq, so what the fuck?"

Dr. Sovia turns back to Lance, "I've been here four months, I haven't heard of Kelly Roberts."

Only happened two days ago, Lance reveals, "this is all highly classified."

"And we're getting her back for one lousy appendix? Almost seems as if they are giving her back for free."

The Humvees arrive at Masoud Mansoor's mountain redoubt. In the daylight it looks like a medieval stone fortress. It probably was at some point in history. Lance continues, "we don't think the bad guys even know who they have. I'm just hoping young Miss Roberts knows to keep her young mouth shut."

The cave had surprisingly high ceilings, most think of a cave as a dark and cramped space but this cave had electric light bulbs, strung up on the high ceiling. Wooden crates were stacked six feet high with Cyrillic words stamped on them. Weapons left over from the Soviet Empire's last folly into Afghanistan were still being sold and used to kill.

Along the wall, six female hostages are up on their feet. Afghan men are untying their hands and giving them water bottles. Kelly Roberts sees Baraat Mansoor a few feet away giving orders in Pashtun. "Abdul, get them ready to transport to my brother's house. We are about to collect our ransom."

Abdul roughly shoves water bottles to the women. Kelly steps towards Baraat.

"It's about goddamned time," Kelly crows, "we are thirsty and hungry. I want-"

Baraat scowls at Kelly, "I can always put the gag back on you young lady."

Kelly looks down and keeps rubbing her wrists, "are we really going home?" Baraat smiles cruelly at her. "Some of us need to pee sir," she says, "you know...use the toilet."

Baraat scowls, "yes I know the toilet." He snaps his fingers at Abdul and points and rattles off in Pashtun, "take them to the shit hole. Quickly, we are leaving for my brother's compound momentarily."

Abdul nods yes and grabs Kelly and another girl by the arm and pushes them further into the cave. Baraat switches back to English, "Follow him, he will take you."

Stacey Baker is left with the other two hostages, hugging, smiling and drinking water. Stacey confides to the girls, "I knew her father would get us out. Thank god he's a Congressman."

Baraat overhears the conversation and his head turns to the girls staring at them. The girls notice him and poke Stacey.

"What did you just say young lady?" Baraat questions her.

"I'm just saying," Stacey drawls on, "thank God Kelly's dad is a powerful guy. I guess he arranged our freedom."

Baraat pauses, looks back in the direction of Kelly and then looks back at Stacey. "Congressman?... Roberts?"... Baraat says questioningly. The look of realization comes across Baraat's face like an epiphany. "Congressman Roberts of course."

"Yeah. Of course," Stacey adds.

Baraat looks sharply back in the direction Abdul and the Afghans brought the girls and screams, "ABDUL!!! Bring them back!"

The Manservant leads Dr. Sovia and three Special Forces soldiers carrying bags of medical equipment to the exam room we saw earlier. Chief M. puts down his bags.

Dr. Sovia sees Ameena on the exam table and turns to Ritchie.
"Get a cuff on her right now, I want a BP and a temperature ASAP."
Ritchie complies and the men begin pulling out medical gear.
"Sergeant Spann, in that silver case you carried is a

portable anesthesia vaporizer. Pull it out and prep the tank of Desflurane with the regulator and hook it up."

Johnny stares at perplexed "Doc I ahh."

"Do your best Sergeant, I'll be there in a minute to help fix it." Dr. Sovia approaches the young Afghan woman sitting on the exam table. She lies back on the table. Dr. Sovia looks in her eyes with a light. "Call out her pressure and temp anytime now Sergeant Long."

Ritchie calls out, "BP 159 over 99 temp 102."

Dr. Sovia lifts up her burka to examine her abdomen, "Oh no good. We gotta move fast people." They all prep faster.

Lance paces in an outside courtyard of Masoud's fortress. It is filled with flowers and a small pond. Soldiers from his team are spread out pulling security around the compound. Masoud Mansoor walks into the garden with his manservant. "You are a man of you word Captain."

"Did you doubt me sir?"

"I doubt all Western promises young Captain," Masoud replies.

"Well sir, in the game "Let's make a Deal", I believe it is your turn."

Masoud pauses and looks at Lance while thinking, "and I will fulfill my end Captain. My daughter is not yet out of surgery. Regardless, the Western guests and Imran Khan, are on their way here of course."

Lance studies the face of Masoud looking for lies but finds none. "I would like to think we can build on this cooperation," Lance says.

Masoud pauses and thinks, "build what Captain?"

"A better Afghanistan sir. A better place for your daughter to grow up, a better place where people don't have to die constantly for nothing."

Masoud smiles for the first time then puts his smile away while gesturing with his arms, "This is the Afghanistan that was here three thousand years ago. It will be the same Afghanistan three thousand years from now. Only the weapons change, Afghans will never change. I do admire your idealism young Captain. Hold on to that as long as you can."

Back in the exam room turned Operating Room, the three soldiers of ODA 666 and Dr. Sovia are masked, capped and have blue surgical aprons over their clothes. Dr. Sovia has a head-lamp strapped to his forehead and is reaching into Ameena's open body cavity.

"BP Sergeant Long?" asks Dr. Sovia.

"140 over 80 Doc. Holding steady."

"Ok Sergeant Long, if you can see this without moving good, if not then too bad. Sergeant Spann do you see that grossly swollen bulb on the end of the long intestine?"

"I do," replies Johnny.

"Watch where I put the clamps you may have to do this one day." Dr. Sovia reaches into Ameena with a stainless steel clamp. "Sergeant Spann I want you to reach in and clamp the other side, I will guide you." Johnny reaches in with a little less precision and Dr. Sovia guides his hand. "No, further up from the colon. She'll still want to hold her poopies in for a few more years."

All four men and the manservant standing nearby laugh. "Be careful to go around the connecting tissue," warns Dr. Sovia, "don't poke it, it may puncture and all those delicious intestinal juices will cause peritonitis."

"What's that?" Chief M asks.

Both Ritchie and Johnny simultaneously call out "Infection." Dr. Sovia looks at the two soldiers approvingly.

"Now watch gentleman," the Doctor demonstrates with the clamp, "at the risk of sounding condescending, we cut on the OPPOSITE side, of the clamp, away from the appendix. The clamps will keep all the juices inside."

The truck bounces down a rutted narrow dirt road. In the rear cargo area of the truck, sit six female hostages and Imran Khan. All the hostages are blindfolded, hands tied, sitting in the dimly lit truck. The hostages sway to and fro. Abdul and other Afghan men sit across from them on pillows on the floor. Abdul cruelly pushes his feet into their legs making them wince or cry out in pain. Kelly Roberts calls out, "Whoever is doing that to my legs stop it now!" Abdul cruelly laughs and presses harder. She screams.

Abdul screams back at her in Pashtun, "Quiet!" Baraat leans into Kelly and starts playing with her hair while he speaks closely into her face. "That was very clever Miss Roberts," Baraat says, "hiding your father's identity."

"I didn't hide anything."

"Nor did you volunteer that information... No matter," Baraat continues, "your true value is much, much more than we had bargained for." Baraat turns to Stacey. "And you, thank you so much for making us aware Miss Baker." A shrill cry is drowned out by truck brakes, everyone leans forward to a stop. Men can be heard walking and talking outside. The cargo truck's rear canvas flaps are pulled open. Baraat's goons scramble to their feet and yank the hostages up.

Baraat begins issuing commands in Pashtun, "Get them out of the truck. GENTLY! Do not damage our merchandise." Baraat points to Abdul. "Be nice! Walk them down the cave and up the stairs to my brother's compound." Abdul nods in agreement. "Wait with them inside the room at the top of the stairs," says Baraat. "Keep them there just in case we have to escape. DO NOT show them to the Americans."

Abdul's eyes widen as he reacts to the sound of Americans and he racks the bolt on his AK-47. The girls scream and shudder at the sound of the weapon. Baraat turns to the hostages and switches to English, "Ladies, Mr. Future Vice President, it is almost over. Relax." Baraat jumps out of the truck and turns back to his men as he walks off he says magnanimously, "I must protect my family's interests."

Back in the exam room turned Operating Room, Dr. Sovia and his soldier/surgical assistants are still working on Ameena. "Blood Pressure 140 over 80," says Ritchie

Dr. Sovia looks at him, "Thank you Sergeant. Good job assisting. We are a GO gentlemen. Chief M, please go inform the good Captain that Ms. Ameena Mansoor is all done and OK." The

Manservant standing nearby comes forward to inspect for himself. Dr. Sovia looks him in the eye, "She's all good. Go tell your boss."

Ritchie and Johnny fist bump each other and simultaneously say, "YES!" The Manservant's nods and exits the makeshift Operating Room.

It is late afternoon in Afghanistan as the survivors from the MP truck walk the dirt road. The sun beats down on Nurse Christina Cruz's face. Christina was never one for outdoor sports or camping or any real stressful endeavor, which made it all the more puzzling to her parents as to why she would join the Army as a nurse. Sure the Army was going to pay back all of her college loans, and they were many, but "The Army Christine?" her astonished parents questioned her.

"I'm not a weakling!" Christine shot back at her parents. "I can be tough and the Army is going to help me." Now lost in the mountains of Afghanistan, her throat in pain from thirst, Christine could not stop second guessing her decision, "What the fuck was I thinking?" she thought to herself. She licks her lips and cries out loud, "did anyone bring any water?

MP Private Terry staggers and sways, looks at her and finally says "I did". Christina's face brightens for a moment, "but I drank it all," replies Private Terry.

"Why can't somebody call for help?" Christina whines. "This is ridiculous."

Maria slugs along carrying a military medical bag looks annoyed but responds, "The radio blew up when it was shot."

"Didn't anyone bring a cell phone?" Christina says looking around the group of exhausted soldiers.

Sergeant Douglas feels compelled to remind anyone of the regulations, "ya know private cell phones are against regulation Ma'am."

Christina looks at the four Military Police Soldiers who were in the MP truck walking along, their faces covered in bandages. "This sucks, what about you guys, a cell phone?"

MP's look back at her, "same regulations Ma'am," says Private Terry.

Christina looks oddly at Maria, "and who thinks to bring a medical bag to Kandahar?"

Maria responds with the authority of her higher rank, "that's why I'm the doctor. Lieutenant Cruz you need to start behaving according to your rank." Christina looks disparagingly at Maria.

Sergeant Douglas gets a surge of courage and walks proudly to the front of the group and announces, "That it people. I am taking charge." A collective groan can be heard in the group as Sergeant Douglas pulls out a map and compass and starts looking around. "Map heyer shows a lil village called Marjan a couple a mahles way. Maybe theys got a phone we kin borra."

Masoud Mansoor is a wealthy man who does a great deal of thinking. He seeks peace in solitude and high up in his stone fortress, in one of the upstairs rooms is a lavishly decorated western style man cave, with all the accoutrements of the Western world, a widescreen television, plush leather couches, a computer work station and best of all, a fully functioning bar. Masoud looks at the setting sun from his mountain redoubt, holding a scotch on the rocks and a cell phone to his ear. The Manservant walks in and whispers to Masoud.

"She is well? It is over?" The Manservant nods, Masoud snaps his cell phone shut slamming the empty glass down on his way towards the door. Baraat Mansoor, his brother walks into the man cave blocking his brother's exit. Masoud stops, "am I late again Brother?" Baraat asks. Masoud stares at Baraat then starts to walk out only to have Baraat put his hand on Masoud's chest. "Is that Alcohol on your breath? Baraat questions his brother, "yet again brother?"

Masoud looks deep into Baraat's eyes and responds, "wait here, I must ensure I am getting what I bargained for. Masoud continues out the door.

"Oh, I have a feeling you ... We... are going to get far more than you bargained for," Baraat says as Masoud spins back around at him.

Masoud looks confused, "what are you saying?"

Baraat smiles cruelly at him, "let me tell you about at least one of our guests. Who knows brother... maybe more than one."

Downstairs and outside, within the stone walled compound, some of the Special Forces soldiers are cleaning their gear, enjoying a moment of rest. Lance stands next to his Humvee, his body armor, helmet and gear are off his body and lying on the hood where he stretches his legs.

Chief M arrives smiling and chipper. "Oh sir Lance-alot, she's all done." Lance smiles and hugs Chief M enthusiastically.

"Yes!" Lance joyfully exclaims, "we're almost there, just waitin on our girls to arrive."

"You sure bout Masoud guy comin through?" Mike questions.

"Who fuck can be sure about any of these Hajis Mike. I get the impression he loves his daughter though." Lance pulls out his cell phone, dials and waits and waits and looks at Chief M, "If they're all done down there get em packed up and ready to rock. I want to vacate this AO (Area of Operations) as soon as we have our girls."

Chief M radios the surgical team but no answer, he starts walking off, turns to Lance who is still on the phone, "No signal Lance, I gotta go back down."

Lance hangs up his phone and looks back at the stone fortress, "Masoud is not answering, I'm not liking this already."

Back upstairs in the fortress, Baraat stands before Masoud pointing his finger and yelling, "you! You and your decadence.

"Shut up! Get out of my way!" Masoud shouts as he attempts to push past Baraat but he is shoved back.

"You think your money will buy you into heaven," screams Baraat, "money is a tool!" Masoud snaps his fingers and his Manservant draws his pistol in a flash. But Baraat draws faster and fires. The Manservant cries out and goes down.

Masoud rushes to his man and kneels, "what have you done?!" Baraat leans over his brother still clutching his gun.

"No… brother," says Baraat, "it is what YOU

have done, selling our family out for the life of one girl."

"Not just one girl, my daughter! Your Niece!"

Baraat pauses and stands up straight and announces, "We hold hostage, the daughter of one of the most powerful politicians in America, we can squeeze them for almost anything we want."

"I already have everything I want," screams Masoud, "I would not lose my only child so you can have a better bargaining position."

Baraat waves his arms in frustration and anger, "a necessary sacrifice towards our ends. You have grown weak! Decadent! Look at you, drinking alcohol, in your palace, counting your money. The money I have earned for you!" Baraat raises his gun and shoots his brother several times, then pulls out his cell phone, dials and speaks in Pashtun, "Plan B everyone. Go. NOW. Everyone!" Baraat removes Masoud's phone from his dead hand and sees a missed call.

Back downstairs in the basement medical

exam room, the three soldiers of ODA 666 are packing up medical equipment. Dr. Sovia consults with Ameena's mother. "I am leaving you two bottles of Amoxicillin to prevent infection, one pill three times a day," Dr. Sovia tells her.

"Thank you doctor, I will care for her," replies Mrs. Mansoor.

"Your English is excellent Mrs. Mansoor. Where did you study if I may ask?"

Mrs. Mansoor studies Dr. Sovia's face looking for sarcasm but only finds compassion. "London School of Economics Doctor, I was not always in Afghanistan," she replies.

A gunshot is heard from upstairs in the house. All the soldiers tense up. "Welcome to Afghanistan gentlemen," Mrs. Mansoor breaks the tension, "someone is always shooting something here."

The soldiers chuckle and look at each other. "C'mon guys, pack! We wanna get upstairs for the exchange," says Chief M.

Dr. Sovia says, "good luck with her Mrs. Mansoor, a-salam-allekium."

Mrs. Mansoor smiles, "a-lekum-salam, thank

you Doctor, I was just-"

More shots ring out in succession above in the house. Chief M drops the med bags and barks out commands "that's not good. Gear up boys, body armor and weapons. NOW." The Special Forces Soldiers drop the bags of medical gear and throw on their body armor and gear and rack their rifles. Mrs. Mansoor hugs her still sleeping daughter.

Back outside in the walled compound, Lance runs and reaches his Humvee and hurriedly straps on his body armor then speaks into the radio handset through the driver side window. "Chris, Bobby pick up. I'm hearing shots."

The radio crackles to life, "boss you there? It's Chris."

"Yeah, go Chris," replies Lance over the radio, "whatta we got?"

In the hills overlooking Masoud Mansoor's stone compound, Staff Sergeant Chris Langan lies amongst the bushes and trees, again he is heavily camouflaged and covered in a Ghillie camouflage suit to look like a bush with a radio handset pressed against his head. "Boss, we got multiple indigenous personnel, possible Taliban or insurgents coming down from the hills towards the compound." Chris Langan holds the radio handset in one hand and looks through his infrared binoculars with the other, "In tactical formation and armed."

Through the infrared binoculars Chris sees fifty to seventy human like shapes, slowly walking. They appear to be carrying a variety of rifles and rocket launchers as they get closer to the walled compound of Masoud's fortress.

Back in the walled compound the sun is setting and it is getting dark. Lance holds the radio handset to his ear while he straps on his gear. "What? How many Chris?"

Over the radio, Chris's voice sounds tentative, "All of Afghanistan... I think. Holy shit a lot of them."

A few meters away from Lance's Humvee sits Staff Sergeant Dan Nuzzi, twenty-six years old and part of Lance's ODA 666. Dan, the team's communications Sergeant, still wearing headphones, hangs his head out from his Humvee. "Lance I'm pickin up a whole lot of radio chatter on the open frequency. Something's happening."

Lance still pulling on his gear yells back, "Goddamn right something's happening. Get on the radio to everyone. Gear the fuck up. NOW!"

Far below Masoud Mansoor's fortress, like so many of Afghanistan's warlord's homes, a series of complex tunnels was dug out and built over the years. Masoud as a business man, whose business consisted of mostly smuggling. He needed safe and hidden areas to store his precious cargo, whatever cargo it might be at the time. Tunnels, some natural, others carved out to form stone stairwells up and down from the fortress, lead into and out of hidden cave entrances. Brother Baraat made use of these tunnels over the years, bringing his brother's often illegal cargo of liquor, drugs, prostitutes, or any Western luxury goods that could be sold at a handy profit. Baraat again tonight made use of his brother's tunnels, now dozens of armed Afghans are climbing up the stairs from the underground tunnel and pouring into the stone fortress of Masoud Mansoor, spreading out and upstairs overlooking the compound.

Back downstairs in the basement medical exam room, the three Special Forces Soldiers stand by the exam room door, rifles at the ready.

"Anybody have their night vision goggles?" asks Johnny

"Yeah mounted to my helmet back in the truck," Answers Ritchie. Chief M responds, "Great fucking place for it... so are mine." He looks back towards Dr. Sovia still standing by Ameena Mansoor and her mother. "Doc unless you are planning on staying here, get in front of me behind Ritchie. NOW doc!"

Dr. Sovia looks apprehensive and hesitates. Chief M goes to grab and drag him but Dr. Sovia intervenes, "I don't need to be grabbed like I'm-"

An overwhelming burst of automatic weapons fire explodes nearby and shreds the walls and doors of the exam room and knocks out most of the hallway lights. Shouts in Pashtun are heard from the dark hallway outside. Chief M attempts to motivate his men, "Well, nothing like a gunfight in a basement."

"Fuck yeah!" Ritchie yells out supportively.

A voice comes out from the dark hallway in heavily accented English, "you die today Yankee! You die!" Ritchie and Johnny look at each other while pulling out, arming grenades and tossing them down the dark hallway. The voice calls out again, "You die you Yankee, you-" The explosion rocks the hallway with smoke and debris.

Ritchie calmly states, "we should get out of here now."

"No, she can't be moved yet!" says Dr. Sovia as he covers Ameena's body with his own.

Chief M turns to see Dr. Sovia covering Ameena with his body. The Chief pulls out his pistol and shoves it in Dr. Sovia's chest. "nothin worse than coming unarmed to a gunfight doc."

Dr. Sovia looks at the pistol while clutching it, "I'm a doctor. I don't kill people."

Far above the basement exam room, inside the stone house of Masoud Mansoor, armed Afghan men are taking up positions in windows overlooking the courtyard where Operational Detachment Alpha 666 (ODA 666) has parked their vehicles. Baraat Mansoor takes charge of his men and the attack. "Everyone hold your fire until I give the command to-" A lone Afghan starts shooting wildly out the window upon sight of the Americans. Baraat pulls out his pistol aims it at the man's head but then all the Afghans begin shooting out the windows. Baraat puts his pistol away without firing it and says to no one in particular, "So much for surprise."

Back outside, within the stone walled compound Lance and the remaining men of ODA 666 are already alerted and armored up. Shots ring out from the stone house in the compound. Lance stars yelling commands, "Bobby, get that 50 up!" Bob, sitting in the turret of the heavy machine gun atop the Humvee is racking and re racking the big heavy gun up in the Humvee roof turret.

"I'm jammed up," yells Bob." Lance returns fire with his M-4 automatic rifle ducking behind the hood of the Humvee.

"Well get it un-fucking jammed!" Lance yells out while attempting to survey the battlefield. Bob racks the bolt on the big gun one more time and lets loose a volley of heavy rounds into the house. The air pulsates like a rock concert from the big gun being fired. The stone walls of the fortress crack and crumble wherever the rounds impact

"I'm up boss," Bob yells over the gunfire. Lance ignores him and kneels down behind the

Humvee with the radio handset pressed up against his ear and mouth, "all units engage at will. Mike, pick up, we're in contact... MIKE pickup!"

Back downstairs in the basement medical exam room, the Special Forces Soldiers stand by the exam room door, rifles at the ready while Dr. Sovia tends to Ameena Mansoor. The sound of heavy gunfire is heard from up above. Chief M. screams into the radio handset. "Lance, Bobby, Danny, any station this net pick up." He puts the radio handset back into its pocket. "No signal down here. Mrs. Mansoor, is there another way out?"

Mrs. Mansoor, sitting a few feet away, holding her daughter Ameena replies, "I'm sorry no there is not."

Chief M. looks at her kindly, "they are not after you or your daughter. They are after us so stay here." The Chief turns around to talk to his soldiers. "Everyone full magazine in and one in hand, we are pushing out of here.

Dr. Sovia defends his patient, "I said she can't be moved!"

"She's not being moved Doc, you however,

are." Chief M hands him two spare magazines of pistol ammo.

Dr. Sovia looks down at the magazines of pistol ammo and back up at the Chief, "I told you I don't-"

The Chief grabs the Doctor by his lapel, "sometimes you gotta stand up and fight for what you want doc. This girl is important. Is she important enough to fight for?" Bursts of machine gun fire are exchanged between the door and the hallway. Dust and debris fly everywhere. "Worry not doc we'll do the fightin, you just point the gun behind us and shoot anything that moves. Ya hear?" Dr. Sovia nods then runs to a far corner and pulls out a surgical blanket and covers Ameena, still lying on the table.

Mrs. Mansoor, keep her covered, says Dr. Sovia.

"We will be fine doctor," she replies. Dr. Sovia clumsily holds the pistol as Chief M pulls him close.

"Stack up boys." Chief M orders as the soldiers line up closely to each other with the Doctor sandwiched in between. "Let's go go go!" The

Special Forces soldiers move into the hallway with weapons at the ready, peering through the dust and dark to acquire targets. At the end of the hall light can be seen. Johnny silently motions with his hand to move towards it.

In the hills overlooking Masoud Mansoor's stone compound, Chris is lying flat on the ground in his Ghillie camouflage suit blending in with the vegetation. He peers through the scope of his long rifle watching the unknown Afghans attack the compound walls. He shoots over and over.

Inside Masoud Mansoor's stone fortress, Baraat looks out the window, down at the trapped Special Forces soldiers in the compound and smiles and turns to his trusted aid Abdul and says in Pashtun, "we will be the first to capture a Special Forces A-Team Abdul." Abdul smiles and slides his finger across his throat mimicking an execution. Baraat pats his back and looks at his brother's phone and dials the most recent missed call. Baraat, now screaming in Pashtun, "cease fire. Cease fire." The shooting stops, Baraat holds the phone to his head.

Down in the compound, inside his armored Humvee, Lance sits in the passenger seat shouting into the radio handset as bullets ping off the armor. "Big Bird One. Big Bird One. This is Red Rhino. Come in, over.... FUCK!" Lance switches radio handsets and speaks again "Mike! Pick up! ...God Damn it!"

Back downstairs in hallway outside the basement medical exam room, the three Special Forces soldiers walk abreast of each other and spread out down the darkened basement hallway towards the light. Dr. Sovia walks behind them with his pistol pointed towards the rear. Baraat's armed insurgents begin rushing in from the dimly lit entrance into the basement.

Johnny is the first to spot them, he calls it out loud, "Contact! 12 O'clock." All three soldiers commence firing and the insurgents fire back. Glowing bullets and screams fill the basement air.

Dr. Sovia takes cover behind a side door but does not fire his pistol. A Major fire-fight ensues, bullets flying back and forth. The smell or cordite fills the air as debris flies off the walls where the bullets hit.

A new scream cries out. Ritchie shouts, "Johnny's down!" Ritchie throws a grenade down the hallway. It explodes and he races to rescue Johnny while firing his weapon as he moves. Bullets come from behind them where they just left. Ritchie screams and goes down.

Chief M yells out, "Ritchie's down!" Dr. Sovia sees more of more of Baraat's men enter the basement and Dr. Sovia fires his pistol at them and they momentarily retreat. Chief M runs to Dr. Sovia, crouched down in a side doorway. The Chief is bleeding profusely from his neck.

"Holy shit Chief." Dr. Sovia starts to treat Chief M to stem the bleeding.

Breathing heavily, Chief M grabs Dr. Sovia's tunic, "I'm gone Doc, shot in the legs too… Go get the girl." Dr. Sovia looks back down the hallway, hears shouts in Pashtun.

"I can't. I don't know how. I'm doctor I'm not a hero."

Chief M grabs Dr. Sovia's collar and pulls him close, "you a soldier motherfucker!" Chief M gurgles on his own blood. Fear sweeps across Dr. Sovia's face as Chief M continues, "can't run away this time Doc... You gonna fight for her Doc... You gonna fight for anything?" Chief M goes limp and silent. We hear boots crunching on debris. Dr. Sovia sees three of Baraat's insurgents at the end of the hallway look into the exam room and walk in.

Three armed insurgents stand over Mrs. Mansoor who is clutching her barely conscious daughter. They point their AK47 rifles at them and shred them with bullets.

From where Dr. Sovia is still sitting, he sees the men begin firing, and is instantly enraged. He leaps to his feet, pistol in hand runs down the hallway. The sounds of his steps are masked by the machine gun fire. He dives into the exam room firing his pistol and kills all three insurgents screaming, "NOOOOoooooooo!" He throws himself on top of Ameena, now lying on top of her mother's bloody body.

Ameena barely alive whispers, "Papa. Papa. Pa-"

Dr. Sovia holds her tight and cries.

In the hills overlooking Masoud Mansoor's stone compound, Chris is lying down, hidden in the underbrush by his Ghillie camouflage suit, killing enemies via sniper rifle. His radio crackles to life with Lance's voice, "Chris pickup!" Chris hears the radio and grabs the handset off his shoulder, "Little busy boss." The radio voice comes back out, "we're sitting ducks in the compound," says Lance, "how we looking from there?"

"You are about to be overrun boss", Chris replies over the radio, "a minute or two... give or take."

Down in the compound, inside his armored Humvee, Lance sits in the passenger seat on the radio when suddenly the volume of fire from the house suddenly drops. He looks outside then his cell phone rings. He looks down at the number and answers the call, "Masoud you fucking scumbag! I saved your daughter and you fuck us like this?"

Inside Masoud Mansoor's stone fortress, Baraat looks out the window, down at the trapped Special Forces soldiers in the compound with

Masoud's cell phone pressed to his head and smiles. "Captain Lance Erikson I presume." Baraat paces while he talks, "I say presume because I have not had the pleasure meeting you face to face."

Back in the Humvee, Lance replies, "Who the fuck is this?" The British accented English comes out of the cell phone very clearly, Baraat responds "but I have a feeling I will be seeing you close up in a matter of minutes."

"This is Masoud's phone" Lance says.

"It still is his," replies Baraat over the phone.

"So he's...?" asks Lance.

Baraat looks down from the fortress out the window at Lance's Humvee parked outside in the compound. "Moved on to the next world, Allah will decide my brother's fate," Baraat smiles as he says.

Back in the Humvee, Lance's face reveals he suddenly knows to whom he is speaking. "BARAAT!" Lance says.

"Oh a smart one," replies Baraat over the phone, "are you the one who ruined my first ransom pickup?"

"Yeah," replies Lance, "and I'm gonna ruin your last one too scumbag!"

Baraat looks down from the fortress out the window, cell phone up to his ear, "well I wish I could have talked you into a surrender. But now I won't even offer."

Lance's voice comes out over the phone, "this isn't over."

"You are right. It is not over," Baraat brags, "I am going to video us dragging your naked dead body across the dirt and release it to the world." Baraat hangs up, signals to his men to open fire and returns to the window to watch.

Back in the Humvee, the automatic weapons fire increases to a deafeningly roar, the bullets pinging off the armor of the Humvee as it rocks every time it's big fifty caliber fires. The windows start to crack from the bullets impact.

Just then, the radio crackles to life, "Red Rhino, Big Bird One Over."

Lance jumps to grab the radio handset and talks into it, "Big Bird one, Red Rhino, how copy over?"

The giant grey four propeller plane is circling above the compound at ten thousand feet altitude. From the plane, the compound below can be seen with rifle fire criss-crossing over it. AC-130 Attack Plane was first used in the Vietnam War. A monster sized cargo plane, mounted with Gatling guns and howitzer cannons along one side of the plane's fuselage. The AC-130 affectionately known as Puff the Magic Dragon in Vietnam now known as Spectre gunships, can circle a target, at night and cover every square inch of a football field with a bullet. The electric powered, rotating Gatling gun fires six thousand, yes SIX THOUSAND rounds a minute. With every sixth round a glowing tracer round, when the Gatling gun fired, it looks like a solid laser beam coming down from the sky. It is a fearsome sight to behold.

Back in the Humvee, the Radio Voice booms "Red Rhino, Big Bird One, read ya five by five, good to be working with you again. We are on station at your position at this time over."

Lance presses the radio handset pressed to his ear and consults his laptop map. More and more armed Afghan men are climbing over the walls and shooting at them. He squeezes the talk button on the handset and tries to act calm, "Big bird One, we are being overran. You see those ass holes climbing over the walls of the big compound? Over."

Up in the plane, the targeting officer looks at his computer screen displaying an infrared video of dozens of Afghans running towards and climbing over the wall of the compound and firing weapons down below on the ground.

Back in Lance's Humvee, the Radio Voice replies, "I see em Red Rhino, Over."

Lance speaks into the radio handset, "smoke their asses."

Radio Voice replies, "That's Rodge Red Rhino."

Outside in the compound, dozens of armed insurgents swarm over the walls of the compound firing AK-47 rifles. A Rocket Propelled Grenade flies through the air and explodes the metal gate of the compound. Armed Afghans pour through the opening. A deafening sound rips through the air as what appears to be a giant laser coming down from the sky destroying everything it's path, as six thousand glowing rounds a minute pour down from the AC-130 Attack Plane circling thousands of feet above.

Above at ten thousand feet, the giant grey propeller plane circles the compound below. Its great Gatling gun belches out a steady stream of fire out of its left side as it circles the compound below.

Back down in the compound, insurgents explode as the flying weapons platform rains hell down from above. The attackers run back to the hills. Outside Lance's Humvee, Bullets are whizzing by and the sound of the fire from the AC130 above is deafening. Lance, now outside and standing behind the Humvee and points a small laser mounted on his rifle, at the house with the radio handset pressed up against his ear, "Big Bird do you see infrared laser target, I'm putting on the house? Over."

"We see it, Red Rhino, over" says the Radio Voice.

Lance takes aim with his rifle mounted laser target designator, "shift your fire to my mark, over," Lance calmly requests.

"Roger that Red Rhino," replies the Radio Voice, "Lighting em up right now."

Baraat is watching the action from the high window of the fortress when the building suddenly begins to rumble and shake. His men coming over the wall outside are instantly vaporized and explode in flashes of light and violence. Baraat is staggered by the shock and awe of the weapons system being used against him and his men. He stares at the carnage, "Holy God what is this?" Baraat says out loud to no one. Suddenly the steady stream of glowing, exploding bullets changes direction and now moves towards him. He runs screaming in Pashtun, "go! GO! Back to the tunnels!" Baraat is the first one out of the room. The roof rips open and fiery hell pours in. Screams are extinguished by exploding bodies as what is left of his men follow him.

Back downstairs in the basement medical exam room, Dr. Sovia holds Ameena Mansoor in his arms. The earth shattering roar of a dragon is heard and the building shakes uncontrollably like an earthquake, the last of the electric lights flicker. His pistol is visibly empty. Dr. Sovia hugs her body and cries. The sound of boots crunching on debris can be heard. He looks up to see several insurgents coldly staring at him.

"You fucks," he says, mustering up what courage he has left. "You fucking bastards." Baraat's men calmly put fresh magazines in their weapons, rack the rifle bolts and begin to take aim at him. The building explodes with debris and partially collapses. We hear the same earth shattering roar of a dragon. The basement is illuminated by thousands of glowing bullets descending from the sky. The building is shredded by the AC-130 flying in the sky above.

CHAPTER 5

CHIAPAS, MEXICO, 2003

The Mercedes sedan is powerful and Jose uses every bit of its horsepower to gain distance from the Chiapas Medical Clinic. The giant stuffed Snoopy doll is still in the backseat. Pedro Garcia, sits bleeding in the front passenger seat, in and out of consciousness while Jose grips Pedro's left shoulder with his right hand to stem the bleeding while he steers intently with his left hand.

"Hang in there man!" says Jose.

Pedro sleepily whispers, "Mama..."

"Suck it up compadre!" Jose orders, "it's only a flesh wound. I promise you, if you straighten up, you won't die." Jose spins the steering wheel frantically in one direction and then the opposite direction as the car's balance is swayed back and forth. Jose, veteran of Mexican Army Special Forces got to do a great deal of counterintelligence training with the American spooks. He learned how to throw off a tail in an urban environment with temporarily aggressive driving. Jose smirks at the thought of the Americans and their classifications for everything.

"Wake up man!" Jose orders, "how are you feeling? Hey!" Once in the road's straight away, Jose steers with his knee and smacks Pedro in the face with his left hand. The whole time, never, ever letting pressure off the Pedro's shoulder with is right hand.

"Pedro! PEDRO!" Jose shouts, "wake up little girl."

Pedro begins to stir, waking up now "Huh? Wha?! OK! Stop smacking me. Okay?"

"Good to see you're still alive," Jose says as he re-grips the steering wheel, "what happened back there after I left you? When I left you Jefe was still alive."

"Shot. Shooting," Pedro mumbles as he rubs his shoulder. "So loud, is Jefe OK?"

"No," Jose says, "Jefe is not OK." Jose kills the cars headlights and makes a sudden turn to see if there are any head lights or break lights he can see in the rear view mirror. As soon as the car turns left, shuts off the engine and lets the car coast in the blackness, never stepping on the brakes so as to show his brake lights. If someone was following them, they would see only a dead black night with no indication of a car.

"It's OK little man," Jose says reassuringly, "I was just messing with you before. Actually not, I'm gonna keep you alive, you owe me money after all." Pedro Garcia is conscious enough to get the humor and snorts, trying to hide his laughter. "See, I knew you were faking it all," Jose quips, "It's OK. As far as I can tell it's just a flesh wound to your shoulder."

Pedro speaks up, "It hurts. OKAY?!"

"I know it's your first time in a real firefight," Jose says, "you held your own and didn't fall apart."

"Did I do OK?" weakly asks Pedro.

"Pretty admirable for a first timer. Very calm," Jose says while he takes a few extra seconds to stare at the young man, analyzing him and his wound.

"Thanks. Can we please go to a hospital now OK? This really hurts."

"We fall back to our last rally point," says Jose, "the place where we said we would retreat to in the event of an ambush."

"Rally point?" asks Pedro, "OK, what the fuck are you talking about?"

"Go to sleep little one. I'll take care of you."

"OK," Pedro says barely consciously. When the car finally rolls to a stop and there are no head or tail lights that can be seen from the car. Jose picks up his cell phone and makes a call.

Back in the Medical Clinic in Chiapas, Captain Raul Benitez walks down the hallway to surmise the situation. He makes it down the hallway to see the body of Jefe Rosa, riddled with bullets and still strapped to the gurney. His Kabili soldiers are already positioned outside the exit door so as to provide security against retaliation. The Captain barks out "MARTINEZ!" Martinez, who had already been near the forefront of the action with the other soldiers but was now taking account of the damage, chimes up.

"Si Capitan," says Martinez as he trots over to the Captain.

"I want a preliminary sit-rep (Situational Report) on our dead and wounded in sixty seconds," orders the Captain.

"Si Capitan," Martinez sharply replies as he speaks into his hand held radio, "Squads one through four I want a status on your downs and outs right now."

Martinez goes on to hear the radio chatter while Captain Raul Benitez, formerly of the Guatemalan Army Special Forces, walks out the door to the parking lot, where the last of Jefe Rosa's men made their escape. Raul thinks to himself, "If only we had more time to plan". He turns to one of his soldiers who is on his knees pointing his weapon out to the parking lot. "Kabili!" shouts the Captain, "Where is your team leader.

A soldier with more communication gear strapped to his helmet than the others steps forward with confidence. He is the Alpha Team Leader, twenty-six years old, he presents himself to the Captain at the position of attention, "Alpha Team Leader, first squad, here senor Capitan!"

"Alpha Team Leader," Captain Raul says, "I want to hear it from the people who were at his particular location in the clinic first. Would that be your team?"

"Si Senor!" The Alpha Team Leader energetically replies.

"Tell me exactly what or who you saw go out this door and get away," commands the Captain.

"Sir we had-" suddenly the radio goes off in the Alpha Team Leader's headset and due to repetitive training he immediately addresses the radio.

The Radio voice over the radio asks, "Alpha team leader gimmie your sitrep."

The Alpha Team leader presses the radio button over his ear and speaks into the hands free microphone protruding from his helmet near his chin, "we are five up up." The Alpha Team Leader quickly refocuses on the Captain, "we saw two men, one firing his weapon while moving in a tactically proficient manner sir. He was buddy carrying another man, who may or may not have been wounded."

The Captain's face registers a sudden realization and he senses the urgency created by the presence of another professional, this one on the opposing side. The Captain begins moving, looks around and turns to the Alpha Team Leader, "snap pictures of the dead. Lots of them."

"Si Senor."

The Captain grabs the Alpha Team Leader by the shoulder ad looks him in the eyes, "and Alpha Team Leader, I need intel fast, so I will brief your team on the way out. Make sure I know which truck you are in as we exfil." (exfiltrate/leave)

"Si Senor," replies the younger soldier.

Captain Raul Benitez switches the frequency on his hand held radio and speaks into the overall command channel on his radio, "OK everyone, standard EVAC (evacuation) off this objective. Fall back to the trucks and exfil. Back to the last rally point."

Commands start to fly amongst the subordinate commanders and down to the men as they withdraw from their positions, in a tactical manner, always walking backwards, keeping their rifles up and seeking out potential threats.

Stuck in the laundry room of the Medical Clinic, Dr. Sovia and Isabella Perez huddle as they peak out of the side of the small window in the door to the laundry room. They stare down the hall at the many men with guns dressed in a mixture of civilian clothes and army camouflage. They duck for cover when a large group starts walking back down the hallway towards the scrub room.

"Oh Dios Mio! Isabella says too loud for comfort, "what are we going to do Robert?"

Dr. Sovia quickly puts his hand over her mouth, "Shhh! Let them pass us by," *he whispers.*

Isabella looks at him and tries to say, "Roberto I-"

Dr. Sovia plants his mouth over Isabella's really just to keep her quiet, and after a couple of seconds of resistance she succumbs to her desire for him. Dr. Sovia clearly does not dislike the long silent kiss she passionately returns to him.

In the town of Chiapas, the sun's rays are just rising above the thick Mexican Jungle. In the Sovia home, rays of light begin piercing through the yellow curtains of the window just above the kitchen sink. Valeria Torres is in the kitchen as always and has already been up before sunrise to prep the coffee and breakfast in her daughter's house. She is as always at the kitchen stove when her husband, Diego Torres, fifty-four years old, comes into the kitchen. "Coffee," he growls.

"On the counter" his wife Valeria informs him.

"In 34 years of marriage, is it too much to ask for you once in a while to have my coffee ready for me, the way I like it?"

Valeria takes a second to think and snidely replies, "but Senor, your likes keep changing."

Diego Torres smirks at his wife with the

humorous contempt indicative of a long successful marriage and replies, "I'll be back late tonight, I'm collecting rents on the Northern properties today." Diego Torres in his younger years, spent his time amassing a small empire of rental properties throughout the state. They did not live with their daughter out of necessity, although Diego always claimed poverty, they lived with them out of love.

Valeria smiles at the love of her life, "you Mexican men are all the same. Roberto was supposed to be home last night and only god knows where he is off to."

"He's being a man Valeria!" Snaps back Diego, "he's out being a man! Whether he is earning a living to pay for our daughter's home or whatever else he chooses to do. He is a man."

"I hate you," she says.

Diego Torres gets up and starts walking to the kitchen sliding door. "I hate you more, just hate me enough to have my dinner ready. I'll be home at 7:30." Diego Torres walks out the sliding door.

Mexico City, Mexico

In the Federal Building in Mexico City, which serves as the headquarters of the Policia Federal Ministerial (PFM), Mexico's version of the FBI, Chief Rivera is huddled with a group of men in suits all nervous about speaking to the throngs of media people swarming the place. Among the near one hundred journalists shouting questions and shouting at each other.

A single voice is heard is heard over the din, "do we know if it was gangs or foreign military?" shouts out one reporter.

"Early reports say such a small amount of shell casings left behind and such accurately fired rounds indicate a military level expertise," yells another reporter, "any comments?"

Deputy Inspector General Gabriel Hernandez, fifty-eight years old, makes his way to the podium.

Some men need not wear any uniform for others to know, they are the Commanding General. Deputy Inspector General, Gabriel Hernandez, fifty-eight years old was such a man. Deputy I.G. Hernandez moved to the podium through the crowd slowly, because Deputy I.G. Hernandez did not have to move fast for anyone. He steps up behind the microphone and the questions are shouted by the dozen. Deputy I.G. Hernandez simply stands there waiting for quiet. Finally, when, most of the voices were silent, did he speak, "Quiet! QUIET!! I'm here to tell you what you will report."

    A collective aaahhh goes through the room and Deputy I.G. Hernandez looks over the crowd with disgust on his face. "If you don't like it you can fuck off and scrape the streets for scraps of information," he disrespectfully says to the crowd of reporters. The room is silent as a tomb. "One call to any of your respective bosses and we'll shut your station down. Comprende!?!? Assholes?!" The mass of journalists remains silent. They know this old prick might actually make it happen they are silent. The Deputy I.G. continues to speak, "Ladies and gentlemen of the press and others in attendance, it is with the greatest regret that I must inform our country that a great tragedy, in two parts, has plagued our great land yet again".

    A lone voice from the crowd shouts out an unintelligible question.

    "Please! NO QUESTIONS! Until we are finished distributing the basic facts." Deputy I.G. Hernandez waits calmly while the masses of the media quickly subside. "In the mountainous border to our South with our neighbor Guatemala," says Deputy I.G. Hernandez, "yet another incursion into our sovereign territory has occurred and Mexican civilians have been slaughtered. This is a preliminary report. We do not know if it was a foreign government or gangs. Chief Inspector Hugo Rivera of the PFM will be flying to Chiapas to personally head up the investigation to this crime."

Chief Rivera's head picks up as he hears this sudden news. "Chief Inspector Rivera would you like to say a few words," asks the Deputy I.G..

Caught off guard and not prepared Chief Rivera clumsily approaches the podium. "Yes, thank you Deputy Inspector General," says Chief Rivera, "this atrocity will not go unpunished I promise you and the people of Mexico. This investigation will be the very definition of swift justice."

The first reporter from earlier yells out his question, "Senor Rivera, do we know how many victims were murdered at the clinic."

Chief Rivera fumbles with his words as he is not as polished a public liar as the others. "Ahh... as the Deputy Inspector General already quoted, this is a preliminary news conference. We will give *you more details as they come in. Good day people."* Chief Rivera leaves the podium and walks off the stage struggling to contain his fury as reporters continue to shout questions.

Back in Chiapas nearly a dozen sets of police cars parked outside the clinic bathe the waiting room with flashing red and blue lights. The debris of crushed walls and glass litter the floor mixed with blood and flesh of last night's carnage. Isabella Perez sits on a bench in the waiting room with a blanket over her and surrounded by investigators of the Polica Federal Ministerial (PFM), Mexico's version of the FBI.

"I... I... really don't want to talk right now," Isabella Perez says as she stares blankly out into space, still in some level of shock she holds a cup of coffee without drinking any of it.

One young Agent keeps pressing her for answers, PFM Agent Martin Chavez, twenty-seven years old tries to question her, "Senora Perez," says Chavez, "can you tell me what you saw here?"

Isabella continues staring straight ahead when she speaks, "It was horrible. The screams, Dr. Cruz is dead, Camila, Mariana, Daniella." Isabella begins weeping, "they're all dead. Oh my god."

There is a female PFM Agent there and she feels bad for Isabella, she takes a kind tone in her questions, "did you know them well?"

Isabella looks blankly at them with a thousand-yard stare so many combat veterans have, "yes. I worked with them. They were... they were laying in a pile... on the floor. Like bloody meat on a kitchen counter."

"I'm sorry for your loss," Agent Chavez says. Isabella begins to convulse and vomit.

"They were piled up like meat!" Isabella is screaming now, "Oh my God. OH MY GOD!" The Female Agent takes pity on her and holds Isabella while she cries.

Twenty feet away but in a different hallway, crime scene technicians are snapping photos, others are bagging evidence. Dr. Sovia is speaking to an agent of the Federal Ministerial Police (PFM) AGENT Tomas Reyes, thirty-three years old, and he is not believing what he is seeing or hearing. "And how is you are still standing here alive Doctor?"

Dr. Sovia is visibly shaken up and exhausted from the night before, "excuse me?" he asks with disbelief.

"I said explain to me why you are still alive and with not a scratch on you," says Agent Reyes, "yet your entire staff and patients that were here are all dead."

Dr. Sovia looks exhausted, his eyes are swollen from lack of sleep and stress, "we were hiding, all night, in the Laundry Room," he answers.

"Who is we Doctor?"

"Myself and one of our surgical technicians, Isabella Perez."

"And how is it that you and Isabella Perez were safely together in the laundry room?" asks the Agent.

Dr. Sovia stares with exhaustion straight through PFM Agent Tomas Reyes and asks, "is Ms. Perez OK?"

The PFM Agent cocks is head like a puzzled puppy. He does not know what to make of the Doctor. "Are you being problematic Doctor? Confrontational? Because if you are-"

"I'm wiped out Agent Reyes," Dr. Sovia interrupts, "It's been a long night."

Agent Reyes looks at Dr. Sovia and tries to pull a power play, speaking harshly, "this is a blood bath Doctor. You and your associate lived through it and I need-"

"I need to call my wife," *interrupts Dr. Sovia again.*

"I want to hear more about what happened," *Agent Reyes rebukes the Doctor.* "Now what? Where the fuck are you going?"

Dr. Sovia walks to one of the clinic phones on the wall, not caring whether the Agent likes it or not. Agent Reyes hears a sudden commotion down the hall and stops mid-sentence. He begins to trot down the hall. "Doc, wait right there, *he says as he moves towards the commotion,* "I'll be right back. Don't go anywhere."

Dr. Sovia watches him walk briskly down the hall and then reaches for clinic phone on the wall and dials.

It is morning at the Sovia home, the sun's rays are lightly illuminating the master bedroom through the curtained windows. The phone rings on the night table, shaking Sofia Sovia out of her slumber. She quickly answers the phone, "Sovia."

"It's me. I'm OK," *says Dr. Sovia's voice over the phone.*

Sofia rubs her face and her whole demeanor changes, "how dare you stay out all night-"

"Hon-" *he starts to say before she interrupts him.*

"We were expecting you twelve hours ago-"

"Honey!" *Dr. Sovia shouts louder this time in his attempt to get his wife to calm down and listen. Sofia is having none of it.*

"Is this starting all over again? Because if it is-"

"SOFIA!" *Dr. Sovia shouts loudly now into the phone,* "have you not seen the news?

"No. I-"

"Haven't you heard what is going on?" he asks.

"You know I don't watch the news!" she shouts back, "It's depressi-"

"Turn on the TV! Please"

Sofia starts looking for the television remote in the bed while holding the phone to her head. She continues griping, "plus I have this whole house to run and kids and mama and god only knows what YOU are doing. I-"

"Would you please give it a rest?! Hector Rosa is dead."

Sofia freezes at the news, "Oh my god." Sofia frantically searches the blankets for the remote control and clicks on the TV.

"And so is Dr. Cruz and almost all my clinic staff."

Sofia is stunned into silence, her mouth open. "Are you making an excuse Roberto?"

"Turn on the TV Sofia."

"It's on, I'm looking," Sofia says as she clicks through the channels. "Some B.S. story to make me feel bad for-"

"Turn on the TV already!" he snaps, "it's a blood bath! And I am right in the middle of it."

Sofia doesn't have to search for long, the story is on every station with live shots of the clinic partially in ruins and pictures of the dead bodies lying in various locations. "OH MY GOD!" Sofia says into the phone," "what... What is happening? Oh ROBERTO are you OK?"

"I don't know just yet Sofi. I'm not wounded but I think... I think everyone else is dead."

"Come home Roberto! Come home now."

Before Dr. Sofia can respond, a voice is heard throughout the clinic, "we've got a live one here!" cries out a fireman. Agent Reyes returns from around a corner and waves to Dr. Sovia to come and help. "I gotta run Sofi, I'll call you later." He hangs up and heads towards the commotion.

In the lobby, under the debris from the collapsed wall and furniture piled up by the impact of the truck, a whimper is heard and an arm in now visible. More fireman rush to the pile and begin a human chain to remove the debris carefully off the survivor. The Fireman barks out some orders, "Ok, OK everybody, lets slow it down pulling at the pile could cause a collapse on the victim." The removal of debris reveals the face of the survivor; Francisco Rosa. His face is covered in ash and dried blood with streaks of wet tears running down his face. The Fireman tries to calm the victim, "hey buddy, we got you. You're gonna be OK. Can you hear me? What's your name compadre?"

A weak whisper leaves Francisco's mouth, "Frank. Frankie... my friends call me... I am Francisco Rosa." Upon hearing the fireman loudly repeat the survivors name, a hush falls upon the crowd of fireman and police followed by nearly everyone getting on their cell phones or texting.

"Well, Francisco Rosa it's your lucky day," responds the Fireman.

Still whispering, Francisco replies, "you could have fucking fooled me!" The Fireman smiles and pats Francisco's arm. The front waiting/reception area of the clinic where the truck crashed through is a disaster zone with piles of building debris. Upon hearing of a survivor dozens of rescue/police/medical personnel scramble to help the survivor.

The Fireman, still taking the lead asks loudly, "can we get a stretcher over here?" Dr. Sovia moves to help the survivor when PFM Agent Reyes puts his hand on the Doctor's shoulder.

"Doc, you're doing too much in your condition," says Agent Reyes, "let our people handle this."

Dr. Sovia responds as any good doctor would, putting others health and safety before his own health and safety, "I'm the only doctor here that I know of. If he dies because he had to wait to get to a hospital to be treated, I will be sure to make it known that YOU were the one who forbade me from treating him."

Agent Reyes knows the Doctor has him by the balls, "go! See if you can help."

Dr. Sovia in typical command fashion begins calling out orders as he walks, "Someone get me a trauma kit from behind the desk. It's in the white case with the red cross." Some anxious policeman grabs the case and brings it to the doctor who now squats down next to the still buried survivor whose face is covered dust and begins to check his blood pressure and pulse. "Hey now, Frank, you said your name was?

Francisco weakly answers, "yeah."

"This will sound like a stupid question right now Frank, but what hurts on you? What specifically?"

"Nothing hurts really," Francisco weakly replies, "I can't feel a thing right now. So weird. Just tired."

"Stay awake, stay with me Frank. My name is Dr. Sovia."

"Ahhh... Pretty boy. It's you," says Francisco managing a small laugh. With all the debris and dust and dirt caked onto the survivors face, Dr. Sovia did not recognize the son of Jefe Rosa

"Francisco?" Dr. Sovia asks, "Francisco Rosa?"

"Yeah," he weakly answers, "you better save me asshole!"

Dr. Sovia waves over a group of rescue personnel with the stretcher and issues orders, "Ok everybody grab a piece of Francisco's clothes. We are going to all lift him at the same time." They all manage to lift Francisco onto the stretcher while Dr. Sovia pumps a blood pressure cuff and listens with his stethoscope to Francisco Rosa's vitals. "OK people he may be going into hypovolemic shock." Dr. Sovia points to medic nearby, "you there, grab me two bags of the blood expander in that upper cabinet. They look like clear balloons with water in them, marked in blue."

Agent Reyes appears and questions the Doctor, "what's going on Doc?"

Dr. Sovia puts his hands up and announces authoritatively, "step back please. He's lost a great a deal of blood, his pressure is way down." Dr. Sovia reaches back into the trauma kit and starts the IV on Francisco's arm, "I'm going to start two IVs before we put him in the ambulance to get his pressure back up." The medic we saw earlier hands Dr. Sovia the bags of blood expander who starts connecting them to Francisco. "Don't worry Francisco," Dr. Sovia says to reassure him, "you are in the best of hands. You're going to be fine."

"That's fucking great," Francisco tries to answer with bravado, "I didn't think I could get any worse."

The rescue workers carry the stretcher over the pile of debris out through the giant hole in the wall to a waiting ambulance while Dr. Sovia is *holding two IV bags over Francisco's head.*

Agent Reyes comes running out to the ambulance, "Dr. Sovia, you can't leave yet. This is still an active investigation."

"I am escorting this patient to the hospital," says Dr. Sovia as he climbs in the back of the Ambulance. "If you have a problem with that, jump in and you can come along." Dr. Sovia owes everything to Jefe Hector Rosa. The bad guys may have killed him but he would be damned if he let his son die. "C'mon," the Doctor adds, "ride along with us."

Agent Reyes, like so many other government employees looks around for his boss for permission or to see who might see him, pauses to think for an extended few seconds and remains silent.

The ambulance driver looks out his window towards the rear and yells, "Hey back there, we're moving out. NOW!"

"Fuck it!" Says Agent Reyes, "let me in." Agent Reyes climbs in the back of the ambulance and they shut the doors of the ambulance just as it starts driving away.

Several miles away in Chiapas, the family home of Jefe Hector Rosa is an enormous sand colored stone hacienda, infused with Spanish and Native American influences, rustic touches with colorful hand painted tiles built into the walls. The hacienda is bustling with Chiapas Cartel men cleaning weapons, preparing food. Pedro Garcia is sprawled over an easy chair with his arm in a sling watching television. Jose Canale, the ex-Mexican Special Forces soldier turned Rosa family sub-commander, walks over to check on his man recovering from the gunshot wound he received at the Medical Clinic.

"How are you holding up Pedro?"

"Ahhh, OK. My arm is still killing me OK," Says Pedro. Jose smiles and Pedro shakes a prescription bottle of bills. "Thank god for Vicodins. Is that doctor from the clinic still alive? I want my shoulder looked at. OK?"

Jose smiles and shakes his head yes, "yeah he made it out last night, surprisingly for a doctor. Word is he was banging a nurse in the laundry room when we got hit." Pedro shudders at the memory. That was the doctor's face in the door's window. Dr. Sovia knows his secret.

"OK," Pedro continues, "I'm guessing the clinic is closed for now."

"Good guess kid,"

"OK. Can we get him over here later?" Pedro pleads, his face twisted in pain. "Maybe he can fix up my arm. OK?"

"Not now," says Jose, "just stay here at the house and be around in case you are needed. Don't get drugged up."

Pedro Garcia sits back comfortably in his easy chair and grabs his TV remote control. "OK don't worry. My ass is glued to this chair. Ok did you know the Jefe had so many channels on TV?"

"Enjoy," Jose says and he walks into the garage while Pedro clicks through the television stations, pondering his next move.

The garage is dimly lit by a single light bulb. Colonel Luis Escalera is tied to a chair in the garage and looks like he took a beating all night. "Did he talk yet?" asks Jose. The man Jose speaks to, could extract any secret from any man, Mateo Morales, thirty-one years old but with the tired eyes of a man who has had to do horrible things and keep his guilt inside. Morales is also formerly of the Mexican Army but a more secretive branch. Mateo Morales had trained at the famed "School of the Americas" at Fort Benning, Georgia in the United States where he learned advanced techniques of extracting the truth from resistant confessors.

"I've been working on him all night," Morales admits to Jose, "I've run different approaches, I know he broke more than once. He's told me more personal secrets than I wanted to know."

"I'm not interested in his personal life," retorts Jose.

"His story does not change, no matter how many tricks I pull on him," admits Morales, "I'm professionally inclined to say... he's telling the truth."

Jose takes a minute to study the Colonel, slumped over in the chair, bloodied, bruised and quite undignified for Colonel in the Guatemalan Border Police. "Let me talk to him. Alone," Jose says. Without answering Mateo Morales walks out of the garage while wiping his hands on a rag. Jose pulls a chair up to the Colonel and begins cleaning his face with a clean cloth. "I'm so sorry this had to happen Colonel Escalera."

Colonel Escalera attempts a smile but the bruises on his face cause pain and he stops smiling. "Not as sorry as I am... I presume," he says.

Jose grabs a nearby can of moist wipes and continues to clean the dried blood off the Colonel's face. "Please understand Colonel that after the ambush in the jungle and half the men we had on that deal died, we have to go through all the suspects."

"How about my men?" *asks Colonel Escalera,* "how many did I lose?

"We don't have any info on any of your people. Once we survived the initial artillery barrage, and we all high tailed it out of there. We lost contact with everyone on your side."

"Can I make a phone call please?" *The Colonel asks,* "I am sure I am missed.

Jose finishes wiping the Colonel down and cuts the ropes that restrain him. "Yes, you can make a phone call, but not just yet." *Colonel Escalera looks at Jose suspiciously. Jose hands him a cold beer and the Colonel holds it to his bruised cheek.* "First I would like to go over your deal with Jefe Rosa," *says Jose,* "perhaps something can be worked out from here to make up for lost profit and bruised egos."

Colonel rubs is bruised and still bloody face and says, "egos are not the only thing that are bruised young man."

Chief Inspector Hugo Rivera of the PFM (Policia, Federale Ministerial), is comfortably ensconced in his first class passenger seat taking a well-earned nap. He had enjoyed his first class steak dinner and of course the complimentary scotch they served. Living high on the tax payer's money was a tradition in Mexican law enforcement, especially amongst the Federales. Life was good for the law man approaching middle age. The stewardess taps him on the shoulder to wake him.

"Senor, you must move your chair to the upright position and put your seat belt on," the Stewardess informs him. "The Captain is going to land soon."

Chief Rivera, groggily shaking off the sleep manages to answer in his usual manner full of hubris, "About time.' Chief Rivera looks at his expensive watch as he presses his phone power button on.

The Stewardess sees this and returns to his seat, "The Captain still has the no cell phone signal on," she informs the Chief.

"Yeah, yeah," Chief Rivera flashes his badge and the Stewardess turns and walks away. Hugo loves the perks of being a big shot. But big shot or not, he still could not get a cell signal in the air. "God Damn these phones to Hell. I need to know what is going on." As the plane continues to descend, as if on cue, the little phone chirps to life and reveals 16 voice mails and god only knows how many text messages to answer. He begins to click the buttons to see the texts.

PFM Agent Reyes: TEXT MESSAGE: Call me.

PFM Agent Reyes: TEXT MESSAGE: Call me. It's important.

PFM Agent Reyes: TEXT MESSAGE: You have to CALL ME!!

Chief Rivera could wait with the Agent and his bumbling. He got to the names he wanted.

PEDRO :TEXT MESSAGE: Don't text me back, I'll be unconscious, hopefully in surgery. There was a witness. Dr. Sovia, the doc who owns the clinic.

PEDRO :TEXT MESSAGE: Saw everything. Might come back on us. I'm deleting my messages and turning phone off. Passing out. TTYL.

RAUL: TEXT MESSAGE: Mission accomplished. We are back over the border. Call later for details.

    Chief Rivera thinks to himself joyfully, "Maybe not as accomplished as you thought soldier boy." Chief Rivera dials a number and speaks into his phone, "Where are you?"

    PFM Agent Reyes answers the phone, "Tuxtla Hospital in Chiapas with Jefe Rosa's kid, Francisco."

    "He's alive?" asks the Chief incredulously.

    'Miracle," says Agent Reyes, "looks like whoever did this, lead the way with a Ford 250 pickup truck right through the wall of the clinic. Ran right over little Frankie and buried him till this morning."

    Chief Rivera is grimaces with rage and says through his teeth, "yes a miracle."

In Tuxtla Hospital, in Chiapas, PFM Agent Tomas Reyes is standing in a corner holding his hand over his phone to hide the voice. "The big shit Doctor down there, Sovia, him and some young hottie, Isabella Perez also came out of there without a scratch."

The voice comes through the phone with a serious tone from the Chief, "there's a problem, there's a witness. The Doc, Sovia may have seen something he shouldn't have. Now listen to me very closely..."

In a different wing of the hospital in the Emergency Room, orderlies and nurses wheel Francisco Rosa on a gurney back to his curtained off corner of the emergency room while three of Jefe Rosa's Thugs walk behind. Dr. Sovia sleeps in a chair in the curtained off section.

A hospital Emergency Room doctor, walks up to wake Dr. Sovia, "Dr. Sovia. Dr. Sovia. Wake up."

"Yeah, yes I'm up," *he replies sitting up in the bed and rubbing his face.*

"You asked to be briefed on Francisco Rosa's

condition," the E.R. Doctor reports.

"Yes," Dr. Sovia groggily replies, "What is it?"

The E.R. Doctor puts an X ray up on the x ray illuminator light board so they can both look at the x ray. He points at a spot with his pen. "Mr. Rosa suffered a severe spinal impact to his number 5 and 6 vertebrae."

"Prognosis?" asks Dr. Sovia.

"His life is not in immediate danger from this," replies the E.R. Doctor, "I've made an appointment for him to see the Nuero/Ortho department. He has use of his arms but he is weak still."

"The legs?" asks Dr. Sovia.

"I've seen this before from such impact," the E.R. Doctor replies, "sometimes they recover, sometimes they don't. The Neuro/Ortho Department will know better than I."

Unbeknownst to anyone in the room, Francisco Rosa is awake and listening, "will that make you happy pretty boy?" Francisco asks snidely, "If I can't walk again?"

"Mr. Rosa," replies a surprised E.R. Doctor, "you're awake, how are you feeling?"

"Fuck my feelings! Doc, give me and Roberto here a minute alone." The ER Doctor grabs his clipboard and leaves them.

Dr. Sovia starts to talk, "Francis-"

"Shut the fuck up!" he rudely interrupts, "my father is dead."

"Yes I know. I'm sorry for your loss."

"Fuck you and your apology! That doesn't bring my father back."

"I know."

"We spent a lot of money on your stupid clinic! I fought with my father against it. But no, he had to support his little pretty boy!"

"Don't call me that. I'm a surgeon and I operated on your father for hours. We saved him. He was going to recover."

"Well he didn't. Did he?" Francisco questions rhetorically.

"No he didn't," replies Dr. Sovia, "some of

your asshole enemies killed him. They killed him along with my people. My friends."

Francisco looks at Dr. Sovia with suspicion, "my guys picked you up at the airport yesterday. You were in Guatemala?"

"Yes," I was with Doctors without Frontiers."

"Can you prove that?" asks Francisco suspiciously.

"Many Doctors and nurses from other countries were there with me. We operated on very poor people in a poor region."

Francisco glares at Dr. Sovia, "what a coincidence that you are out of Mexico, in Guatemala when a hit team from Guatemala attacks us."

"I do not dictate when your associates don't like you anymore Francisco," says Dr. Sovia.

"You being funny now pretty boy?" Francisco angrily snaps back, "you think this is a time to joke do you?" Dr. Sovia is silent. "Who approached you?" Francisco asks.

"What do you mean who approached me?"

"Nah, fuck that! You know exactly what I mean. Your MIA, my father gets hit, then you're there and you come out of it without a scratch."

"Are you seriously asking me if I am somehow involved in this?" says Dr. Sovia.

"I may not be a fucking brilliant doctor but I'm smart enough to smell a rat pretty boy. There had to be somebody on the inside."

Upon hearing the idea of an inside job, Dr. Sovia considers telling Francisco what he saw in the hallway last night. But sensing treachery he keeps it to himself. "If there was, it was not me. I assure you," he tells Francisco, "I owe your father everything. He paid my way through my undergrad so I could get into medical school. He sponsored the clinic."

"Yeah, yeah he did. Little Roberto, my father's favorite pet. Do you know he always compared you to me?"

"Stop it Frankie."

Mimicking his father's voice, Francisco mocks Dr. Sovia, "Why can't you be more like Roberto? Look at Roberto, he worked his way through college and then earned scholarships to Medical School".

"Don't do this Francisco, he loved you."

"I'm his son! HIS SON! His flesh and blood and I could never measure up to you. Some little son of a nobody."

"A nobody who died for your father," snaps Dr. Sovia

"Fuck you and fuck your father too!"

"We're done here." Dr. Sovia begins to walk out of the room.

"Robert," Francisco begins crying as he calls out but Dr. Sovia does not stop or look back but keeps on walking.

Francisco begins screaming now, "don't you walk away from me! I am FRANCISCO FUCKING ROSA!! You don't walk away from me!"

One of the Jefe Rosa's Thugs, looks in the room at Francisco Rosa and points to Dr. Sovia walking away. Francisco shakes his head no and waves his man away then quickly changes his mind, "No, hombre! Come back in here," Francisco calls out. The Thug walks to Francisco's bedside while Francisco quickly wipes away his tears to hide his shame. "Get on the phone to our cops and find out *where that prick was last week,"* orders Francisco.

"Got it boss!" says the Thug as he pulls out his cell phone and makes a call.

PFM Agent Reyes is furious that he has lost one of his witnesses to the crime. He is furious that events seem to be happening to fast for him to control the investigation. He stands one hand against the wall and the other pressing the phone up to his ear listening to the ring. The phone call is answered by Dr. Sovia's voice.

"Sovia", Dr. Sovia answers the call.

"Dr. Sovia," Agent Reyes says angrily, "I did not give you permission to leave the hospital. Where are you?"

Dr. Sovia is in the back seat of a car being driven. "Permission? PERMISSION?" Dr. Sovia angrily reacts. "Let's get one thing straight here government servant, I do not need your permission to come and go as I please."

"You are a material witness to a slaughter that

occurred within the past twenty-four hours that I am investigating," says Agent Reyes into his telephone.

"Am I being charged with a crime?" asks Dr. Sovia.

"Should you be?" Agent Reyes replies.

"Fuck off Agent Reyes!"

"All right," Agent Reyes says after taking a deep breath, "let's dial it back a few notches.... Dr. Sovia. I was not supposed to allow you to leave the clinic. It is a murder scene and you are a witness."

"Thank you for letting me know what I already know," responds Dr. Sovia.

"In order to save a survivor and you were the most qualified medical professional on the scene, against my better judgment, I let you leave. Yes doctor, I LET YOU!"

"Dr. Sovia leans his head back on the car seat and rolls his eyes. "I do not recall being told I was being detained or arrested Agent Reyes. As far as I know I am still living in a free country and I am free to come and go as I please."

"So where are you going Doctor?"

"I am going home Agent Reyes, I am on my way home to see my wife and family. I promise you I will be there all day probably into tomorrow."

"Probably into tomorrow? Asks Agent Reyes.

"If you need me, call or stop by but please give me some time to rest and see my family." Dr. Sovia turns off his phone and looks at the driver, "are we almost there?" The driver glances at Dr. Sovia and nods yes.

Dr. Sovia walks from the car that dropped him off and nearly staggers through the front door. It's a Saturday and his daughter Ariana Sovia, runs up and hugs him.

"Daddy! I missed you!" squeals Ariana Sovia.

Dr. Sovia bends to pick her up and kiss her cheek, "I missed you too my little pumpkin. Where is your brother?"

"Sleeping late like always. Daddy, did you bring me a present?"

"I did my little princess, but I left it at the

clinic yesterday. I will give it to you tomorrow."

"Promise daddy?"

"I promise pumpkin," Dr. Sovia puts her down and walks into the kitchen and is greeted coldly by his wife Sofia.

"Hello Robert," she says, he walks over to hug and kiss her. She pulls away.

"Really?" he asks with disbelief.

"Nice of you to make it home," Sofia adds sarcastically.

"It's been an eventful twenty-four hours Sofia."

Sofia simply stares at him from across the kitchen, "I'm not even going to ask you to lie to me this time."

"About what Sofi?"

"About why you are feeling so guilty. You only make small talk when you are guilty about something."

"I am guilty of working hard Sofia. I am guilty of establishing a clinic so poor Chiapas people who *never had health care can live without disease."*

"Let's not forget Hector Rosa's thugs can get their gunshot wounds treated without being reported to the police," Sofia quips.

"I owe him Sofia. He paid-"

"Your father paid. Paid for everything the Rosa's gave you. He paid with his life Roberto. Don't forget that."

"Sofi don't-"

"Am I wrong? There wouldn't be a Hector Rosa if your father were still alive," Sofia says.

"After my father died, they were my family."

"Does your obligation die with Hector Rosa? Because he is gone now Roberto."

"I don't know just yet."

Sofia begins to cry. "Where are we going Roberto? Are we going backwards? I Don't want-" Dr. Sovia rushes to her and sweeps her up in his arms and kisses her. She melts for no more than a second before hitting his chest over and over yelling, "No. NO! NO!! Get off of me. Sofia pulls away and wipes her eyes as Dr. Sovia lets go of her.

Sofia takes a minute to compose herself. She turns to Dr. Sovia, "No. No. It is OK Roberto. It is OK. We all get what we deserve...Eventually."

"Really?" Dr. Sovia asks, "we are doing this again?!"

"Did she go with you? To Guatemala?"

"I told you. It's over. I love you. I thought we were past this now."

"Yes. Yes you did... Robert. You did say that. You know something you never said though. Dr. Sovia stares at her in silence. "You never said you were sorry." A sudden knock on the door shakes Dr. Sovia out of his stare. Sofia uses the opportunity to walk to the door, away from her husband before he can see her tears. Sofia opens the door while wiping her eyes to see a giant black and white Snoopy doll instead of a person.

"Hello Senora." The Snoopy doll moves aside so he can make eye contact. "I'm Pedro, I work for Senor Rosa. OK?" Pedro struggles with the Snoopy dolls girth with only one arm to wrap around it. He drops it so now his face is visible over the five foot stuffed animal. (This is the Snoopy doll from earlier at the airport & car) "OK, your husband Dr. Sovia

left this in Senor Rosa's car yesterday."

Sofia motions for Pedro to come in with the doll. *"Well that was very nice of you to bring it over, if you would carry it in please."*

Pedro squats, wraps his one arm around the stuffed animal and picks it up to walk it in. His face is hidden by Snoopy's giant mass. *"Ok... Sure thing,"* says Pedro.

"Follow me please," Sofia says as he leads Pedro down the hall to the kitchen. Sofia has no idea that this was the man who murdered all of her husband's co-workers and Jefe Hector Rosa the day before. Sofia walks Pedro right into the kitchen where Dr. Sovia now has his back turned while he pours a cup of coffee. *"Just put it on the table please,"* Sofia says.

At hearing his wife speaking Dr. Sovia turns to see the giant Snoopy dropped off in his kitchen for him. Dr. Sovia smiles at the stuffed animal and begins walking towards it, *"Oh, great, thanks for bringing-"* Dr. Sovia's blood runs ice cold and his eyes grow wide the second he sees it is Pedro who drops the oversized Snoopy on the kitchen table.

Sofia speaks as she exits the kitchen,

"Somebody is dropping off your bribe to your daughter." As Sofia is walking away from them, Pedro holds his finger up to his mouth and stares at Dr. Sovia.

"You must have left this in the car yesterday doctor. I wanted to make sure you got it. OK? Pedro Garcia was still not one hundred percent sure that the doctor saw everything. Not until just now when he saw the good doctor's reaction.

"Yes," Dr. Sovia says, "thank you." They continue to stare at each other both minds racing. "Will there be anything else young man?"

Pedro's head is on a swivel scanning the house for witnesses or potential danger, "Ok... Terrible attack last night, huh? OK yeah."
Dr. Sovia is frozen looking at Pedro. There is a moment of silence that is agonizing.

"What now?" asks Dr. Sovia.

"The Rosas and Chiapas Cartel are regrouping at Jefe's hacienda," Pedro informs Dr. Sovia. "They want you back at the house. OK?"

Dr. Sovia glances towards the hall listening for his children. "I can't go anywhere right now."

Pedro pulls out a pistol, "Ok let's go Doctor. OK?"

"I'm not going anywhere."

A gunshot explodes throughout the house. Pedro goes down. A voice booms out behind Dr. Sovia.

"That's right Doc. You're not going anywhere." Dr. Sovia spins around to see the Federal Police Agent, Agent Reyes, he had spoken with earlier and rode in the ambulance with. Dr. Sovia puts his hand on his chest and reacts immediately.

"Jesus holy Christ, you scared me. Thank you," Dr. Sovia says sounding exasperated. "I believe he was going to kill me."

Sofia runs into the kitchen after hearing a gunshot, "What is going on here?" Upon seeing Pedro's crumpled and bleeding body Sofia screams. Agent Reyes grabs her with his free hand and shoves her towards Dr. Sovia.

"Oh, I'm so sorry Senora Sovia, you were not supposed to be mixed up in this."

Sofia looks to the Agent, still wearing his blue

windbreaker with PFM emblazoned on the front and back. Agent Reyes is still wearing his badge around his neck on a chain. She looks over the Federal Police Agent with astonishment. "What are you doing?" she asks.

"What the Hell going on?" demands Dr. Sovia.

Agent Tomas Reyes motions to Dr. Sovia to shhh with his finger over his lips but the Doctor ignores him.

"That was the man that murdered Hector Rosa," booms out Dr. Sovia, "last night at the clinic."

"What?" Sofia excitedly asks with disbelief.

"He murdered Hector Rosa while he was still strapped down to a gurney after surgery and still unconscious," yells the doctor.

"Oh my God!" screams Sofia.

"And he also killed my entire surgical staff at the clinic, machine gunned them like it was nothing."

Sofia is near hysterical now, "OH MY GOD.

And I let him in our house!"

"I saw him do it through the window in the Laundry Room."

Tomas Reyes looks at Sofia and smiles, "Oh yes, you mean while you were in the laundry room. Alone... with Isabella Perez?"

Sofia looks at her husband with hurt and disbelief. "Yes, we hid from the gunman in the laundry room," says Dr. Sovia.

Agent Reyes laughs out loud, laughing he says, "Oh yeah, hiding."

The voices of the children are heard behind Agent Reyes, "Mom? Dad? Mom, what's going on?" asks little Alberto Sovia.

"Holy shit?!" asks Agent Reyes as he spins around to address the voices, "who the fuck else is here?" Agent Reyes shoves the kids into the kitchen towards the Sovias. "Get in there with your parents." Ariana sees the body of Pedro Garcia lying on the floor and screams.

"Shut up!" orders Agent Reyes as he walks into the kitchen, around the Sovia family clustered in the middle and over to the body of Pedro and

takes the gun out of his hand. "Oh I'm so sorry about bloodying up your beautiful home Senora Sovia, but Pedro had to go. We can't have such an inept assassin, could come back on us."

"Us?" Dr. Sovia asks.

"Yes, us Doctor," Agent Reyes answers. "Oh are you surprised? Forces are arrayed against your former patron Hector Rosa or did you not see that already." PFM Agent Tomas Reyes, with a gun in each hand, enjoying tormenting those soon to die.

Sofia begins to plead for the lives of her children, "Please just let the children go, plea-"

"Shut up or I'll kill both of them right in front of you," Agent Reyes interrupts her. He looks Dr. Sovia directly in his eyes, "you do know the Chiapas Cartel is going to kill you Dr. Sovia? Right?"

"Francisco and I have a long history," replies the Doctor, "but he would not stoop so low."

"Take the blinders off Doc. They think you were in on this assassination of the Jefe."

"That's not true. I was performing surgeries all last week in Southern Guatemala."

"Well it sure looks suspicious to the new Jefe Rosa, Francisco Rosa, that his dad gets ambushed on the Guatemala border by who? Guata-fucking-malans!"

Sofia comes to the defense of her husband, "but he wasn't involved, he was helping people."

"Yeaaahhh. Where?" Agent Reyes says to torment her, "in Guata-fucking-mala!"

"Don't beg him for anything Sofia."

"Oh no!! Not only do the Rosas and the entire Chiapas Cartel want you dead," Agent Reyes adds, "but my boss needs you to be gone as well."

Sofia screams out, "what are you doing? You are the Police."

"Mommy, I'm scared," Ariana cries out and Sofia picks her up to console her.

"Yeah, what are you doing? You're the Police," says young Alberto Sovia.

"Agent Reyes smiles cruelly at the family. He points Pedro's gun at them with is left hand and says, "too bad that Pedro Garcia single handedly killed the entire Sovia family. But the Doctor, oh he

was so brave and strong. He did manage to shoot and kill Pedro." Agent Reyes shakes the other pistol in his right hand to display different guns for each shooter in his story. "But not before Pedro shot him. And in Greek tragedy style, they all died. Too bad so sad." Agent Reyes makes a sad face.

Sofia shrieks in horror and cries out more, "Please. Please, please."

Agent Reyes points Pedro's gun at her. "Shut up! That's one possible scenario of how this could play out doc. The Chiapas Cartel thinks they got their rat; you. They lose one of their own but hey it's only Pedro, who gives a fuck."

"One possible scenario," says Dr. Sovia, suddenly getting loud and confident. "Am I to guess that you have an alternative ending to this story?"

"Oh you are soooo smart Doctor. I love dealing with men I don't have to spell everything out to."

Sofia gets frustrated and loud with Agent Reyes, "What are you talking abou-"

Dr. Sovia grabs his wife around the mouth to stop her from talking. "What are you looking for Agent Reyes?" Dr. Sovia asks.

Agent Reyes smiles and thinks for a beat. "Are we going to be honest with each other here Doc?"

"You're the one holding the gun. You tell me."

Agent Reyes smiles again at Dr. Sovia, "Where is your little stash Doc?"

Dr. Sovia looks at the curiously at Agent Reyes.

"Stop fucking around Doc."

"I'm not. I don't know wha-"

"We are the government," says Agent Reyes, getting angry now, "we know about your little side arrangement with the Jefe. The whole reason he sponsored the clinic."

Sofia looks angry and hurt at her husband, "what is he talking about Roberto?"

Agent Reyes is smiling at Dr. Sovia, "He knows what I am talking about."

"No. No I do not know what you are talking about," replies Dr. Sovia sharply.

"You don't have a future here in Mexico Doc. At least not in Chiapas you don't. Give me what I

want and I will help you resettle in a different state."

The nervousness in Dr. Sovia makes his voice cracks as he begins to plead, "I don't have-"

Reyes holsters the 9MM that was in his right hand and grabs Ariana out of her mother's arms and shoves Pedro's gun into her head. Ariana shrieks in horror. Sofia screams out "No."

"I am not fucking with you doc," says Agent Reyes trying to regain the situation, "my boss, a senior official in Mexican Federal Law enforcement gave me strict orders to kill you." Sofia shrieks again.

Dr. Sovia cries out, getting frantic now, "please don't hurt my little girl."

"The Rosas and the Chiapas Cartel want you dead," Agent Reyes says in a louder more serious voice, "give me what you got and I will let you go. You can go South, go North, I don't give a fuck."

"I don't have anything," Dr. Sovia screams desperately. Agent Reyes squeezes Ariana until she screams.

"Daddy!" screams Ariana.

"Give it to me!" Screams Agent Reyes.

"NOOOOooo!" screams Sofia

A gunshot rings out and the screaming stops. Agent Reyes opens his mouth but no sound comes out. A red stain on his chest appears and grows for a few seconds before he falls over and drops Ariana. She runs to her parents and hugs them.

Pedro, still lying on his back behind Agent Reyes, smoking gun in hand whispers loudly, "I fucking hate cops. OK? Especially the dirty ones I hate OK." Pedro, barely alive regained consciousness enough to reach for his backup weapon in his boot and shot Agent Reyes though the back.

Agent Reyes lies on the floor, two feet from Pedro, blood spreading in an ever expanding pool underneath him. Pedro Garcia who just fired the fatal shot is himself slipping into shock after being shot by Agent Reyes a few minutes earlier. Dr. Sovia rushes over to check the pulse of Agent Reyes then Pedro.

"OH MY GOD! Roberto what is this? We have to call the police. Sofia rushes towards the phone but Dr. Sovia blocks her.

"No. Sofia, no." Dr. Sovia says.

"What do you mean no?" she asks, Sofia tries to push past Dr. Sovia but he blocks her again.

"No Sofia."

"Two men are shot on our kitchen floor," Sofia screams, one of them is a Federal Agent. Sofia goes to pick up the phone to dial again and Dr. Sovia pries the phone from her hand and slams it down.

"The police belong to the Chiapas Cartel," Dr. Sovia says, "Jefe Rosa's organization. You call them, you kill us."

"Don't be ridiculous," Sofia says as if she knows for certain, "this man is obviously a bad cop, but he's a Fed. What do you expect. But not our local cops."

"What are you out of your mind Sofia." Did you not hear what both of them said? The Feds want me dead because I am a witness. Francisco thinks that I'm a rat."

"You're not a rat. You have been like a son to Hector Rosa almost all your life."

"Yes Sofia, that is the problem, Hector is gone now. There is no one to stop Francisco from doing what he has always wanted to do. Get rid of me." Coughs behind Dr. Sovia make both of them pause to look down on the ground at Pedro Garcia.

Pedro, still weak from his gunshot, whispers softly, "he's right Senora. OK, Francisco hates Dr. Sovia. He will kill him, maybe all of you. OK?"

"Why are you telling us this?" Sofia asks.

Pedro coughs up blood and catches his breath, "Ok... I was going to kill your husband. I'm sorry... OK?" Pedro puts his head back down on the tile and tries to breath, gurgling blood.

Valeria Torres walks into the kitchen and sees the blood of Agent Reyes and reacts rather coldly, "Uh oh, what is this? Sofia what is happening.

"Mama, take the children to their rooms please."

"Mom!" yells out Alberto, "I want to stay"

"Now mama, please." Sofia suddenly snaps with authority, "I will be there in a minute."

Valeria Torres stares for a bit then escorts the

children against their will to their bedrooms. "The Feds are going to kill you," Pedro lifts his head up off the tile and informs them, then goes into a coughing fit, coughing up blood. "OK? I told them you saw me in the hallway. Sorry, OK."

Sofia looks at her husband. "Roberto?"

"Sofia, as fast as you can, pack a bag for the kids and one for us. We have to leave."

Sofia reacts with shock, "leave? to where?"

"Sofia we have to leave here. NOW," he says strongly.

"Leave? I'm not going anywhere. This is our home Roberto. We've worked years to-"

"WOMAN! Go pack a bag for you and the kids. Quickly! We are leaving." Sofia stares again at her husband and then marches down the hall to the children's bedrooms. Dr. Sovia kneels down by Pedro.

"I'm sorry Doc. OK?" says Pedro, "don't take it personally. It was just busin"... Pedro Garcia passes out mid-sentence leaving Dr. Sovia staring at his would be murderer. Dr. Sovia quickly walks out of the kitchen calling for his wife.

"Sofia!"

CHAPTER 6

VILLAGE OF MARJAN, AFGHANISTAN, 2004

In the village of Marjan, all is quiet. The villagers have buried Akhtar Sherzai who was burned to death earlier by Baraat Mansoor. The homes in the village are dark, there is no electricity and all have gone to sleep after evening prayers. The survivors from the earlier ambush on the Military Police truck straggle into the Afghan village made of stone and mud. Christina Cruz limps to the nearest house and starts pounding on the door, yelling uncontrollably, "Hello. HELLOOO! Can somebody help?"

Maria shouts for her to come back, "Lieutenant Cruz come back here!" Christina ignores her and continues pounding on the door of a stranger's house.

MP Private Terry leans over to Sergeant Douglas, "she's an officer in your unit?"

Sergeant Douglas looks condescendingly at

Christina Cruz and replies, "Army needs nurses. They'll take anyone they can git."

Christina continues to pound on the door. She starts crying, "Somebody please... I need water."

Dogs in the village start barking. A candle is lit in more than one house. The front door creaks open.

"Oh my god, please help us," Christina cries as she pushes the door and rushes in to their home. All the Afghani inhabitants scream, run or kneel on floor with hands on head and behave in a terrified fashion. They have previously suffered a few night time coalition raids on their homes.

Ullah Dostum, forty-five years old, ancient for an Afghan man, a father and grandfather fears for his family. He yells out in broken English, "No Taliban. No Taliban."

Maria, Judy Tonas, Sergeant Douglas and the four MPs, all US soldiers in uniform, run to the door to retrieve Christina, causing the family to scream even louder. "It's OK. OK, "Maria says trying to calm the villagers and extract Christina from the home.

"It's NOT OK! I need water!" Christina yells

while crying.

Sergeant Douglas of course feels the need to input his opinion, "Ah think theys might be Taliban." This causes the frightened villagers to increase their screams and protests.

Ullah Dostum, screaming now, "NO TALIBAN. NO!" More candles are lit in more houses, some villagers come out of their front doors to see. Christina motions with her hands to drink something trying to communicate her need for water to the villagers.

The MP's take notice of the activity, "We're attracting attention here," says MP Private Terry.

"Ah used to be infantry," Sergeant Douglas exclaims, "fore mah knee got all busted up. Ah'll handle this." An Afghani hands Christina a plastic water bottle and all the Americans start drinking from it. Sergeant Douglas steps back towards the street to meet the now gathering villagers. "All right yall, nuttin ta see heere. Lessin one a yous got a cell phone we kin borra." Sergeant Douglas pantomimes a phone to his head while looking around waving his other hand. Villagers stare at him. "A ceeel phone, ta cahl. We'ze lost." Across the street two of Baraat's men he left in the village earlier are watching the melee and already dialing their cell phone.

The stone fortress of Masoud Mansoor had stood for hundreds of years. Money earned by Masoud's business endeavors had paid for upgrades like electricity, plumbing, etc. Now the building lay in ruins, still smoking from the gunfire and debris blown to pieces by the fight. Lance and several of his soldiers are carefully patrolling through the remnants of the building. Lance's radio crackles to life. "It's Sovia, is anybody left alive?"

Lance quickly pulls the radio handset to his head, "where the fuck are my guys?"

Back downstairs in what is left of the basement medical exam room, Dr. Sovia, covered in dust and dried blood kneels over the body of Chief M. and pulls the radio off of his gear. "They're gone" he says into the radio... "Somebody come get me the fuck out of here." Dr. Sovia rubs blood, sweat and soot off his face and sighs.

Lance, back upstairs, pauses, grimaces his face

in a flash of sorrow then recovers his composure. "The girl," he says into the radio, "where's the girl?"

Back downstairs Dr. Sovia starts to breakdown, he coughs, smacks the wall and shakes his head to gather his composure. He puts the radio back up to his mouth. "She's gone too." We pan out to see Dr. Sovia still in the basement but whole section of the house that was above the basement is gone and he can see up into sky. "I'm in the basement. What's left of it....I can see the stars."

Back in the village of Marjan, Maria, Christina, Judy Tonas, Sergeant Douglas and the four Military Police soldiers are seated outside the home of Ullah Dostum. "Why these folks is just like folk from mah hometown, hospitable." Sergeant Douglas proclaims. The MPs are grouped in twos and attempting to be alert. Villagers bring them food and water. Other villagers just stand around and watch.

"Oh, yes. Yes. Thank you," says Christina as she greedily sucks down what the villagers have brought her. Ullah Dostum who we met in the home earlier tries to communicate with Christina in his broken English.

"Danger!" whispers the old villager to Christina.

"Oh God yes it was soooo dangerous. We had no food, no water, it was horrible," Christina wails.

Ullah Dostum tries to discreetly point toward the MPs, "Danger!" Maria hears him and is quickly alerted.

"What? What did he just say?" Maria questions. Ullah turns to Maria and points towards some Afghans.

"DANGER!" Ullah says louder now. The men Baraat left behind earlier who we saw on the phone pull AK-47s from under their clothes and simultaneously gun down the nearby four Military Police Soldiers. Screams from the villagers and the soldiers mix together to form a cacophony of terror.

"Noooo," Screams Maria as she jumps up but does not know where to run.

"Holy shit! What is happening?" screams Christina Cruz as Baraat's men run to the dead MPs and quickly take their weapons. Sergeant Douglas jumps up only to be kicked in the chest onto the ground by Baraat's man who now points his AK-47 directly at the prone Sergeant. He raises is hands in surrender.

Maria puts herself in front of Baraat's men, her hands raised in surrender, "No. Don't shoot!" Maria starts pointing at herself and her group. "Doctors, we are Doctors! We help! We help!" Baraat's man, his foot still on Sergeant Douglas's chest, smiles and pulls out his cell phone and makes a call.

Back in the ruins of Masoud Mansoor's fortress, Dr. Sovia and Special Forces soldiers find the man cave where Masoud was drinking earlier. It is surprisingly untouched by the carnage on the other side of the building. They look down at the dead body of Masoud and his Manservant. "Somebody want to tell me what the fuck just happened here?" Dr. Sovia asks loudly.

Lance walks around the bodies looking down at them, "Masoud's brother, the kidnapper."

"His brother?! Did all this?" says Dr. Sovia, "Why?"

Lance shrugs and shakes his shoulders, "who the hell knows, sibling rivalry maybe. Islamo-fascism, argument over money, this is Afghanistan; nobody needs an actual reason to betray and destroy everything.

"So much for getting the hostages back without firing a shot," Dr. Sovia says as he angrily throws a piece of debris against the wall. "If we don't get that girl back, I am beyond fucked."

Lance, still in a state of shock replies, "Hey Doc, what do you want from me? I am up shit's creek right with ya."

Dr. Sovia scowls and grabs Lance's shoulder spins him around, "Yeah and me? What, I get Court Martialed anyway? God only knows what more charges I'm gonna have because of this little stunt!"

Lance backs away rubs his chin, pauses a moment, "I gotta call this in, this is too big now, can't hide this."

The Communications Sergeant we met earlier, Dan Nuzzi walks in to the man cave, "Can't call anyone boss."

Lance turns to Dan, "What? Why?"

"Chief M's truck's burned to a crisp," replies Dan, "and the other satellite transmitter on your truck is shot to shit."

"No radio or satellite contact to higher authority?" asks Lance.

"Not unless a plane or a chopper is flying overhead by accident and picks up our short range radio signal," replies Dan.

"Fucking great," Bob White, standing nearby says, "we are cut off from support?"

"Are we fucked Captain?" Dr. Sovia asks, "tell me are we?" Lance gets lost in his own thoughts. "What about your cell phone?"

"It's not military," replies Lance, "It's a local cell system and it's compromised by the other side."

"Fuck you it is!" yells Dr. Sovia.

"We're not even supposed to be on it," replies Lance, "even if I could reach them through it. I won't. Can you imagine a US Army unit calling for help on a compromised system, the Taliban would be flying here in minutes to kill us.

Dr. Sovia looks around and gestures at the carnage and debris around them, "Didn't they just do that?"

"Look I've pushed way past the point of no return," says Lance, "I lost three men. Chris is MIA and no manpower to look for him.

Dr. Sovia angrily kicks over some debris, "well what the fuck do we do now? Give up? Drop me off at Kandahar so they can lock me up."

"No," Lance says.

"Of course not," Dr. Sovia responds angrily, "you'll be locked up right next to me." The two men stare at each other and Lance's phone chirps with a message.

"What the fuck? Message from Masoud's phone," Lance says as he holds up the phone and clicks on the text message which opens into a video message. The soldiers gather around to watch.

On the video, from the point of view POV of a Camera Phone: Baraat is wearing a bandana over his face, stands before three uniformed, US Soldiers on their knees looking bloody and bruised. "Hello world," Baraat says joyfully", I am not sure when you will be receiving this but my name is... well my name is not important right now." Baraat proudly displays the soldiers. "I now hold four US Army soldiers from the...

"What is your unit?" Baraat turns the camera so we see Sergeant Douglas trying to look brave, he tries to give the four pieces of information he allowed to as per the Geneva Convention, "Douglas, Doug R. Sergeant, 12/12.79, US Army, Four Five Four-"A rifle but smacks Sergeant Douglas unconscious, he drops to the floor.

"We shall talk more when he wakes," says Baraat into the camera as he moves to Christina and squeezes her shoulder.

"OOOWwww!" Christina howls, and Baraat puts his masked face up to the side of Christina's, "What unit are you from sweet miss?"

"I'm a nurse with the 313th Forward Surgical Team," she replies.

"And your name young lady?" Baraat kindly asks her.

Lieutenant Christina Cruz, I'm a nurse, oh my god they killed the MP's, that helped us, somebody please help us, we need-" While she is talking, Baraat pulls out his pistol and shoots Christina in the head. Blood and brain matter flies everywhere. Screams are heard off camera.

Baraat looks straight into the camera while walking and talking, "oh worry not, we have more American girls. We are chocked full of American patriots ready to die." The camera pans around to show Kelly Roberts who is bloody and writhing in pain and being tended to by Maria. The camera pans back up to Baraat's masked face, "I hold Congressman Roger Roberts daughter, Kelly Roberts. Say hi Kelly. The camera pans down to Kelly Roberts, on the ground, clothes bloodied and tattered being tended to by Maria. The camera pans back up to Baraat.

"She is injured but as Allah would will it," Baraat melodically says, "we have a doctor." The camera pans down to Maria on her knees working on stemming the bleeding. Baraat grabs the back of Maria's hair and shakes her head before the camera.

"We did not hurt her, she was injured by one of your own aircraft. We will try and keep her alive. My people will make contact with a list of our demands." Baraat stares at the camera, "...Ok... Turn it off... No the other button!" Baraat walks forward and the picture shakes as the terrorists try to figure out how to stop recording. We hear cursing in

Pashtun, "IDIOT! NO NOT THAT BUTTON. IDIOT." A gunshot rings out. From the cameras POV, the camera falls on the floor, the screen goes black.

The Special Forces soldiers and Dr. Sovia are stunned into silence, "Fucking scumbag." The light before the sun breaks over the horizon, the rays of the sun begin to illuminate the air above the earth comes through the shattered great window we saw earlier in the man cave. The early light shows Dr. Sovia holding his head in his hands.

"I knew that woman, she worked in the Operating Room at the 313th. She assisted me in saving your friend Craig."

Bob White, who normally remains silent, breaks the silence, "Shit… What do we do now boss?" as he looks to Lance for guidance.

"She is dead because of me." Dr. Sovia shoots a look at Lance and lunges towards him. The professional soldiers catch and hold him before he can get near Lance. "And you! It was your harebrained scheme got her captured," Dr. Sovia rants, "she'd still be alive if-" The ODA soldiers break them up.

"If what? Huh? If this if that," Lance rages back, "this is war doc. It sucks. I lost my best friend an hour ago, plus two more of my guys, another one's missing!"

"If you weren't so driven on your career," Dr. Sovia yells, "and me so focused on getting out of trouble… she'd be-"

The cell phone chirps. Lance looks at the number, scowls, looks at Dr. Sovia and answers it. "Oh now you need me scumbag!?"

"Did you like my press release?" says Baraat Mansoor over the phone.

"Is that what low level terrorists call a cell phone video?" asks Lance.

Miles away in the village of Marjan in the home where Baraat's men hold hostage Maria, Christina, Douglas and Judy, Baraat paces back and forth while holding a cell phone to his head. He whacks Nurse Judy Tonas with a stick while she is on her knees. "If you want Congressman Robert's daughter alive," Baraat says into the phone, "I need some things."

"You want a doctor?" Lance says over the phone.

"I have a doctor, I want surgical gear."

"You can have want in one hand and shit in the other. See which one fills up first," says Lance, snidely over the phone. Dr. Sovia tries to rip the phone out of Lances hand, Lance spins away.

We hear Maria yell out through the phone loudly, "It's a two-man job. I need another Doctor."

Baraat turns away from her and speaks into the phone, "I will give you coordinates. You send that wetback doctor you're chauffeuring around with my list of surgical equipment."

"Wetback huh?" We hear Lance over the phone, "your American is improving."

Baraat laughs, "I am learning much from my guests." Baraat pats Sergeant Douglas's bruised head. He looks away ashamed.

"Go fuck yourself," retorts Lance.

"I'm going to put my doctor on with your doctor, she will give him the list, commands Baraat. "Do not even think of getting near us, I will wipe out the hostages, film it and release it before you can stop me." Baraat turns to Maria as he hands her the phone, "do not be clever. Give him the list of what you need."

Baraat lets go of the phone and Maria speaks into it, "Hello?"

Back in the ruins of Masoud Mansoor's fortress, Lance hands the phone to Dr. Sovia, "hello? Who is this?"

"Sovia? Is that you?" Maria's voice comes through loud and clear. "This is Captain Paredo… Maria."

Dr. Sovia cradles the phone as he speaks, I'm glad you're ok. I'm so sorry-"

"How is this happening?" Maria cuts him off. "I thought you were kidnapped- OW! Stop!" Maria snaps at Baraat who just hit her with his stick.

"No small talk! Give him the list of things you need to operate." Baraat commands her.

Maria takes a beat to compose herself. "I am told to give you a list of things I will need to perform a Hemothorax drain for bullet wound. Maria proceeds to run down the list of items and Dr. Sovia writes them down.

Baraat grabs phone back and brings it to his

ear, "you are the illegal alien doctor turned US soldier yes?"

"Yes, that's right I'm a doctor," Dr. Sovia says.

"Good. You... alone be at this grid coordinate," Dr. Sovia copies down the information, "And do be alone," Baraat continues, "we will be watching." Baraat snaps the phone shut, kneels down to Maria who is treating Kelly Roberts. "Worry not, American princess help comes for you," Baraat then looks at Maria, "for you... maybe not."

Lance has his ear pressed up to the side of Dr. Sovia's head, listening to the conversation. He pulls out his map onto the bar and the soldiers all gather round. "Alright Doc, where are we going?"

"Grid coordinate, 2452-4833," says Dr. Sovia. Lance traces the map with is finger, "2452-4833 is right here" says Lance, "base of these two mountains, this guy's not stupid."

"He can cover the approach from the mountains and see you guys coming from a mile away," says Dr. Sovia after looking at the map.

The ODA soldiers look impressed.

"Someone's been studying tactics," says Bob White.

"I'm not stupid, he said come alone," replies Dr. Sovia, "I'm sure he's got some of his guys already there watching with radios."

"And how exactly would you know that doc?" asks Bob.

"It's what I would do," says Dr. Sovia, "he's going to grab me, the gear and get us back to the girl, wherever she is."

"You think you're up to going in there alone.... He might kill you," says Lance.

Dr. Sovia looks crestfallen. "The Army was prepping for my court martial. That prick Goldstein was gonna see to it that I'm out of the Army."

"Worse things than being sent back to Mexico have happened Doc," says Bob

"Not for me, not for my kids... We can't get sent back to Mexico we can't."

"What's so bad about Mexico Doc?" asks Bob.

"Not bad for you guys, you're Americans, but bad for me. My kids, we can't go back."

"All right, high time to come clean Doc," says Lance, "What the fuck happened in Mexico to make a doctor, a surgeon into a wetback illegal?" Dr. Sovia looks enraged at the insult. "Hey Baraat Mansoor's words not mine." Dr. Sovia goes silent, looks down at the floor.

CHAPTER 7

CHIAPAS, MEXICO 2003

Back at the Medical Center in Chiapas, the Federal Police (PFM) Chief Inspector Hugo Rivera steps out of the federal sedan that drove him from the airport to the clinic along with three local Federales. For a moment he stares incredulously at the damage he helped to set in motion. "Wow," says the Chief, "some action here huh?"

PFM Agent Chavez, has been on the scene since early morning and is right on top of Chief Rivera within seconds of his arrival overhears as he walks over, "understatement of the year sir." Chief Rivera turns to confront the stranger's voice. Agent

Chavez realizes he should not be so familiar with a superior from Mexico City he does not know and he immediately takes a serious military bearing. "Good morning sir. I am Agent Martin Chavez."

Chief Rivera takes a long minute to silently size up the Agent then turns back to the devastated building and speaks without looking at the young Agent. "Yeah yeah… We got anything yet on who did this?"

"No identity as of yet, but they were clearly very good," replies the Agent.

"Ya think?" the Chief sarcastically replies.

"All the bodies we recovered so far were either clinic staff or members of the local drug gang. The Chiapas Cartel," says Agent Chavez.

"Yeah I know all about the Chiapas Cartel Chavez, I'm from headquarters remember?"

"Yes sir. What I meant was none of the bodies are unknown so if the bad guys lost anybody, they took them with them when they left."

Chief Rivera nods, "got away clean indeed."

"Excuse me sir?" Agent Chavez asks.

"*A very professional job,*" *Chief Rivera clarifies then his phone rings. He motions to Agent Chavez to go away,* "*Give me a minute,*" *then he turns away to take the call.* "*What?*" *The Chief says into the phone,* "*No, no get your people over there now. Before the Rosas get their people there. Go now!*"

Back at the Sovia home, the kids are resisting the idea of travel and refuse to cooperate with their mother. Sofia and Dr. Sovia are hurriedly packing suitcases with their clothes. The children are screaming and crying while their grandmother Valeria Torres packs for her and the children and yells down the hall to her daughter, "*Sofia, I must call your father to tell him where we are going.*"

Sofia hears and yells from down the hall and yells back, "*Call from the road mama. We have cell phones now.*"

Ariana sits on the bed next to the suitcase, "*where are we going grandma?*"

Valeria Torres, still packing doesn't look at

her granddaughter yet answers, "on a fun trip little one."

Alberto Sovia runs in to the bedroom, "I'm not going if I can't bring my toys."

Valeria exasperated gives in to get children's cooperation, "OK, if you promise to be good, go quickly pick some toys, it's only a short trip."

Dr. Sovia walks briskly into the bedroom, "that's it, close it up, were done." He takes charge and closes the suitcase for his daughter and grandmother and carries it to the car.

Sofia yells down the hall, "Alberto get your suitcase." Alberto Sovia comes out of his room with his giant sized army backpack and web-belt with canteens and toy rifle and presents himself to the family.

"I'm ready."

"Are you going off to war Alberto?" asks his mother.

"It looks that way in the kitchen mom."

Sofia puts her hand to her mouth so as not to scream, crosses herself and calms down. "That is what our home is now, isn't it? All right let's go. Go!" She ushers the children and her mother out to the car. Where Dr. Sovia is quickly packing the trunk of the car then waves the family over.

"Let's go everyone," Dr. Sovia says nervously," we have go. NOW!"

Sofia gets into the front passenger seat, closes the door, then starts to open the door, "Oh my God. I'll be right back. I forgot something."

"We don't have time for this Sofie," her husband yells." Sofia runs back to the house and returns carrying her jewelry box.

"I'm not leaving my jewels," she says when she gets back in the car. The family is packed, the car doors close and Dr. Sovia like a stunt driver backs the car out of the driveway not even slowing down to turn to change directions. The car speeds off.

"Where are we going Robert?" asks Sofia.

Dr. Sovia remains silent for a long moment, his eyes glued to the road before he finally speaks, "I did my undergrad with a friend of mine. He's high up in the Justice Department in Mexico City. He'll know what to do."

Sitting in the backseat with the children, Valeria says with surprise, "Mexico City? All the way up there? Sofia give me your phone, I must call your father."

Sofia dials her dad and hands the phone to her mother then turns to address her husband, "Roberto, is it that serious? How much trouble are we in?"

"Were you not in the same kitchen with me ten minutes ago when men came to kill us?" One of them a Federal Agent?"

"Why is this happening Robert?"

"Dr. Sovia takes a long silence then speaks, "The Rosas."

"I never wanted this Robert," Sofia says.

"Don't start this now... You wanted everything that came along with it. Nice house, nice clothes." Dr. Sovia pokes the little jewel box on his wife's lap that she ran back to get. "Nice jewels too."

Suddenly Valeria's conversation with Diego can be heard, "you are sure?...... Well of course I have to ask that? You know your memory these days... Yes I love you too." Valeria hangs up and hands the phone back to Sofia and says, "We have to go back to the house."

"We are not going back to the house," says Dr. Sovia.

"We have to go back to the house," counters Valeria.

Getting stern now, Dr. Sovia says, "we do not have to go back to the house."

"How much cash do you have on you?" Valera asks with a "holier than thou" attitude.

Dr. Sovia suddenly realizes his dilemma and takes a long breath before answering, "not much mama."

Sofia chastises her mother, "Mama!"

"I told your father what's going on," says Valeria, "and like the good tightwad he has always been with money, he has some stashed away, but it's back at the house."

"We will stop at an ATM," Dr. Sovia calmly says as he drives.

"Diego says that if the Feds are involved in this, and they are actually looking for you, they will

track you and us by the ATM, "says Valeria, "If they haven't seized your bank account already."

"Fuck," Dr. Sovia quietly says under his breath as he uncomfortably shifts around in his seat.

Sofia looks closely at her husband, touches his arm, "we need the cash Robert."

Dr. Sovia nods in agreement, "we need the cash."

Dr. Sovia pulls the car over and does a U turn, then races the car faster than normal to race back to the house.

"Mommy is everything going to be OK?" Ariana asks from the backseat.

"Yes of course baby," answers her mother with not so much confidence.

Dr. Sovia slows the car to turn the corner and sees down the street, two cars screech to a halt at the Sovia home and armed angry looking men swarm the house. "Oh no," says Dr. Sovia.

Sofia holds her hands to her mouth, "Oh NO. No, no."

"No cash for us. Sorry mama," Dr. Sovia says

as he smoothly turns the car away from the house and begins driving away. Suddenly in his rear view mirror Dr. Sovia sees unmarked police cars rapidly pull up to his house. The unmarked police cars are mixed with the Chiapas Cartel cars only distinguished by their single little red spinning light in their windshields. Dr. Sovia pulls his car over to the side of the road to watch.

Sofia and the rest of the family turn to see the plain clothed Federal Agents of the PFM hurriedly exit their vehicles, draw their weapons and begin firing on the Chiapas Cartel men still on the Sovia front lawn. They are cut down like ribbons while the Chiapas men who had already entered the house begin shooting back at the Agents through the windows. The Sovia family silently turns face forward again and Dr. Sovia calmly lets his foot off the break and the car slides back onto the road. Inside the car all is silent as they drive out of the neighborhood away from the bloody shootout at their home.

MEXICO CITY, MEXICO

The sun rose an hour ago and the streets of Mexico City are already baking hot. Dr. Sovia stands in front of a bank of pay phones, nervously tapping a phone with his hand while glancing across the street at the ominous, giant Federal Building we saw earlier where Chief Rivera and the Federal Police work.

"Man you look like crap," *Dr. Sovia nervously spins around to see his old college friend, Benjamin Herrera, thirty-three years old, dressed in an expensive business suit. With a giant smile he walks up and extends his hand to Dr. Sovia.*

Dr. Sovia shakes hands and says, "That's the nicest thing you can come up with after all these years?"

"Get over here knucklehead." *Benjamin Herrera pulls Dr. Sovia in and gives him a big bear hug.* "How the hell have you been Robert?"

"Usually or lately?" *replies Dr. Sovia.*

"I want to hear everything", *Benjamin says,* "where is that beauty you married, Sofia?"

"She's back at the motel with the kids and her mother."

"You brought the whole family?"

"Almost, my father in law has some rental properties he is looking after. He opted to stay behind... Can we go to your office?"

"Yeah sure," says Benjamin, "you want to get some breakfast first. You look like you could use some coffee Robert." Dr. Sovia stares blankly at Benjamin who quickly senses Dr. Sovia's distress. "My secretary makes a great cup of Joe. Let's get upstairs and we can talk." Both Dr. Sovia and Benjamin walk off.

The motel was a discount motel, cheap little rooms with old thin mattresses. It was all the Sovia family could afford. Alberto and Ariana Sovia are sound asleep in one bed while Sofia sits by the cracked open window smoking a cigarette talking to her mother sitting with her at the little table.

"I don't know why I put up with him mama."

"He is your husband Sofia. That is the only reason you need."

"Look where we are mama. All these years and we are hiding in a fleabag motel."

"Look at where you were yesterday. You have a nice life Sofia."

"A man came to our house to kill us mama. Two men came... My children mama."

"Your husband is a very smart man Sofia. He is out handling it now is he not?"

MEXICO CITY, MEXICO,

Inside a moderately large office for his mid-level position, Benjamin Herrera types away at his computer behind his desk. Dr. Sovia flips the pages of pictures of known criminals by the Mexican Department of Justice. "Are you freaking kidding me?" says Benjamin while looking at the computer screen, "Robert, you are in a lot of trouble my man."

Dr. Sovia holds his head in his hands. "Well don't sugar coat it Benji, tell me what you really think." Benjamin turns away from his computer towards Dr. Sovia.

"I think you're fucked Robert!" Dr. Sovia's head drops out of his hands. "Ok. Let's go over

what we know," Benjamin says, "the Kingpin of the South, Hector Rosa died two days ago in your clinic."

"Murdered in my clinic," Dr. Sovia corrects him, "after I saved him."

"Yes. Murdered by assailants still unknown but reports as of now say it was a very professional job," Benjamin reads off of his computer screen. "Mercenaries most likely."

Dr. Sovia takes a breath and says, "The agent who came to kill me was-"

"Was, is and forever will be protected by forces on high in the PFM," Benjamin says by interrupting him.

"The guy shot and killed a man in my kitchen in cold blood."

Benjamin, playing the attorney, quips back "Would you feel better if he was heated up when he did it?"

"Please don't make jokes right now Benji, I can't handle much more."

Benjamin looks seriously at his friend, "I

wasn't really joking Robert."

"He was a Federal Agent Benji. One of you guys."

"Not one of mine," counters Benjamin.

"Before Pedro Garcia shot and killed him," Dr. Sovia says, "the Agent said his boss, someone high up in the PFM, the Federal Police Ministerial wanted me dead."

"Do you think he was telling the truth?"

"How should I know?"

"Or was he using that fear to persuade you to do something else Robert? What else if anything did he try and get from you? Money? Drugs?"

After days on the go and with little sleep, Dr. Sovia was still suspicious of everyone's motives. The past forty eight hours had shown him to question every relationship now. Dr. Sovia silently stares at his friend, an attorney for the Mexican Department of Justice.

"He tried to get money out of me."

"Maybe he was using the big scare tactic to squeeze you for money before he killed you."

"How the hell is that supposed to make me feel better Benji?"

"Let's forget about feelings right now Robert. I am NOT here to make you feel better and I don't think you came here for a therapy session."

Dr. Sovia hangs his head again and says, "you're right Benj. But I have to know the full scope of what is going on. Are they after my family or just me?"

"Look Roberto, it appears as if you are caught in the middle of a big power play here."

"How am I am part of this?" Dr. Sovia asks incredulously.

"Robert stop acting like a babe in the woods. Hector Rosa headed the Chiapas Cartel, they move cocaine, up from Central America all the way to Northern Mexico." Dr. Sovia looks at the floor as he cannot bring himself to look at his longtime friend. "And now that pipeline, long established and making tons of money, is itself the target of a hostile takeover."

"By whom Benj?"

"That remains to be seen. But whoever

knocked off Hector Rosa was obviously well trained, well armed and no doubt, well financed. They really wanted him out."

"I should not have left," Dr. Sovia says. "I have an obligation to the Rosas."

"Are you kidding me? No really are you? You said yourself, the kid, what was his name?"

"Pedro Garcia."

"He wiped out all of your staff. You saw him do it."

"Yes."

"He came to your house. He was trying to get you to go with him. Do you really think you would have lived if you had gotten into his car?"

"No. He would have killed me."

"Too bad we can't talk to him." Dr. Sovia shoots his friend a dirty look. "Francisco Rosa hates you," Benjamin continues, "he always has. And now he has a legitimate question about your loyalty and no one to stop him."

"I know," says Dr. Sovia regretfully

"You have a family, a wife, two kids, a mother in law. You are a Doctor Robert. You can get past this and live your life." The stress of the past two days has finally broken his iron will. Dr. Sovia has tears beginning to well up in his eyes.

"What am I going to do?"

Benjamin Herrera sits up in his chair and clears his throat. "Your loyalty to the Rosas ended with the life of Hector Rosa. You do not owe Francisco Rosa squat. Whether or not you know it, you possess information on the workings of the Chiapas Cartel."

"What?... What are you saying?"

"Information Robert. Information that my Department, the Department of Justice, will reward you handsomely for." Benjamin raises his eyebrows at his old friend. Surprised he is not catching on.

"What?" Dr. Sovia asks with shock, "No. NO!"

"This is the only way."

"No. I can't! An informant?! You want me to become an informant against the Rosa's? I can't do it Benji."

"The Department of Justice has been gunning for the Chiapas Cartel for years," Benjamin says. "Have you ever heard of the Witness Protection Program?"

"Yes I have and-"

"We can set you and Sofia and the kids up in a different part of Mexico."

"And do what?"

"You can still be a doctor Robert."

"Oh? If what? I help you ruin the lives of the people that have helped me all my life?"

"Ruin their lives? They tried to take yours. And will try to take again if given the chance."

"I can't Benj. I can't do it."

"Probably your wife's and children's lives as well. How much more do you owe them Robert?"

Benjamin Herrera and Dr. Sovia stop talking and just stare at each other, neither wanting to break the silence first.

Back in the cheap motel a few miles away from the Federal Building, Sofia Sovia still sits by the open window holding her cigarette up so the smoke is carried away from the room. Her mother still concerned for her. "When did you go back to smoking?

"When two men were shot dead in my kitchen yesterday Mama."

"Oh, well then it is excusable," *Valeria says.*

The two women fall silent while they stare at each other. Sofia's eyes begin to well up with tears. "Speak," *Valeria commands. Sofia turns away from her mother.*

"This is all his doing mama. Again, he's at it again."

"You don't know that," *Valeria says.*

"Yes. I know it."

Valeria gets up to put her arms around her daughter. Sofia resists. Valeria persists until her daughter surrenders and tears fall. "He can't stop himself mama."

Both Assistant Attorney General Benjamin Herrera and Dr. Roberto Sovia are still staring at each other, neither one wanting to break the silence first. Fortunately Benjamin's computer does it for them by chirping with a new e mail which he immediately reads.

"Oh this is interesting," Benjamin says.

"What's interesting?" asks the Doctor.

"You say it was a PFM Agent who came to your house yesterday?"

"Yes. PFM Agent Tomas Reyes."

"Tomas Reyes," says Benjamin.

"Yes."

"And you are sure it was yesterday that he was shot in your kitchen?"

"Yes, I was there. We all were."

"Well then something smells fishy in Denmark," says Benjamin.

"Will you always speak in riddles?" asks Dr. Sovia.

Benjamin is looking at different screens on his computer, "he is coming up as being freshly shot today. And you my friend are listed as a Person of Interest."

"What is that?" asks Dr. Sovia.

"Oh don't worry, you are still boring and uninteresting."

"My life is falling apart by the minute and you want to tease me?"

"A Person of Interest, is the first step to becoming a suspect. The authorities want to speak to you about it."

"No really," says Dr. Sovia, "aren't you the authorities? That's why I am here."

"You have to come clean Robert," Benjamin takes a serious tone now. "I mean about everything. I do this all the time, it works, you can live your lives. But there are conditions, you have to tell everything Robert. There can be no surprises."

"I trust you Benji. But the man in my kitchen

who shot and killed a man in front of my wife and children was himself, a Federal Agent."

"I know."

"How can I trust these people when they can clearly be compromised?"

"Living out in the jungle in Chiapas, maybe Agents can get compromised. You are in the capital now Doctor, Mexico City. This is the big leagues. They don't play that shit up here."

Dr. Sovia looks suspiciously at his friend.

"There is a program Robert."

"What program?"

"A secret one," Benjamin says, "it's not discussed or made public. Almost all agents of the PFM and even Justice Department employees don't even know it exists."

"What are you talking about?"

"I'm talking about something the Yanks up North have had for years to protect important government witnesses." Benjamin says.

"Everybody knows about the witness

protection program says," Dr. Sovia.

"But nobody knows about this," Benjamin replies, "It's similar to witsec, you get to start over someplace else, new name, new identity. Any electronic or paper history of you as Dr. Robert Sovia and pictures of you and your family all go bye bye. It'll be a clean slate for you and Sofia and the kids."

Dr. Sovia stares off past Benjamin's head, the thousand yard stare of a man who has been to battle, seen death, exhaustion from days on the go nearly losing his life three times. He is breaking and Benjamin sees it, he has done this before with witnesses.

"I know very powerful people here Robert, the power players. I will get you and Sofia and the kids out of danger. I promise you Robert."

Dr. Sovia visibly sinks just a little bit physically a sure sign he is capitulating in his head. "You are sure you can trust this secret Witness Protection Program?

"Yes I am absolutely sure. But more importantly I sure as hell trust the man who created and runs the program."

"Who's that?"

"The Deputy Inspector General himself, The Legend as he is known."

"And you can trust him?" Dr. Sovia asks.

"Of course," smiles Benjamin, "he's my father in law."

Another silent staring match ensues. This time it is Dr. Sovia who blinks first, "make the call," he says.

Benjamin almost smiles but doesn't. A simple nod of understanding to his friend is enough as he picks up the phone, "Juanita, get me Deputy Inspector General Hernandez." Benjamin Herrera smiles comfortingly at his friend Dr. Sovia.

Benjamin Herrera's SUV is packed with the Sovia family and him at the wheel driving while talking on his cell phone. The brown Chevy SUV's color almost matches that of the desert sands along the highway. Benjamin is driving and speaking into the phone pressed up against his head. "We'll be *there in a few. Ok... I'll see you later."* He shuts the flip phone.

Dr. Sovia, still looking nervous speaks, "Tell me again why we are meeting all the way out here."

Benjamin is navigating the SUV around the long winding desert highway and does not take his eyes off the road to answer, "there is a safe house here that the Justice Department uses to keep witness far away and safe from prying eyes and ears."

"Oh really?" asks the Doctor.

"It's a special branch of the Justice department," says Benjamin, it's the one that does these top level deals with informants." Benjamin pulls the SUV off the two lane road onto a crushed stone driveway and pulls up to a modest, white one story ranch house. There is already one car in the driveway. "He's here. Just like I said he would be."

Sofia leans forward from the backseat, "I need a shower, the kids do also." Sofia reaches across the sleeping children and wakes her mother. "Mama. Wake up. We're here."

Out from the side door of the house steps the tall, rugged Deputy Inspector General of the PFM,

Gabriel Hernandez. He strides boldly to the SUV window. "Everybody all right?" he asks.

"Just tired and dirty Pop," replies Benjamin, "The ladies would like to get in there and take a shower."

Deputy Inspector General Gabriel Hernandez opens the rear driver side door and extends his hand for the passengers, "Ladies, right this way, it is a pleasure to meet you. You must be Mrs. Sovia."

"Yes. Pleasure," Sofia says as Gabriel Hernandez holds her hand as she dismounts the vehicle.

"I wish we were meeting under better circumstances," says Deputy I.G. Hernandez, "but believe me, I have helped a great many people through what you are going through right now."

Valeria Torres steps out after the children and is already surmising and analyzing the old cop. He sees Valeria and tries to make her feel better, "It gets better," he says.

"I bet you say that to all the ladies," replies Valeria.

Gabriel Hernandez smiles at Valeria and is

quickly interrupted by Dr. Sovia, "Can we talk?"

"Yes of course," Gabriel replies as he motions towards the house, "Sovia family, please go inside, use the bathroom, the shower, there is food in the fridge. Take a nap if you need. The three men walk towards the back of the house and the rest of the family goes inside.

"What can I expect for my family?" asks Dr. Sovia

"Whoa, hold on, not so fast," Gabriel Hernandez says. "My son in law says you may hold some vital information regarding drug trafficking."

Dr. Sovia looks at Benjamin with suspicion. "It's OK. He's one of the good guys," Benjamin says reassuringly.

Gabriel continues, "now, I need to know, what have you told Benji here or any other law enforcement personnel about what you know?"

Dr. Sovia is aghast with disbelief and his voice quivers as he speaks, "whoa whoa whoa... My first concern is my family and their safety, let's talk about that first."

Gabriel Hernandez quickly shifts gears, "yes

of course. How rude of me. Please understand I have been after these guys almost thirty years."

"Thirty years?" asks Dr. Sovia.

"Yes, well nearly, almost my entire career in law enforcement."

"Hmmm," Dr. Sovia says, "well you're doing an outstanding job. Thirty years he has gotten away from you and he dies, murdered in my clinic. Gabriel Hernandez grimaces, clearly holding in his anger. "Benjamin painted for me a very rosy picture of the safety and security you could provide for my family."

"That is true," continues the old law man, "yes we can."

"I'm not feeling so safe right now," Dr. Sovia says, "I mean what kind of organization is the PFM that you have Agents sent to kill me, Agents on the take working for drug cartels. And then Benji has to drag us out to the desert to a secret PFM safe-house."

Hernandez tries to console him, "Becau-"

Dr. Sovia, tired and fed up interrupts, "and what kind of organization is it that can't trust its *own people so much you've got Deputy Inspector General's running around like some secret agent." Dr. Sovia is pacing back and forth alongside the gable wall of the house, the side of the house that has no windows.*

Benjamin tries to calm his friend, "Robert, please calm dow-"

"Don't tell me to calm down Benji, I haven't slept in nearly 3 days. I'm at my wits end over here with all this bullshit. You bring me out here, promise me the world and this guy wants to start drilling me for information. I'm done! Take me and my family out of-"

Gabriel Hernandez pulls out his pistol and clunks Dr. Sovia in the head with his pistol butt. Dr. Sovia falls to the ground unconscious.

"Holy shit!" Gabriel Hernandez says, "I thought he'd never shut the fuck up."

Benjamin is shocked and speechless, he stares silently with his mouth open at his sleeping friend and back to his father in law, "What the fuck?! Pop what did you do?"

Gabriel Hernandez pulls out a fat cigar calmly and quietly cuts off the end and proceeds to light and smoke a cigar while Benjamin stares at him. "Benji," he says, "my daughter loves you. I love you. I do wish however you would take better care of my little girl."

Benjamin kneels down to check his friend to see if Dr. Sovia is still breathing. "What are you talking about? Why did-"

"Benji," *Gabriel Hernandez interrupts,* "I've been in this business a long time. I've accomplished a lot of good. Stopped many bad guys."

Benjamin, now kneeling and checking Dr. Sovia's pulse, can't pay close attention to his father in law's prattling. "Yeah Pop, I know."

"My family has a comfortable life. I drive a nice car, nice house. I have plenty of subordinates to do most of my work."

"What the fuck are you talking about?" *Benjamin says finally says forcefully.*

Gabriel takes a long pull on his cigar and puffs out a giant cloud of smoke into the air. "Haven't you ever wondered why you have been at the Justice Department for seven years and you are still at your level?"

"I'm working on cases. We are-"

"Shut up kid and listen to those who have lived this life longer than you have been around. You want to advance? You want to make changes? Well you need to have friends. Friends and power are what gets you ahead."

"Well I'm married to your daughter. I-"

"That has gotten you nowhere professionally, the old man scoffs, "I told you years ago I would look out for you but no guarantees of advancement. You had to do that on your own."

"I'm doing-"

"But now I am going to hand you friends and power, friends and power on a silver platter Benjamin."

Benjamin quietly stares at his powerful father in law, trying to absorb it all, "what are you trying to say?"

"You remember all those times I told you about one day you will have to make tough choices, well this is one of them. You don't rise to the top without getting a little dirt on your hands. Well that day is today. You get to decide whether you remain *a mid-level assistant Justice Department Attorney or are you leadership caliber Benjamin?"*

Benji, unaccustomed to corruption is slow to realize what his Father in Law is talking about. He doesn't go for it. "I just brought you the crown jewel of witnesses, a witness who has known Jefe Hector Rosa all his life, who knows the Chiapas Cartel. And what do you do? You knock him out?"

"Son in law," Deputy Inspector Hernandez says sternly, "how far are you willing to go when hard work is not enough? This man, this friend of yours... he has to go Benji."

"What?" replies Benjamin.

"He saw something that could and will lead to our people, could lead to us, to me Benjamin."

"What the fuck are we talking about here Pop?"

"We arranged for Jefe Hector Rosa's death Benji. The PFM, la Policia Federal Ministerial."

Benjamin Herrera's jaw drops and he cannot formulate words fast enough, "What? What the-"

"Yes Benjamin we did it. I watched that piece

of shit operate with impunity for nearly thirty years and now I got his ass."

"Why?" asks Benjamin, "why would you do this?"

"We cannot and never will stop the drug trade from the outside Benji. We need to be in it."

"Benjamin's head is spinning, the information is coming in to fast. Am I losing my mind or did a Deputy Inspector General for the nation's police just tell me he wants to be IN the drug trade?"

"Not only me Benji, there is a core group of senior strategists, officials. We have mapped this out and planned this for two years. It has been classified."

"Is it even fucking legal?" demands Benjamin.

"Legal illegal, these are nuanced terms Benji," Hernandez replies.

"No. No they are not Deputy Inspector General. We either obey or break the law. Which one are you."

"Benji, can we at least agree that as long as our Northern neighbors or the Europeans will pay

such a high price for drugs, there will always be someone to supply them?"

"No. No we cannot agree," says Benji.

"Well they can, do and will pay. And we will control it. We will regulate it. We will have dramatic drug seizures of our competitors to show the world we are cracking down on drug trafficking."

"As you line your pockets along the way."

"How do you think a civil servant like me affords the houses, the cars, I sent my daughter, your wife, to Yale Benji."

"You won't get away with this."

"Benji, were past that now," the old man says as he puts his hand on Benjamin's shoulder. "You are my son in law, my family, I love you as such."

"Get away from me," Benjamin says as he shrugs off the hand.

"Do you love my daughter Benjamin?"

"Of course I love your daughter. What does that have to do with-"

"If you love my daughter, you are going to

have to evolve."

"Evolve?"

"Change, adapt," snaps Gabriel, *"you are family and I am going to bring you in on this, whether you like it or not."*

"Fuck you Gab. Fuck-"

"Do you realize we are about to make history here?" his father in law asks.

Benjamin Herrera, never a street cop and not very adept at weapons begins to draw for his pistol he keeps on the small of his back. Gabriel Hernandez thirty plus years as a cop, knows from his body movements what Benjamin was doing before Benjamin even knew it himself. Gabriel Hernandez has his gun up to his son in law's head and knocks him to the ground before Benji even slipped the gun from its holster.

"Are you kidding me?" Gabriel asks, *"you were gonna draw on me?"*

Benjamin, lying on the ground with his father in law kneeling on him to keep him down, starts speaking loudly, *"Gabriel Hernandez, you are under arrest."*

"Shut up Benji."

"You may consider yourself under OWWWW!"

Gabriel drives his knee through Benji's back while he handcuffs Benji's hands behind his back. *"Sorry kid, I tried."*

Benjamin, ever the honest lawyer turned lawman replies, *"Fuck you again."*

Several minutes later, inside the safe-house, Deputy Inspector General Gabriel Hernandez is staring at the situation, trying to come to terms with what he has done and is going to have to do. Benjamin Herrera, his son in law who refused to be bought or betray not only his friend but his oath as a Justice Department Attorney, is handcuffed behind his back sitting in an easy chair. The Dr. Sovia and his family are sitting on the couch across from Benjamin in the recliner.

"Here, let me recline you," *offers Gabriel,* *"you'll be more comfortable that way."*

"Fuck you," *is Benji's reply. Gabriel reclines him all the way back and walks back to where he*

was standing by the window, peaking out the curtain at the long desert road. "Help is on the way," *he says.*

"Did you hear me? Fuck you Gab!" *screams Benjamin,* "Really? All these years? A fucking sellout."

"Oh wake the fuck up Benji," *Gabriel spins away from the window back towards everyone.* "Or grow the fuck up, what do you think runs the world."

"You're a cop. You're a fucking legend. You were my hero!" *Benjamin says almost crying.*

Gabriel Hernandez quickly walks over to Benjamin lying down on the reclined chair and lightly smacks his face. "Time to wake up little boy! No more dreaming of fantasy land where you're gonna come in and change it all from the inside."

Ariana Sovia, sitting next to her mother on the couch across from Benjamin in the recliner, cries out to her mother, "Mommy."

Gabriel Hernandez points his finger, "Shut those kids up." *Gabriel walks back to the window and looks out again and begins talking to no one in particular,* "It was all gonna be so great, so *freaking great!"* He shakes his fist while talking, *"but that god damn greedy pig Rosa!"*

Gabriel spins around to look at Dr. Sovia, "and you, Doctor, great job on getting those medicines out to the needy."

Dr. Sovia's head picks up when he hears this, "what?"

"Oh yes, you're such a hero, heading up that Charitable Foundation. It was all so perfect." Gabriel looks out the window again. Then back at his room full of hostages. *"Did you know doctor, that lovely Charitable Foundation Hector established was actually my idea?"* Dr. Sovia looks silently at Gabriel Hernandez. *"No, really it was,"* Gabriel continues, *"you were so passionate about helping others who were helpless. What greater ambassador to the world than a Doctor part of Doctors Without Frontiers, saints who travel the world to operate for free on poor people."*

"What is he talking about Robert?" asks Sofia.

"I don't know," replies Dr. Sovia.

"And the good Doctor got to distribute tens of thousands of dollars in medicine," continues Gabriel. *"Shots and inoculations everywhere he*

went, he established receiving centers for our donated medical supplies didn't you doc?"

Dr. Sovia does not respond so Gabriel Hernandez leans over him so as to intimidate him and his family. "Didn't you Doc?"

"Yes." Replies Dr. Sovia.

Dr. Sovia was not only volunteering in Doctors Without Frontiers, he personally escorted donated medicines that went to inoculate and treat poor people, Deputy I.G. Gabriel Hernandez says. "Dr. Sovia was to be the director of not only that shitty little clinic but a global charitable medicine donation foundation."

Benjamin is disgusted by his father in law's revelations, "you're a piece of shit Gab."

Gabriel does not look at his son in law and continues, "all orchestrated by Jefe Rosa to build an infrastructure so well run and so above suspicion that eventually they would be shipping our cocaine worldwide through this Charitable Medical Foundation that donated tons of pharmaceuticals to poor regions, all facilitated by the good doctor here and Doctors Without Frontiers."

Benjamin turns to his friend, "Robert, you

were part of this?"

Sofia, sitting next to her husband, holding on child in each arm looks to him for answers, "Roberto, did you know this?"

"I... I... Didn't know," says Dr. Sovia, "I never saw any drugs, not the illegal kind anyway."

"No, of course the good doctor didn't know about Hector's plans," Gabriel boasts, "he was just so happy to get a pat on the back." Gabriel slowly turns his head towards the Sovia family and gives the Doctor a dirty look. "Like any good dog, he just wanted to please his master, Hector Rosa." Dr. Sovia gives a hateful look at Gabriel Hernandez. "Always searching for that daddy figure you lost Hector used to say, always anxious to please."

Benjamin is looking at his longtime friend Dr. Sovia and his family, all captive on the couch, "are you gonna kill them yourself Gab?"

Gabriel turns to his son in law, still lying handcuffed on the recliner, "actually I was hoping somehow, before or during our conversation outside... That you would volunteer."

"OK. I changed my mind," Benjamin confidently says, "I'll volunteer. Uncuff me and give

me the gun. I'll show you loyalty."

"It's too late for that Benji," Gabriel Hernandez looks away in shame. In that one second to two seconds Gabriel was looking away Benji swings his legs up and then sharply down pivoting his body up and with legs spread over the recliner, on his feet. He charges his father in law who is looking out the window. The glass smashes as Benji, with his hands still cuffed behind his back, rams his head into his Father In Law's lower back, driving Gabriel's body and especially face partially through the glass.

"Robert!" Benjamin screams.

Dr. Sovia needs no more invitation and he explodes off the couch and into the melee. The Deputy Inspector General was indeed one of the toughest cops of legend who used to beat armed men to death with his bare hands. He spins pushes Benji back with one hand and shoots his gun into Benji's chest with the other.

Dr. Sovia is right behind his friend and the bullet passes through Benjamin's body narrowly missing Dr. Sovia who jumps onto the two and hits Gabriel Hernandez in the head with the frying pan that Sofia had left on the kitchen counter. More shots ring out as Dr. Sovia grabs Gabriel's gun hand as he fires the pistol until it is empty. Dr. Sovia, like a madman hits Gabriel over and over again in the head with the heavy cast iron pan. All three men fall on the floor.

"Fuck you! FUCK YOU!! FUCK YOUUUUU!!!" screams Dr. Sovia. The blood splatters with each impact of the pan until Dr. Sovia stops hitting Gabriel's head. He is heaving and coughing and finally notices the screams of his family behind him. He turns to see Sofia on the couch, covered in blood, next to the children on the couch. Valeria is holding her, "Oh my darling dear no, no, no!" Dr. Sovia jumps off of Gabriel and onto the couch with his wife. Benji's near lifeless body slides off Gabriel onto the floor.

"Sofia! Dr. Sovia screams as he cradles his wife while checking her for a pulse. Alberto and Ariana scream and reach to hold their mother. "No. NO. NO! No Sofia. Sofia!" he strokes her face and hair as he looks at the single bullet hole in her forehead and puts his hand in the back of her head to feel the exit wound. He holds her face close to his and screams.

Valeria, slowly lets go of her daughter. "Oh no. No, my sweet baby, no!" The four sit bunched on the couch hugging the dead body of Sofia.

Dr. Sovia strokes her hair and kisses her cheek, "I'm so sorry Sofia. I'm so sorry. He squeezes her hard. The sound of coughing and gurgling from Benjamin is heard in the kitchen nearby. Dr. Sovia turns his head to see then stands up and kneels down to examine Benjamin. "Benji, it will be OK. Alberto!" Dr. Sovia screams to his son, "run out to the car, get my medical bag out of my suitcase."

"What about mom?" the eleven year old boy screams, still holding on to his dead mother. "Dad what about Mom?"

Dr. Sovia gently slides his friend onto the floor and rips Benji's shirt open to address the wound. He speaks over his shoulder to his son, "she's gone Alberto, she's gone."

Valeria screams at the reality of her daughter's death, "OOOoooo! my daughter."

Ariana shakes her mother trying to wake her, "mommy! Mommy! Wake up! Alberto lets go of his mother and walks up see bloody Benjamin and gasps aloud.

"Alberto! Go out to the car, in my suitcase

now. Go get my medical bag!"

"But mom," says Alberto.

Dr. Sovia looks over his shoulder at his son and screams, "NOW Alberto!" Alberto runs out the front door. Dr. Sovia turns back to his friend, "you're gonna be fine Benji. I know just what to do."

Benjamin, gasping for air and drowning in his own blood, manages to say, "Robert, I'm sorry, I'm so sorry, I did not know about Gabriel."

"It's OK, don't talk Benji," Dr. Sovia says.

"I trusted him Robert. I trusted..."

Dr. Sovia picks his head up to look out the window and yells at his son, "Alberto hurry up!"

Benjamin, still gasping, says to his friend, "take my car, key's in my pocket... Go."

"Shhhshhh," Dr. Sovia says while trying to stop the bleeding.

"He's got guys coming! Now Robert. Get your family out of here. Go North, to the states." Dr. Sovia on his knees, grabs kitchen towels off the counter to staunch the bleeding looks back at the *couch.*

"Valeria go to the bathroom, get me whatever towels you can find," The Doctor yells and Valeria runs to the bathroom.

"Don't take the car across the border," Benjamin whispers, "It's a government car, they'll be on the lookout for it. Get out of Mexico. Go to Texas."

"Be quiet Benji."

In a final burst of energy, Benjamin Herrera grabs Dr. Sovia's shirt with his teeth to pull him closer, "Go now! They will kill you. They will kill all of you." Benjamin stops talking and exhales his final breath. Dr. Sovia stares at his friend's lifeless face then shifts his gaze to Gabriel Hernandez bloodied and battered face. He checks the pulse of both men and grabs the pistol lying on the floor beside them.

Valeria returns and asks, "Roberto. Is he... Is he dead?"

"They're both dead Mama."

"What are we going to do Roberto?" she asks.

Dr. Sovia stands up, puts the gun in his pocket just as Alberto runs in with the medical kit.

"Sorry it took so long. I had to find-" Alberto stops mid sentence as his gaze falls on the very bloody head of Gabriel Hernandez."

"Valeria, go in the fridge, the cabinets, get everything we can eat and drink and take it with us," says Dr. Sovia. He looks around the corner and points at his daughter who is still sitting on the couch too terrified to move. "Ariana get in here and help your grandmother, you too Alberto, NOW. Dr. Sovia moves to the bedroom and comes back with a blanket, wraps Sofia in it and caries her out to Benji's car while the kids and grandmother ransack the kitchen for food and water.

"I'm scared Nana, says Ariana.

Valeria puts a comforting hand on her granddaughter, "Don't be scared little one. Your father will fix everything."

Dr. Sovia comes back in the house. "Should we call someone Robert?" Valeria asks.

"Someone is already on the way Mama, let's go. LET'S GO!!" Dr. Sovia looks at his dead friend lying on the floor. Then kneels down and starts

searching his pockets for money. "Sorry Benji, we need it more than you." Then he searches Gabriel Hernandez pockets for money as well. The Sovia family runs from the house, piles in the car and drives off into the Northern desert towards the US-Mexico border.

CHAPTER 8

WASHINGTON DC, 2004

He came up the hard way, had to earn everything he ever had. After the bank foreclosed on the farm, dad took off to the big city. "Gotta earn some real money to take care of you and your mom," Dad told him, "You're the man of the house now." Those are the words Roger Roberts remembers most, even until today, most mornings when the Chairman of the House Armed Services looks in the mirror before he leaves for the day, he quietly repeats dad's last words, "You are the man of the house now". Roger Roberts had to join the Army at seventeen years old; right out of high school, mom's job carrying plates at the local diner was not going to pay for college. No, Roger Roberts suffered the abuse of semi-retarded NCO's (Sergeants as they are called nowadays) and of course the indifference of the commissioned officers who were at the top. The senior leadership of the Army never gave a hoot about the poor low ranking soldier, who suffered the cold, the heat, the degradation of being yelled at daily with the least pay and the worst living conditions.

After the Army, Roger Roberts used his GI bill to pay for undergrad and earned his scholarship to Law School, graduating at the top of his class. It was a long road of deal making, fund-raising and underhanded living to make it to the head at the seat of the table. "Chairman of the Armed Services Committee," was the title he now held. Most voters do not recognize how much money the Pentagon spends every year, over five hundred billion in 2004 alone so far, a half a trillion dollars. And every single penny had to be approved by his committee. With Roger Roberts at the head, most, no, ALL contractors, and suppliers and of course recipients of those tax payer funded toys, "the Generals" kissed his ass in ways one could not imagine.

Sitting behind a giant polished oak desk, Congressman Roger Roberts, fifty years old, sits with an office phone pressed to his head. His aid

Thomas Wernham, twenty-seven years old, frantically walks in to Robert's office ad clicks on TV. CNN is emblazoned on the screen below the newscaster.

The newscaster barely raises his mundane voice, "Congressman Roger Robert's daughter Kelly captured in Afghanistan." On the TV appears video footage of Baraat Mansoor holding the head of Dr. Maria Paredo while she tends a wounded and bleeding Kelly Roberts, lying on her back.

Baraat Mansoor appears alone on the screen and speaks, "We will try and keep her alive. My people will make contact with a list of our demands."

The CNN newscaster drones on, "no word yet on their demands or from Congressman Roberts Office."

Congressman Roberts stands up behind his desk staring at the TV, drops the phone he was holding as more and more phones ring. "Kelly? KELLY?!Noooooooo!"

AFGHANISTAN, 2004

The Special Forces soldiers of ODA 666 listen to Dr. Sovia's tale, "bad guys came. Bad guys came and killed a man who was like a father to me. He was a bad guy too. Not to me but... his enemies... did not stop with him. They went after everyone who was loyal to the Jefe. Drugs money, bribery, Federal Police, everyone was corrupt. Not my wife though. She just wanted to be a mother to my kids and a wife to me. I was fighting for our lives when a bullet meant for me killed her instead. My kids and my mother in law have been hiding ever since. I joined the Army to get legal status for us all... I got nothin, if I get kicked out of the Army. I'll be deported out of the US along with my kids. They will kill us if we go back."

"Wow, that sucks," Lance comments.

"If I die in the line of duty they're not gonna deport my kids are they?" asks Dr. Sovia.

"That's probably true, they won't, bad publicity," answers Bob.

"My kids are my whole world," Dr. Sovia goes on, "as long as they don't get deported back, nothing else matters."

"The Pentagon hates bad publicity Doc, I mean really hates it," says Bob. "If you die in the line of duty, there's no way they would deport your kids."

Dr. Sovia stands up straight, full of sudden confidence, "we are doing this! Let's do this!"

Lance scoffs at Dr. Sovia, "Look who's turning into the big hero. Twelve hours ago you just wanted to coast along and finish your enlistment."

Dr. Sovia looks at Lance silently for a while before he speaks, "before my wife was shot we were running, we were betrayed. She was shot dead, right there next to the kids. They were wearing their mom's blood and brain tissue." Dead silence falls over the group. Dr. Sovia starts to break down and cry leading to more dead silence. He wipes his eyes and gathers himself, "I ran again to the US. I ran away again, this time to the Army. I'm done running away. I'm not standing by while more women die that I could have saved."

All the ODA soldiers stare at Dr. Sovia. Lance is the first to break the silence, "fuck it! We're doin this." Cheers go through the group.

Dr. Sovia wipes his face, "we've still got the

bags of surgical equipment downstairs," he says.

"Get down there and find them," orders Lance.

The soldiers begin to sound off their approval, "let's do this!" is heard, "Fuck Yeah," Dan Nuzzi says as soldiers fist bump each other.

"Let's go get the girls back" Dr. Sovia says, the all begin to head out to prep for the next attack. Lance grabs Dr. Sovia's shoulder and spins him around.

"Hey, this scumbag knows the terrain, the local villages. He has the home turf advantage."

"I know," replies Dr. Sovia.

"You're walkin into an uncertain future Doc."

"Only death is certain Captain," Dr. Sovia replies coldly, "life is not."

"We still have to wait for his next contact," says Lance, "we don't know where he's got them holed up." Right on cue, at that moment, the Radio crackles to life.

"Red Rhino, Devils child seven, over?" Chris's voice comes out of the radio and the group looks.

Lance grabs the radio handset and speaks into it, "Red Rhino Devils Child 7, nice of you to check in."

Several miles away in a wooded area, Chris Langan is connecting a copper wire strung from tree to tree to create a makeshift long range antenna system that he has wired to his communication radio. Chris speaks into the handset, "had some problems with my comms."

Lance's voice emanates from Chris's radio, "where are you?" Chris looks down to his map and compass. Holds up binoculars in one hand with radio handset pressed up to his head.

"Using my tracking skills the Army invested so much money in," Chris smartly replies, "I got eyes on the objective."

"Get the fuck out," Lance replies.

Chris, still consulting the map and looking around replies over the radio, "if you are still at the previous location, objective is 3 klicks Southeast of your position. Village of Marjan according to the map."

Lance scrambles to locate the point on the map, then speaks into the radio handset, "Chris, you say you've got "Eyes On" the objective. You can see them?"

"Holed up in a little stone house in a little village of stone houses," replies Chris while looking through binoculars.

"All right, stay put and hidden we need you to send us intel as we make a plan... Thanks Chris."

"Doin my job boss," relies Chris.

Lance puts down the radio handset and looks around at his men. "Let's get ready."

The soldiers all know how to prep for an op (military operation) and few vocal directions are needed. Dr. Sovia and Dan pull out Medical Bags from the debris. Bob White cleans and preps weapons while Lance pours over electronic map in his truck when his radio crackles to life. "Lance, pick up," comes Dan Nuzzi's voice, "you gotta see what's down in the caves.

Down a long set of stone stairs, carved out of the mountain, Lance is guided by Dan into a monster sized cave filled with rows of stacked crates of consumer goods. "OK," says Lance, "we know he was a smuggler. And why are the lights working down here?"

"No wonder this Masoud guy was so rich," replies Dan, "he thought of everything. I mean everything. Look over here." Dan points to a series of Bar-B-Q sized propane tanks all piped together and feeding into a quiet running generator. "Look at this," Dan marvels, "A near silent generator that runs on propane."

Lance getting annoyed now, "OK so besides this, what am I down here for?" Dan smiles and walks away motioning for Lance to follow, they come around a wall and are greeted by four shiny new 4x4 Toyota Hilux pickup trucks.

Dr. Sovia walks out from behind one, "I'm claiming the red and white one."

Lance smiles, "covert vehicles, nice."

Dr. Sovia rubs his truck lovingly, "we'll look just like the Hajis," he says.

"All right, everyone, go back into the courtyard and grab some clothes off the dead guys," Lance orders, "we're gonna drive their trucks, we're gonna blend in and look like them."

Deep in the bowels of the Pentagon in Washington DC, sits a war room, a ready room with giant computer monitors and all the intelligence and data coming in from conflicts around the world. In an anteroom with glass walls, sits Congressman Roger Roberts at the head of a long table among high ranking officers on phones. Their aids are running notes and conversing with superior officers. The room is abuzz with activity. Four Star General Ricardo Gomez, fifty one years old, steps up to and points at a wide screen computer screen on the wall.

"Sir," begins General Gomez, "we have all our theater wide forces on alert. We are-"

"What the fuck does on alert mean?" The Congressman interrupts.

General Gomez spins back to the table, "Sir it means-"

"Why the hell am I just learning about this now?" Roger Roberts interrupts again, "how long have they had her?"

"We are ascertaining that information right

now sir," General Gomez says as he is handed a paper by an aid walking by.

"I gave you goddamned Army guys the funding for that shit you asked for," Roger Roberts says loudly. "And now you're telling me you can't find a kidnapped American girl in postage sized shithole like Afghanistan."

"Sir I-"

"What the fuck are the American tax payers paying for if you guys can't find shit!" the Congressman rails on.

"Congressman Roberts, give us a chance," pleads the General.

"You've had your chances, how long have you known she was captive?"

General Gomez reads the paper he was handed. "We are focusing on what we are doing now and how we will be aligning our forces to find and retrieve her sir," the General chides the Congressman.

Roberts pauses, breaths deep, "You are confident you can get her?"

General Gomez looks up at the Congressman, "all our forces on alert, geared up and we are in a forward leaning posture at this time congressman."

"What does that even mean, forward leaning," asks Roberts.

"Forward Leaning," the General explains, "it means we are not attacking yet, but leaning forward just before we attack."

"Well why the fuck are you NOT attacking?"

General Gomez sternly replies, "The SECOND… we have a possible location on her, we launch."

The Congressman pauses to think and breath, "Whoever you have on this, better not fuck it up."

On an Afghan dirt road, overlooking an intersection of bigger dirt roads, Dr. Sovia stands with Lance and Bob behind the open tailgate of one of the Toyota Hilux pickup trucks. Its rear cargo area is filled with the bags of medical equipment we saw earlier. Dr. Sovia puts his hands to his eyes and gazes.

"Alright," says Dr. Sovia, "I drive down to that intersection and wait for our new friend to come get me?"

"You'll be waiting for a while," replies Lance, he will want to make sure-"

"I'm not followed, yeah I get it," interrupts Dr. Sovia, "I'll bet he doesn't make me wait." Dr. Sovia takes a look around the hills. "I'll bet you he's got spotters out here already watching us."

Bob's curiosity is piqued, "what makes you say that doc?"

"I grew up around smugglers," The Doctor replies.

Bob feigns shock, "well aren't you full of surprises. All right, let's gear you up Doc."

"No gear, they'll frisk me."

"Oh no doc," Bob says laughing, "we are the experts in smuggling in gear."

"Yes, they are going frisk you." Lance says, now these boys might be killers but they're also devout Muslims."

"Meaning what?"

"Means they won't search your junk Doc."

"Junk?" Dr. Sovia asks.

"Yeah Doc, your junk," Bob says as he grabs his groin to demonstrate and laughs.

Lance pushes him away, "now let me show you where you are gonna put this," Lance holds up a small pistol turns it upside down. "Pistol handle goes up alongside ya nutsack and the barrel points at your bunghole between your cheeks."

Dr Sovia looks aghast with horror, "c'mon now I-"

Bob steps back in to help, "not IN your bunghole doc. That transport space is reserved for me." Bob holds up what looks like a white tampon. "Plastic explosives Doc," Bob says while smiling.

"Get the fuck out. I am not shoving that up my ass."

Lance interrupts them and shows Dr. Sovia the pistol and clip of bullets, "now Doc you get a full clip in the pistol but don't chamber a round until you pull the weapon out."

"What?" Dr. Sovia asks incredulously.

Lance shows the Doctor the pistol while explaining, "an accidental discharge may hit the plastic explosives up your ass." Bob holds up the explosive tampon and points at it.

"And since the primer is already in the explosive," explains Bob, "we could have a premature detonation while it is still inside you. Dr. Sovia's mouth is ajar but Bob and Lance are deadpan serious. Bob asks, "now, do you think your gonna need lubricant?" Dr. Sovia grabs the exploding tampon and gun, slides back the bolt to check it for a chambered round.

"I'm gonna need more firepower," says the Doc. Dan Nuzzi appears and clips an electronic device to a piece of medical equipment in the bag on the truck's tailgate.

"Now these Hajjis are gonna search you but aren't too up on modern technology," Dan explains, "this little device here is getting clipped to your lovely anesthesia machine."

"What is that?" Dr. Sovia asks.

Dan holds up a small rectangular box with a scope. "This Doc is a GPS laser target designator.

We use this to call in pin point air strikes. The GPS knows your location at all times."

"Just in case you guys lose me?" Dr. Sovia tries to joke. Dan laughs as he holds the tubular device to his eye.

"I point at what I want to get bombed, press this button, Dan says as he shows Dr. Sovia the buttons on the device. "The laser loads that exact grid coordinate into the computer and when it chirps press send on the keypad."

"Who am I sending it too?" asks Dr. Sovia.

Dan laughs again, "no you're not calling in air strikes doc. It's so we can track your location. Just leave it clipped to... Dan points at the Medical Equipment, "what is this called again?

Lance steps in, "don't worry what it's called. Doc, get rollin. We got a low altitude drone tasked to keep watch on you. Move out everyone." All the soldiers get in their vehicles and drive away.

Several miles away in a stone house, Nurse

Judy Tonas sits on the floor holding Kelly Roberts head in her lap while Dr. Maria Paredo treats Kelly's bullet wound. Judy looks at her watch and says "three hours now. She gonna make it?"

"I don't know," Maria replies, "her pulse is weak."

Kelly stirs and whispers, "don't count me out yet. Daddy didn't raise no sissy girl." Judy strokes her head and smiles.

Back at the intersection we saw before, Dr. Sovia stands in full US Army uniform, by the tailgate of the pickup truck. Occasional Afghan Jingle trucks and cars packed with pilgrims slow down and stare as they pass him. "What was I thinking?" he says to himself as he looks at a picture of his kids and wife. Two Toyota pickup trucks pull up and four Afghans jump out and walk towards him pointing AK-47s.

One of the men is Abdul, Baraat's right hand man. He yells in Pashtun, "Hands up! Hands up." Abdul motions up with is rifle, Dr. Sovia raises his hands as he is thrown on the ground and searched then lifted up. The attention of the men is shifted to the cargo area of the pickup truck as they look through the bags. Abdul looks up and in his best English asks, "meedeecaleeekweepmant?"

Dr. Sovia shakes his head, yes. The men grab the gear, march Dr. Sovia to their truck and drive away. Two more pickup trucks of identical make and near identical color meet them, they drive off the side of the road in circles creating a dust storm and the trucks can't be seen.

A mile away, in a small clearing in the woods, the men of ODA 666 stand at the back of their Humvee watching the video feed from the drone above Dr. Sovia and the trucks. Their view of Dr. Sovia's truck is blocked by the dust kicked up by the driving trucks. Dan Nuzzi is suddenly unnerved, "Uh oh. Which one am I following here boss?" On the video monitor they watch all four trucks drive off in separately.

Bob White rubs his chin and looks to Lance, "this guy ain't stupid boss."

"Dan what about that GPS designator," Lance asks.

"He's got to activated it first," says Dan.

Lance shakes his fists and stomps on the ground, "FUCK!!! Follow whichever one is NOT heading towards our location. Fifty-fifty chance we catch up to him." Lance walks away from the monitor talking to his men. He points out the village Chris Langan pointed out earlier. "All right let's get ready to assault this objective. We're goin in quiet. Gear up!"

Baraat's men drive their pickup truck through the heavily forested mountain roads. Dr. Sovia is lying flat in the backseat with a smelly Abdul sitting on Dr. Sovia's back holding his AK-47. The truck stops, doors open, Abdul drags Dr. Sovia out and to his feet where he tries to act authoritative. "Who is in charge here?" Dr. Sovia barks out. The Afghans silently stare and give no response. "Anybody here speak English?" A shape walks out from the darkness. Baraat flashes a sinister smile as he comes forward.

"For both questions," Baraat replies, "me... doctor." Baraat snaps his fingers and waves to his men continuing in Pashtun, "get the medical equipment." Baraat's men start gathering the bags of gear and he turns to Dr. Sovia, "I hope you brought everything."

"Yeah, me too, where is the girl," Dr. Sovia asks. Baraat smiles again.

Less than a mile away from the village of Marjan, the Special Forces soldiers are prepping for what is next. Lance now wearing a head wrap to look like an Afghani, stands behind a tree, binoculars up to his eyes, scanning the village. A pickup truck we saw earlier pulls up to the house. Afghans get out and start pulling out gear and the vehicle moves behind the house. "That's it, he's in," announces Lance.

Chris Langan, still concealed in his sniper's Ghilli suit is lying nearby. "Lance, I'm not seeing the doc," he says.

Lance puts his binoculars back up to his eyes, "they moved the truck behind the house. Smart fuckers." Lance walks back to his civilian pickup truck waving his finger in a circle. "Warning order! We're goin in five minutes. Chris will cover us from a forward sniper position.

Chris responds, "roger boss."

"Everybody else," continues Lance, "we're dressed like Hajjis and driving their pickup trucks, we'll drive right in." Lance points to a white board propped up on the back of his pickup truck with a diagram of the village and target house. "Look here campers, no shooting till be get on the objective and only those of us with sound suppressors. We don't want to alert the whole village."

Lance points at locations on the white board while speaking, "Team two keep eyes on us. When we take the guard house, you move up and take position. Dan, you're up."

Dan. Dan Nuzzi walks before the soldiers and produces an electronic device, "Stealth and surprise are our friends. No radio contact between us. I managed to salvage the signal jammer from Chief M's Humvee." A collective groan goes through the group. "But that also means they, the Hajjis will not be able to call on their cell phones or radios for help. Not even to each other."

"We're on our own and so will they be," Lance advises his men, "speed, silence and death. Kill everyone you see. And keep it quiet as long as possible."

Back in the village of Marjan, inside Baraat's now lair turned operating room, Dr. Sovia walks alongside Baraat as multiple Afghan men carrying the medical bags further into the house. Baraat turns to Dr. Sovia and speaks in a genteel manner, "Thank you for coming doctor.

Dr. Sovia does not look at Baraat as he answers, "My job." They arrive at an anteroom where Maria and Judy are on their knees working on Kelly Roberts to stem the bleeding. Maria looks up to see Dr. Sovia. "Sovia!" she calls out, happy to see a familiar face. Baraat raises an eyebrow as Dr. Sovia grabs a medical bag and kneels next to Maria.

"That's ""DOCTOR" Sovia," he corrects her. "What's her BP?"

Nurse Anesthetist Judy Tonas is the first to answer, "BP is low Doctor."

Dr. Sovia speaks while unpacking equipment from the bag, "has anyone got a blood type yet?"

Judy reaches into the medical bag that Maria brought and pulls out a test card, "AB positive."

Dr. Sovia reaches into the medical bag and pulls out an IV bag and tubes, hands them to Judy. "Get her started on blood expander. Either of you AB positive? Both women shake their heads no. Dr. Sovia turns to Baraat, "Neither am I, we need someone from your people to donate blood." Baraat stares at Dr. Sovia then at the women without comment. Dr. Sovia breaks the silence, "Do you want your prize to die? Then I need someone's blood."

Baraat steps forward and rolls up his arm sleeve, "I am AB positive," Baraat says. Grumbles and reactions are heard from the Afghans. Baraat waves them off. Dr. Sovia stares at Baraat. "Take my blood…Now" Baraat continues, "she had better live."

Dr. Sovia looks to Maria, "Dr. Paredo, start the transfusion." Dr. Sovia looks back to Baraat. "Can you get some of your guys to lift her onto that table?"

Baraat snaps his fingers and barks and order. The Afghans carry Kelly Roberts and lay her on a wooden picnic table inside the house while Dr. Sovia starts digging through the bags. "Let's get to work people," Dr. Sovia says, "nurse Tonas, I'll help you set up the anesthesia tank."

Along the dirt road, two of the pickup trucks from Masoud Mansoor's compound, now driven by the Special Forces soldiers of ODA 666 race towards the village of Marjan. From the road, the occupants of the vehicles look like bearded Afghan fighters. They stop for a Taliban check point at a house in the edge of the village. "Oh shit," says Bob, "what are we doing boss?"

"Get that jammer going Dan," Lance orders and Dan flips the switch on the jammer.

"Done,"

A Taliban soldier struts up the pickup truck with a smile, as he approaches what he thinks are friendly forces. He grabs his hand held radio and speaks into it but no one answers. He walks to the driver side window and speaks in Pashtun, "hey, nice of you guys to finally show up.

Lance waves from the driver seat and answers in Pashtun, "yes. Yes. Thank you. The other Taliban fighters approach the vehicle, their weapons still slung over their shoulders. Lance calmly looks at his men in the vehicle and calmly says, "now." The Special Forces soldiers produce silenced pistols in the blink on an eye and drop all the Taliban fighters with only the thuds of bodies hitting the ground to break the silence.

"Chris go!" orders Lance.

"On it!" replies Chris as he quickly exits the truck and drags the bodies into the house. "Go! GO!" Chris says in hushed tones and the pickup trucks continues driving into the village.

Inside the makeshift operating room, Dr. Sovia, Maria and Judy Tonas are surgically masked and leaning over Kelly Roberts on the table. Dr. Sovia is about to cut Kelly's body open when several of the Afghan fighters surge forward to watch. Dr. Sovia stops and looks at Baraat. "Sir, please, conditions here are already unsanitary enough. Please ask your people to stay back."

Baraat waves his men away and they grumble their dissatisfaction but go back to other side of the room and entertain themselves. "Nurse Tonas," Dr. Sovia says, "start the anesthesia please. Dr. Sovia looks hard at the women and they all discreetly pull plastic tubes from inside their surgical smocks and insert them under their surgical masks. Dr. Sovia starts cutting open Kelly's belly near the bullet wound.

Outside on the road, the Toyota pickup trucks slowly pull up next to the target house, the Special Forces Soldiers leap from the vehicle and kick down the door and enter quickly firing silently before the unaware Afghans can get their weapons or bearing. As he leads the way Lance calmly calls out, "clear front." The house is quickly and silently cleared. Lance sees out a window Bob White standing over several dead Taliban in the back of the house. "Clear here boss, Bob says as quietly as possible.

Dan Nuzzi comes running into the room where Lance is, "no doctor Lance, they're not here."

Lance looks around perplexed and asks furiously, "where the fuck are these people?"

Dr. Sovia leans over Kelly Roberts as she lies on the makeshift operating table as he and the team finish with her, "suture here Dr. Paredo," Dr. Sovia says to Maria as she looks around to see all the armed Afghans sound asleep in their chairs. Some have fallen to the floor, unable to remain conscious. Baraat who was donating blood is also passed out in his chair.

Maria mumbles with the breathing tube in her mouth, "can I take this tube out of my mouth, I'm gonna puke."

Dr. Sovia looks around the room then to Nurse Judy, "that's enough, turn off the gas." Judy bends down and starts twisting the vaporizer's valves. "Keep oxygen going until we leave," he adds, "Maria finish closing her up, fast." Dr. Sovia takes a deep breath from his tube, disconnects it, then leaves the operating table, he looks out all the windows and says "alright, it looks clear," Dr. Sovia says as he runs to the unconscious Afghan who drove and searches his pockets, comes out with a set of keys, the runs back to the table and re connects the air tube.

Breathing heavily, Dr. Sovia warns them, "OK, look around and decide what we are grabbing on the way out. Maria grab the Med-bag, Nurse Judy grab a couple of those guy's rifles."

Nurse Judy shakes her head no and says, "no, I can't."

"Listen, I have to carry this girl to the truck," Says Dr. Sovia, "Maria almost done? "

"Yeah, all done here," Maria replies.

"Let's move," Dr. Sovia says as he scoops up Kelly from the table and starts carrying her towards the door. He is tripped up by the tube coming out of this surgical smock still connected to the oxygen tubes. "Fuck! Judy un-hook me please!" Judy fumbles her way to disconnecting the tubes. "Oh no," Dr. Sovia exclaims and puts Kelly Roberts down and grabs the GPS Target Designator Dan had clipped earlier to the Vaporizer.

"What is that?" asks Maria. Dr. Sovia runs back to Kelly, scoops her up and all three quickly exit the house dragging the air tubes behind them.

"Tell you later", Dr. Sovia says has he struggles to carry the still unconscious but alive Kelly Roberts to the pickup truck he arrived in. "Maria get in back and make sure the girl is OK."

They all climb into the truck, Dr. Sovia jumps in the driver seat and fumbles with the keys to find the right one. Maria releases a piercing scream, "Aaaaaaahh!"

Dr. Sovia looks up to see one of the Afghans staggering out of the house, trying to fire his AK-47 at the truck at near point blank range. "Judy, shoot him!" yells Dr. Sovia.

"With what?" screams back Nurse Judy, "I didn't take any guns."

Both Dr. Sovia and Maria react with shock at the news, "What?!"

"Oh my god!" Judy yells, "I'm a pacifist. I don't believe in-"

Dr. Sovia quickly reaches into his groin produces a pistol aims and pulls the trigger. Click.

Nothing happens. "Fuuuuucckk!" Dr. Sovia screams and he quickly chambers a round and fires twice out the open passenger window and puts the Afghan down just as he is aiming his AK-47 at the pickup truck.

Now Judy is screaming, "Oh my God! Help us Lord!" The silence of the village is broken from the gunshots and Dr. Sovia starts and revs the engine, then screeches away from the stone hut leaving a dust trail.

"Get us out get us out of here Sovia," Maria yells from the backseat as the truck speeds away.

"I don't know where the hell we are," Dr. Sovia yells back.

"Just drive drive! Drive!" Maria yells louder now. Baraat's men from the other houses, now alarmed by the gunshots begin rolling out of those other houses and shooting wildly at the truck as it escapes the village.

Nurse Judy crosses herself in the front passenger seat and cries, "Oh my god I am dizzy, Lord help us please. I'm dizzy from the gas"

"Me too," adds Maria.

"We breathed in too much of the gas," says Nurse Judy, "that was brilliant by the way Sovia."

"What?" Dr. Sovia says while taking his eyes off the road for a second to look at Nurse Judy.

"Using the gas to knock out the room," says Judy.

"Well, we're not out of the woods yet," says Dr. Sovia while driving and frantically searching the surround area. "Where the fuck is the team?"

Maria leans forward from the back seat, "What team? They still have the other girls!"

"Where? Here?" Dr. Sovia asks.

"I don't know," Maria replies, "they moved us to a different house after you called. And how are you even here? What is going on?

"The kidnapper called I didn't call," Dr. Sovia responds.

Judy frantically looking out the rear window for bad guys snaps, "Oh who gives as shit who called who! Just get us out of here! Drive!" The truck begins ascending up a mountain road overlooking the village of Marjan. Dr. Sovia pulls the truck over to view the village through a gap in the trees.

"Sovia," Maria asks incredulously, "what are you doing? Why are you stopping? Dr. Sovia pulls out the little box with the scope he pulled off the vaporizer and turns it on and looks through the scope, out the passenger window at the village.

"I don't know where we are," Says Dr. Sovia while looking through the little scope, "but I know where they are.

"Can we just get out of here?" Judy asks angrily.

"Is that the house we just came from?" asks Dr. Sovia. Both Maria and Judy look out the window down to the village. "Ah the one with all the hajjis running out the door and jumping into trucks?" Quips Maria, "yeah I think so." Dr. Sovia lines up the house in the scope and presses the button Dan Nuzzi showed him earlier. The device beeps that it has a lock on the GPS coordinates.

Judy, getting very nervous and searching for bad guys, takes notice of what Dr. Sovia is doing with his little device. "What are you doing? Why aren't we driving out of here? What is that thing?"

Dr. Sovia finishes following the procedure he just learned. "It's a GPS laser target designator."

Maria looks at him incredulously, "who the fuck are you?"

Dr. Sovia fumbles with the device before pressing send. "I'm the idiot who had one lesson on how to use this thing," he replies.

Back in the Village of Marjan, in the house that the Special Forces soldiers of ODA 666 have just raided, Captain Lance Erickson looks out the window at the village. "Where the fuck are these people? His men stare at him in silence. "Dan, turn the Jammer off," Lance orders. Dan Nuzzi pulls the pack off his back and turns it off. Lance presses a button on his chest and speaks into his helmet microphone. Chris, pick up.

Lance's helmet mounted earphones fill with Chris's voice, "yeah go for Chris"

"You sure this is the house?" Lance asks over the radio.

On the rooftop of the first building, where the soldiers silently shot the guards, lays Chris Langan on his belly watching the target house through is rifle scope. He puts the radio handset up to his mouth and speaks, "yeah, my eyes haven't left it.

Two gunshots in rapid succession ring out nearby. All the ODA soldiers bring their weapons up instinctively and scan the area for threats. Lance speaks again into his helmet microphone, "anybody got eyes on? Chris?"

Still on the rooftop, Chris replies, "a pickup truck just pulled out two houses behind you boss. Can't see who's shooting." From Chris's hidden vantage point we see swarms of Afghans exit a neighboring house and shoot at the escaping truck. Some run into the house where the pickup truck just left. They come out screaming and helping drag their semi-conscious friends who were gassed. "Holy shit boss," Chris says into the radio, "three houses away from you is an angry beehive a hajjis.

"What are they doing Chris?"

Chris is watching the pickup truck drive away through is rifle scope. "Shooting at a runaway truck," Chris reports, "and take a guess who's driving it? Through the scope of Chris's rifle see Dr. Sovia at the wheel of the pickup truck speeding away with all the windows down.

Back in the house Lance reacts with a smile, "the Doc?

"Yep," replies Chris, "we got a few trucks peeling out to chase him. Whataya want me to do boss?"

"Cover him while he escapes," says Lance just as bullets start cracking past him from outside the house.

Bob White is peering out a different window nearby and yells at Lance, "were made boss! I got multiple hajjis shooting in our direction." Lance rushes to the window and sees swarms of Armed Afghans running towards them. He talks into his helmet microphone.

"We're made gentleman. GO LOUD! NOW! Team two get the 50 up here." The Special Forces soldiers all start shooting out of any window or door they can find. Enemy rounds snap past them.

From the edge of the village, near Chris's sniper hide site, the two remaining Humvees of ODA 666 pull out from where they hid earlier. The massive fifty caliber machine gun blazing away and knocking back the Afghans and vibrating the air with every shot.

Back in the house with Lance, over the roar of gunfire Staff Sergeant Dan Nuzzi hears his radio crackle to life, "Devils Child nine, this is Fast Mover come in over. Dan clumsily puts his radio handset up to his ear.

Fast Mover, this is Devil's Child Nine. Holy shit it's good to hear your voice Fast Mover." From inside the house a sonic boom of a passing fighter plane rocks the buildings.

Two thousand feet up in the air, a fighter pilot sits in the tight confines of a cockpit as he flies in a circle nearby the Village of Marjan. "I got a digital bomb request just sent from the satellite with your clearance code on it," says the fighter pilot over the radio, "yours? over."

Back down in the house, Dan shakes his fist in delight and smiles at Lance. "Doc must have called in a bomb run," yells Dan, should I confirm it?

Lance looks out the window, shoots and looks back to Dan, "send it."

Dan speaks again into the radio handset, "fuck yeah its mine. What type of ordinance you carrying over?"

"I got two-two thousand pounders and 4 five

hundreds," replies the fighter pilot, "what's the status of civilians in the area over?

"No civilians," replies Dan over the radio, "send me the two thousand pounder over." Lance looks at Dan and Dan shrugs and smiles. "Fuck it," says Dan, "we're surrounded right. The men all laugh and the radio sounds off again.

The fighter pilot's voice comes out of the radio, "weapons released Devils Child, put your heads down, this is gonna be a big one."

Up on the mountain road overlooking the village, the pickup truck is still parked on the side of the road. Dr. Sovia, Judy and Maria are looking down at the village. Maria asks, "what are we waiting for? Can we just get out of here?"

Nurse Judy tries to stretch and asks, "yeah what are we waiting for? What's supposed to happen?"

Dr. Sovia looks at the device in his hand then the village, "a bomb is supposed to drop on the house I pointed at.

"What are you a forward air controller now?"

asks Judy.

"What's that?" Dr. Sovia asks.

"Never mind that," Maria snaps and leans forward from the backseat, "how did you get kidnapped and wind up at that house with all the medical gear.

"Listen, this has been incredible twenty-four hours," Dr. Sovia exclaims, "I'll tell you later-"

"No!" interrupts Maria, "you tell me now Sovia! We were-"

The rear window of the pickup truck shatters. Judy's head explodes and blood and brain are scattered inside the truck. Maria screams in fear, "Aaaaahhh!!!!" Dr. Sovia looks out the rear where the window used to be and sees more pickup trucks racing up the mountain road. He immediately puts the truck into gear and starts driving away. "Go! GO!" yells Maria. More bullets whiz by as the truck accelerates. Suddenly an earth shattering roar is heard from the two thousand pound bomb exploding a half a mile away. Dr. Sovia and Maria look at the village. "Holy Mother of god," Maria cries.

The bomb lands exactly where Dr. Sovia had aimed the laser at from the truck. The stone house disappears in what looks like a volcanic eruption as tons of earth and stone shoot skyward. The seemingly endless swarm of enemy Afghans are instantly vaporized or fly away as debris lands all over the village and mountainside.

Dr. Sovia holds up the GPS laser designator with one hand while steering the truck with the other, "I can't believe it, I guess it did work." The pressure wave from the explosion sends debris and falling trees on the road blocking the pickup trucks a half a mile behind them. Dr. Sovia sees them stopped in the rearview mirror and hoots and hollers, "Hahaaa! Fuckers! We made it." He looks at Maria in the rearview mirror and ties to assure her, "we're gonna make it! We're gonna-"

Maria screams again, "Watch the road!" Dr. Sovia looks back at the road just in time to see a massive tree, fall across the roadway and the pickup truck slams into it causing the passengers to fly forward. "Aaaah!! Screams Maria, "Oh my god! I'm just a doctor, I'm not in the infantry. Get me out of here!"

Dr. Sovia rubs his head after hitting the steering wheel, "You OK? He asks Maria, Is Miss Roberts OK?"

"Ow, yeah," Maria replies while checking on Judy. "Oh my god. Judy's dead!" The crack of bullets is heard and they both look back down the mountain road. Two thousand feet away the pursuing pickup trucks are blocked and angry Afghans are approaching up the steep mountain road on foot.

"Oh shit," he says aloud, "we've got our own problems," Dr. Sovia says as he looks out the back of the truck.

"Oh my god," Maria sounds scared, "we have to run, we have to get out of here."

Dr. Sovia brings the GPS Laser Target Designator up to his eye and looks through the scope down at the approaching men. "Where you wanna go Maria?" he says, "we're alone on a mountain road in Afghanistan."

Maria looks at him incredulously, "so what now? Let them capture us again, they'll kill us for sure."

Without taking his eye away from the scope on the device, Dr. Sovia hands Maria his pistol, "fire a few shots to slow them down. "This GPS fucker worked once, let's hope it works twice."

Maria sniffs the pistol, looks at Dr. Sovia and says, "this gun smells like ass!"

"Don't fucking ask!" Yells Dr. Sovia, "just shoot a couple of times."

Maria shoots rapidly and the distant Afghans throw themselves on the ground. Dr. Sovia grabs the gun with his spare hand while never taking the scope off his eye. "I said a few shots, save your Ammo." The Designator beeps and Dr. Sovia presses send on the keypad

Maria looks at him approvingly and asks, "when did you become this tactical?

Dr. Sovia gives a look of exasperation, "it's been a real long twenty four hours Doctor."

Back in the house in the village, the men of ODA 666 are groggily shaking off the effects of the bomb blast that exploded too close for comfort. Lance is trying to sit up from the ground and rubbing his head, "no more two thousand pounders Dan,"

"Yeah. No kidding Lance," says Dan as he is trying to regain his equilibrium.

Lance looks around for is guys through the dust in the air, "Bob you good?"

Bob White is lying a few meters away rubbing his face, "I don't know, I think I'm dead," Bob says, he coughs, "quiet outside though."

"Yeah, hey guys was that bomb big enough?" Lance asks and everyone laughs. Dan's radio comes to life.

The fighter pilot's voice comes out of the radio, "Devil's Child Nine, Fast Mover over."

Dan grabs the radio handset and speaks into it, "go for Devils Child Nine Fast Mover."

The pilot sits in the tight confines of a cockpit as he flies in a circle nearby the Village of Marjan. He is observing the dust settle thousands of feet below him as the jet fighter circles around the village."Busy day huh. I got another bomb request on a roadway bout a mile away from Marjan over."

Back in the house Dan looks to Lance and shrugs, Lance nods yes. Dan speaks into the handset. "Yeah, that us again Fast Mover over."

" Roger that Devil' Child nine, I need audio confirmation from you on nature of your target over."

Dan starts screaming angrily, "Fast Mover we are in heavy contact from multiple angles, in jeopardy of being over ran. I need that ordinance and I need it now. How copy over?"

"Weapons released, sending ordinance now over," comes the voice over the radio.

Back on the mountain road, Dr. Sovia and Maria are looking down the incline as the armed Afghans continue to approach them in the paralyzed vehicle, the pickup truck sits upon a fallen tree and cannot move and bullets are pinging off the truck and whizzing by.

"We have to go," Maria cries out while trying to cover Kelly's unconscious body, "we can't stay here, we have to go!"

Dr. Sovia yells back, "you want to go, go! Carry Kelly out of here. I will stay and shoot at them for as long as I can." Dr. Sovia shoots his pistol and the Afghans duck down.

"I can't carry her," Sovia, I'm not strong enough," cries out Maria.

Dr. Sovia looks at Maria as a piece of

windshield glass falls down on his face. "I'm done running Maria. Live or die, I am done running." Dr. Sovia puts the laser designator up to his eye again peering out the rear windshield.

"You did that already," Maria chastises him, "it didn't work. We have to go!"

Dr. Sovia tries to get a better angle out the back of the shot out rear windshield. "They moved off from where they were before. I have to laze them again." The device chirps and Dr. Sovia hits send again. More bullets began pinging the truck. Dr. Sovia grabs Maria's shoulder, pulls her down and looks into her eyes as more bullets impact the truck. "I really wish I could have met you under different circumstances Dr. Paredo," Sovia tells her. More bullets smash windows as they duck down into the seats.

"Me too… Robert, she replies, "thank you for coming back for us. You have no idea what that means to me."

Dr. Sovia smiles at her, "do you know that is the first time you ever called me Robert? I'm sorry it didn't work out." They stare at each other for a long moment then kiss passionately. Multiple bombs land behind the truck and explosions fill the background as they kiss. The sky above is consumed with fire and rage.

Down the mountain, the men of ODA 666 are spread out, walking abreast of each other through the wreckage and carnage of the Village of Marjan. Scores of dead armed Afghans lie in the dirt. They tactically enter into houses as they progress forward. Bob White sticks his head out of a door and yells, "in here boss," Lance runs into the house where Bob called from. Lying on the floor, hog tied and bound are five female hostages and Imran Khan. All covered in dust and debris. Lance runs to them and begins un-gagging them.

Stacy Baker is one of the first ones found and unbound, She is crying, "Oh my god. Thank you. Thank you," she says as he hugs Captain Lance Erickson.

Lance replies, "it's ok. It's over," as he cuts away her ropes. Stacey cries and holds onto Lance.

Dan runs in, "Boss, the fighter pilot relayed our request for support to Group Command. Help is coming."

Within thirty minutes of the Fighter Pilot's call, helicopters begin landing and disbursing troops. Trucks and Humvees are pulling in to the village as Kelly's father, Congressman Roger Robert's influence is suddenly felt halfway around the world. Stacey Baker sits on the back of a truck being treated by a medic. Lance walks up to her and asks and smiles, "Hey, how ya holding up?"

Stacey Baker, never in love before, suddenly looks at Lance like he is her avenging angel. "Oh my effing GOD!!!" Stacy yells, "I want to go home…You wanna come?"

Lance looks at her for a minute, kisses her briefly and says, "I am home. I'm at war," Lance smiles and walks away to a different Humvee where Kelly Roberts is being pulled out of on a stretcher. Lance runs over and sees Dr. Sovia helping to unload Kelly Roberts, he calls out to Dr. Sovia, "Doc. Doc! You're alive. How is she?"

Dr. Sovia stares back at Lance with hollow exhausted eyes, "Dr. Sovia says, "she'll live."

Maria walks around from the other side of the Humvee and proudly announces, "we are taking her back to the Forward Surgical Team."

A tall officer surrounded by his numerous staff walks into the mix. Colonel Kevin McKenna strides into the situation and announces, "you're not taking her anywhere Captain, we are taking her."

Maria attempts to re-assert her authority over her patient. She walks forward and loudly announces, "My name is Captain Maria Paredo, and I am one of the doctors who operated on Kelly Roberts. She's our patient."

Colonel McKenna points to Kelly Roberts, stretched out on a stretcher and immediately several of his men forcibly take the stretcher from Dr. Sovia.

Captain Erickson walks forward into the mix and Colonel Kevin McKenna greets him, "Lance, great job here son. Thanks, I'm gonna make you a Major."

Lance points towards Dr. Sovia, "don't thank me, thank that guy right there. That's the doctor who saved the day." Doctor Roberto Sovia," Lance yells aloud.

Colonel McKenna looks at Dr. Sovia and shakes his hand. "Nice work Doctor," says Colonel McKenna, "OK doctors, accompany your patient back to our medical facility. Let's move out." The group moves out to a nearby giant Chinook helicopter. Colonel McKenna turns back to Lance. "Gonna need a full accounting for everything that happened here Lance." Lance stares, the exhaustion visible on his face. Colonel McKenna continues pontificating, "every General and Admiral in theater wanted a piece of this one but you got her. You made me look great! I'll make sure you get what's coming to you... Major Erickson."

Lance glumly replies, "I gotta collect my men sir."

The Colonel turns back towards the helicopter which is now warming up. "You'll brief me after you get the other hostages back?" says the Colonel, "I'm getting off that helicopter with her Lance. CNN and FOX news will be there," the Colonel says grinning ear to ear. Lance stares blankly as the Colonel boards the helicopter and it takes off from Marjan.

"Good for you," says Lance as he walks back to where his soldiers are helping load the remaining hostages into vehicles where he sees Bob White.

"We get everybody Bob?"

Bob takes a deep breath and looks around, "Think so boss, I think so."

EPILOGUE

Kelly Roberts was flown to back to the U.S. where she fully recovered.

Baraat Mansoor's body was never recovered.

Dr. Sovia and Captain Lance Erickson were both court Martialed and discharged from the US Army.

Congressman Roberts was instrumental in obtaining a presidential pardon for both of them and US citizenship for Dr. Sovia.

Dr. Sovia went to work full time for the international organization known as Doctors Without Frontiers as a full doctor and continued to help save lives.

Dr. Maria Paredo resigned her Army Commission and joined him.

Lance Erickson went on to create his own Private

Military Company providing security to Non Governmental Organizations (NGOs) in hot spots all over the world.

Lance Erickson's first Security contract obtained with the help of Congressman Roberts; Doctors Without Frontiers.